W9-BAB-746

"I can't protect you, Noel."

"I don't need your protection. I'm a big girl, living and working in a big world that isn't always kind. I do just fine by my own devices."

His dark brows came together, and there was a tightness around his eyes and cheekbones. "Fine, but I still don't want you involved. This guy's crazy."

"Yes, well, a man in your position should know how it works, Jack. More often than not, you don't get what you want."

"No?" For the first time that day, a smile touched his lips. When she tried to open the door, he wrapped his fingers around her neck, tipped back her head and kissed her.

It was dangerous ground for both of them right now. But she didn't pull away. "If you're trying to frighten me off, it won't work. I don't scare easily."

He smiled, just a little. "That makes us even because neither do I. But I do," he said as he leaned in to recapture her mouth, "get what I want."

CHRISTMAS RANSOM

JENNA RYAN

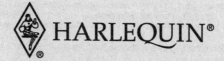

HARLEQUIN®

TORONTO • NEW YORK • LONDON
AMSTERDAM • PARIS • SYDNEY • HAMBURG
STOCKHOLM • ATHENS • TOKYO • MILAN • MADRID
PRAGUE • WARSAW • BUDAPEST • AUCKLAND

If you purchased this book without a cover you should be aware that this book is stolen property. It was reported as "unsold and destroyed" to the publisher, and neither the author nor the publisher has received any payment for this "stripped book."

ISBN 0-373-22884-8

CHRISTMAS RANSOM

Copyright © 2005 by Jacqueline Goff

All rights reserved. Except for use in any review, the reproduction or utilization of this work in whole or in part in any form by any electronic, mechanical or other means, now known or hereafter invented, including xerography, photocopying and recording, or in any information storage or retrieval system, is forbidden without the written permission of the publisher, Harlequin Enterprises Limited, 225 Duncan Mill Road, Don Mills, Ontario, Canada M3B 3K9.

All characters in this book have no existence outside the imagination of the author and have no relation whatsoever to anyone bearing the same name or names. They are not even distantly inspired by any individual known or unknown to the author, and all incidents are pure invention.

This edition published by arrangement with Harlequin Books S.A.

® and TM are trademarks of the publisher. Trademarks indicated with ® are registered in the United States Patent and Trademark Office, the Canadian Trade Marks Office and in other countries.

www.eHarlequin.com

Printed in U.S.A.

ABOUT THE AUTHOR

Jenna Ryan loves creating dark-haired heroes, heroines with strength and good murder mysteries. Ever since she was young, she had an extremely active imagination. She considered various careers over the years and dabbled in several of them, until the day her sister Kathy suggested she put her imagination to work and write a book. She enjoys working with intriguing characters and feels she is at her best writing romantic suspense. When people ask her how she writes, she tells them by instinct. Clearly it's worked, since she's received numerous awards from *Romantic Times* magazine. She lives in Canada and travels as much as she can when she's not writing.

Books by Jenna Ryan

CAST OF CHARACTERS

Noel Lawson—An attorney whose outstanding defense skills have caught the eye of a kidnapper.

Jack Ransom—A corporate raider with a missing sister. He is the president and CEO of Ransom Price Enterprises.

Jacob Ransom—Jack's late grandfather built a corporation and named it for himself and his partner.

Philip Price—Jacob's late partner had no children—that Jack and Noel know of.

Michael Santos—Senior VP at Ransom Price and Jack's best friend.

Helen Stowe—Noel's best and oldest friend. She has designs on Michael.

Caroline Ransom—Jack's half sister. Was she kidnapped for money or revenge?

Harry Dexter—An accountant at Ransom Price. He has a grudge against both Jack and Noel.

Roberto Turano—The only man Noel ever considered marrying.

Matthew Railback—He works for Jack; he dated Noel.

Artie—He owns Artie's Deli—where a certain suspicious blonde hangs out.

Prologue

Dear Jack:

You're going to suffer. As Charles Dickens would say, that must be clearly understood, or nothing I do will serve any purpose.

For what you and your late grandfather did in the past, you will pay in the present. As for the future—well, the kind of suffering I have in mind won't pass easily or quickly.

Have you noticed, Jack? It's been snowing in Steel Town for a full week now. Thanksgiving is barely a day behind us, and already the store shelves are overflowing with perfume, lingerie, tools and toys. There are Santas on street corners and in every mall and department store. Kids have their wish lists ready to e-mail north, and I have mine in my head. Your name tops it this year, with another very close behind.

But that's for later, after I set matters in motion. I know where the instrument of your suffering will be this afternoon, and I know how to coax her out. She loves parties and presents and eggnog with half a shot of brandy. When she sees her living accommodations for the next while, she might want a full shot. Who knows, I might even give it to her. Because she hasn't done anything to me or mine. Inflicting pain is your province, isn't it, Jack Ransom? Yours and your dead grandfather's.

Well, ho, ho, ho, or perhaps, more appropriately, brace yourself for a nightmare like nothing old Ebenezer ever experienced. I've taken my cue from the best. It's time for payback.

Enjoy your Christmas Present, Jack. If it's any consolation, you won't be alone.

Neither will I.

The Ghost of Christmas Past.

Chapter One

Noel,
I have rented out my house for the next several weeks. I'm spending the holidays with my girlfriend in Connecticut. Don't be alarmed if you see strangers coming and going.
Merry Christmas
Fred P. Yost

Noel Lawson pulled a snowy glove off with her teeth, left the note where her eighty-nine-year-old neighbor had taped it to the door and gave the pine tree behind her a settling tug.

"Helen, are you here?" She poked her head into the shadowy hallway. "Helen?"

A sleepy woof greeted her, followed by a dazzling glare of light as a woman in her early thirties strode into the corridor.

"You're back, huh? I was just leaving. It got crazy here all of a sudden. There's a guy charged with arson who wants you to represent him in county court in January, but I'd turn it down if I were you. He's been convicted three times."

"Of arson?" Noel asked when Helen, her friend and weekend legal associate, stopped for breath. Noel dragged the pine across the newly restored floor, glanced up the stairwell and wondered if she should have gotten a smaller tree.

"Arson to cover a break and enter. If you're looking for conscience-clearing cases, this isn't one."

"I'm not—"

"Yes, you are, Noel Lawson, of Faber, Lawson and Kellman fame." Helen pulled a cap over her straight blond hair. "We're all looking for something in the end. In my case, it was serenity, which is why I'm in Winter Valley seven days a week instead of two like you." She wrapped a red wool scarf around her neck and patted her bulging shoulder bag. "I'm loaded with briefs, but I only left three on your desk. I'm thinking we need a full-time assistant."

"You do," Noel corrected. "I'm in Pittsburgh five days a week, remember?"

"It still blows me away sometimes. My college roomie. I thought you'd get gobbled up by the legal vultures your first year out. Shows you what I know." She regarded the tree. "Should I lock up?"

"No, I'll come back down after I get Godzilla here settled for the night. Did you feed Aunt Maddie's dog?"

"Twice, and walked him around the block twenty minutes ago." Helen hesitated. Then with a sigh, she unwrapped her scarf and shed her shoulder bag. "You might be a hotshot in Pittsburgh legal circles, Noel, but you only think with a quarter of your brain outside the courtroom." Grabbing hold of the top branch, she began hauling the pine upward. "How on earth do you plan to keep this thing alive for a whole month?"

Noel removed a large packet from her coat pocket. "The man I bought it from swore a tablespoon of this stuff in the water will keep it alive into the new year."

"Uh-huh, and who'll be watering it every day and getting needles stuck in her hair, not to mention feeding your aunt's dog and probably watering her tree, too?"

Noel sent her a cheerful smile. "Don't break any branches, okay?"

It took them ten minutes to maneuver the tree up the stairs to the second floor where Noel lived. The whole house was hers, purchased in what her aunt, a pastry chef in a Pittsburgh hotel, called a shrewdly sentimental business deal. The sentiment had been Noel's; the shrewdness belonged to the seller who'd pegged her as a big-city escapee the moment he'd set eyes on her.

She'd wanted the hundred-and-fifty-year-old house with a passion that hadn't been satisfied until she'd signed the title transfer papers. Now she had a weekend home, a small town office, her aunt for a tenant and a mortgage that would take her decades to pay off.

She could think of worse places to be.

"Right, good, we're here." Helen plucked a needle from her fingertip. "Do you need me to get it inside?"

"I have to put down plastic first, but thanks."

"No, I should thank your new floors." She squeezed past the frozen branches. "If you want help decorating, I'll be out of town tomorrow. Thankfully."

"Humbug." Noel removed her own hat and shook out her jet-black hair. "I'm coming back early next weekend. Why don't you run an ad for a legal secretary while I'm gone? Winter Valley's small, but there must be someone in town who's qualified."

Helen snickered. "You might not be aware of it, Noel, but you're a bit daunting, or your rep is."

"Luck shouldn't daunt people."

"You've got instincts that work and courtroom savvy, not to mention a very pretty face."

Noel stopped measuring the doorway and frowned. "That's not fair, Helen."

"I know, but both my hands are scraped from your tree. Look, there are lots of pretty lawyers around. Your face wouldn't have taken you far on its own. I'm late. Have fun with your green monster."

Still mildly irritated, Noel shook off her friend's remark, stepped over the tree trunk and unlocked her door.

She owned, or would someday, a house that was a century and a half old. She had neighbors almost that same age who called her "dear" and baked cookies for her. Her favorite aunt lived downstairs whenever she, like her niece, needed to escape the city, and her best friend was her weekend associate. She'd done a smart thing returning to the town where she'd lived for five years as a child. And clearing her conscience had nothing to do with any of it.

"I'm not a bad person," she said out loud. She glanced at the tree as she opened the door. "You're the monster, not me."

The room was steeped in darkness, but it struck her before she touched the light switch—she wasn't alone. A chill crawled down her spine, and her eyes narrowed. She was preparing to bolt when a voice came out of the darkness.

"Don't be frightened, Ms. Lawson." The door clicked shut, and the overhead track light flared. A man in a dark suit and overcoat smiled at her. "Come inside, and we'll have a nice, civilized chat."

Screaming wouldn't help, and running was out of the question. Noel noted a movement behind her and spied the stocky man in jeans and a gray sweater who'd closed the door.

There were four other men that she could see, including the one who'd spoken.

She was accustomed to battling adversaries in court, but her home was another matter. These men had invaded her space, and that made her a victim. It wasn't a word she liked, especially when it applied to her.

Straightening, she met the suited stranger's gaze. "Who are you, and why did you break into my home?"

He almost smiled. "Your door was unlocked, Ms. Lawson."

Her temper rose, but fear and wisdom controlled it. "I'm not an absentminded person. The dead bolt was on. You broke in." With no visible weapons, she was relieved to note. "What do you want?"

The man's hair was long, sleek and dark, tied back in a hip bohemian ponytail. He wore a silver stud in his left earlobe and a diamond in his right. He'd be bald in ten years, but it wouldn't faze him, any more than this confrontation was doing.

He motioned toward her sofa as if he owned it. The gesture brought her hackles up another full degree.

"Please sit down," he began.

"Who are you?" she repeated. The man in gray behind her joined another who was similarly dressed in jeans, a worker's sweater and a baseball cap.

"As you wish." The man in the suit fished inside his breast coat pocket, and for a moment Noel's heart stopped beating. However, it wasn't a gun he pulled out, but a paper. "Read this, then we'll talk. Sit down, Morris," he said in the same calm tone to the man shuffling beside him. "Corporate lawyer," he explained when Noel glanced over. "Bad nerves kept him out of the courtroom."

Another man, also wearing a suit, made a head motion, and finally, the nervous Morris subsided.

Noel opened the note as she swept her suspicious gaze over all five of the intruders. The one who'd closed the door looked Scandinavian. His counterpart was leaner, had long, rather scruffy brown hair and dark brown eyes that she could feel staring at her.

"Read it, please, Ms. Lawson," the slick man directed. "Then we'll talk."

Don't count on it, Noel thought, but she turned her attention to the typed words.

It was straightforward enough—a threat of harm coupled with strong hostility and a certain amount of derangement.

"To Jack Ransom," she murmured. She looked briefly at the man with the ponytail and arched a brow. "From the Ghost of Christmas Past?"

"The guy's a nutcase," the stocky Scandinavian declared.

His dark-eyed counterpart glanced over but said nothing.

Noel reread the note. "Kidnapping," she said. "Who's the 'she' this ghost talks about?"

"Caroline Ransom," the lawyer Morris replied.

"The famous—" under other circumstances, Noel would have said infamous "—Jack Ransom's wife?"

"Half sister," the man with the ponytail corrected. "Only sibling. Only family, in fact."

"You have my sympathy." Noel returned the note. She felt the dark-eyed man staring and shot him a quick look. He wore an earring as well, a silver stud in his left earlobe. She shifted her gaze back to the paper. "This still doesn't give you and your entourage the right to barge into my home."

"I need your help."

Since she no longer feared they would draw weapons, Noel had no compunction about being blunt.

"I choose the people I help. I don't like coercion."

"I'm not aware of any coercion here, Ms. Lawson."

"That would depend on your definition of the word and possibly your point of view. From mine, this is a bullying tactic."

Morris stood. "Mr. Ransom seldom approaches people in your position one on one. You should feel flattered."

His derisive tone rankled. "I count five of you to my one, Mr. Morris, and to my knowledge, Jack Ransom seldom approaches anyone at all. He's been called the Howard Hughes of corporate raiders. His family, meaning, I suppose, he and his sister, own an estate here in Winter Valley, population 12,273, yet I'd lay odds that less than a handful of people in this town would recognize him on sight."

The man with the ponytail gave a small nod. "You'd win that bet. However, we're digressing. I repeat, I need your help."

"No you don't." Turning her attention and her gaze to the man in gray with the stud earring, long hair, lean features and penetrating brown eyes, she tilted her head and smiled. "He does." Her brows went up in a challenge as she held his stare. "Isn't that right, Mr. Ransom?"

Silence followed Noel's question. Morris was the first person to react, and he did so by clearing his throat.

The man who'd done most of the talking studied her with a blend of admiration and bemusement, although the second vanished when the Scandinavian man stood.

"Relax, Talberg." He kept his eyes on Noel. "You're a very observant woman, Ms. Lawson. How did you know?"

"Small things." She continued to regard Jack Ransom, whose own piercing stare hadn't altered. "Was this a test of some sort, Mr. Ransom?"

To her surprise, his lips twitched into a vague smile. "Possibly."

It was the first time he'd spoken, and he had a nice voice, not grating like Morris's or as smooth as the man who'd done most of the talking. Just pleasant.

With nothing more than a faint movement of his head, he motioned the others out. Morris started to object, but stopped when he noticed his boss's expression.

"Who are you?" Noel asked the man with the ponytail.

Unlike the others, he didn't look to Jack Ransom for permission to speak. "My name is Michael Santos, and I apologize for the deception. It wasn't so much a test as a precaution."

"In case I was a groupie or a gun-toting maniac who resented having her home invaded?"

"Something along those lines. Do you want me to stay, Jack?" At the other man's negation, he acknowledged Noel with a wink and ushered his comrades out the door.

"Don't trip over my tree." Noel was watching Jack Ransom again. When he simply watched back, she summoned a pleasant expression. "So, what now? Am I expected to guess why you're here, or are you going to make it easy and tell me?"

"You read the note, Ms. Lawson. What did you think?"

"That you want your sister back, and for some reason you believe I can help you. Does that reason involve a second note?"

For an answer, he pulled a folded paper from the back pocket of his jeans.

She had to move closer in order to take it, and that, she realized in mild surprise, brought her into a sphere of appealing maleness she hadn't anticipated. Scruffy he might be, long-haired and in need of a shave, but he had an aura, and it caused her to take a more assessing look at his dark, dark eyes.

She unfolded the note. "Michael Santos is a good friend, isn't he? Trusted for a long time. Since college?" she guessed.

"Grade school." Jack's gaze flicked to the window. "He was into the school band, art and the debating club. I was into rock bands, graffiti and fisticuffs."

"A match made in heaven." She stopped short as her own name and the phrase *go-between* jumped off the page at her. "The kidnapper wants me to be your liaison?"

"So he says."

"Should I ask why?"

"You can ask. Unfortunately, I can't tell you. It's possible he's heard of you and, wanting a liaison, decided you'd fit the bill. Or possibly he knows you."

"Or he might simply have chosen me knowing we'd wind up asking a question that has no answer."

"Is that what you believe?"

"Not really, but I like to consider all the possibilities." She unbuttoned her coat. "You could have called my office, you know, instead of slinking into my home like a pack of thieving wolves."

Again, he almost smiled. "I could have, yes, but then you might have dismissed me as a crank, and frankly I don't think I'm going to be given a lot of time here. The notes were delivered less than an hour apart. This guy has an agenda, and he's expecting me to keep up."

That wasn't likely to be a problem, but it still didn't satisfy her. Removing her coat, Noel draped it over the arm of the sofa. "You could have sent your friend Michael alone. I would have listened to him."

"This isn't Michael's problem."

Something in his tone had Noel's lips curving. "His idea though, right? Catch the lawyer off guard, and give yourselves the advantage. One thing you should know, Mr. Ransom—I don't like intimidation tactics."

"Meaning you won't help?"

She regarded the snowflakes dancing happily outside her window. "I'm not sure," she said at length. "I don't like your methods, but I sympathize with your problem. And I have to admit, I'm intrigued. What exactly does the liaison between a kidnapper and a corporate—" she smiled "—mogul do?"

He moved forward, his eyes on hers. "You can use the word *raider.* I've heard it before."

What she'd heard was that Jack's grandfather and his long-dead partner had practically invented the word.

At close range, Noel was once again struck by Jack's eyes. They were direct, unreadable and absolutely amazing. In fact, his whole face was rather incredible. Given that, it surprised her that he'd been able to achieve such a high level of anonymity.

"You're thinking something," he said.

"Always. Are you and your sister close?"

"Not especially."

"But she's all the family you have left. No aunts, uncles, cousins?"

Amusement flickered, then vanished. "The Ransoms aren't a prolific clan. My mother died when I was two. My father remarried within six months. Caroline was born a year later. Her mother died when I was thirteen, my father before I turned twenty."

"Your father was an only child?"

He nodded but didn't elaborate. Noel hadn't expected he would. By all accounts, Jack Ransom was a very private man.

Several seconds passed during which they simply studied each other. Then Jack's gaze grew speculative, and he cocked his head. "How did you know?" he asked simply.

She knew what he meant. Her smile was instant and genuine. "Your cheekbones."

When his brows came together, she elaborated. "Just because I've never seen you doesn't mean I haven't heard things. You're big news in Pittsburgh, even bigger here in Winter Valley. One of your grandmothers was a Native American. Navajo, I think. Many of the Navajo people have exquisite high cheekbones."

"So my bone structure gave me away."

"That and the way you watched me. You have the kind of stare that's difficult to ignore. How long has your sister been missing?"

"Since late yesterday afternoon. She left a cocktail party, got into her car and never arrived home."

"How were the notes delivered?"

"They appeared at my corporate office."

"Downstairs or up?"

"Down. The surveillance tapes show nothing out of the ordinary." He shrugged. "I have people reviewing them."

"People." Noel echoed the word. "Not the police or the FBI?"

"Time factor, Ms. Lawson."

"Noel."

"Both the police and the FBI have a vast number of cases on their plates. My people can concentrate all their efforts on finding Caroline."

She smiled. "You don't trust them, do you?"

"We've had dealings in the past," he told her. "They involved my family, and they weren't pleasant. This can be handled without the authorities."

Interesting, Noel mused. Aloud she said, "I'm not entirely sure about you, Jack Ransom. You look more like a construction worker than a corporate raider. You'd rather break into my home than pick up a phone. You have a nervous lawyer, a friend who's your antithesis and you prefer to let your own people handle your problems rather than the FBI. I assume part of that decision stems from the fact that you don't want your sister's disappearance made public."

He regarded her without emotion. "Your point is…?"

She gave a small laugh, mostly because she couldn't really think of one. "No point. Just an attempt to understand you."

Again, something flickered in those deep brown eyes. "Are you going to help me or not?"

Could she say no? She probably should. Noel sighed. "I'm not sure I like the idea of standing between you and a kidnapper, Mr.—"

"Jack."

"Jack. I also happen to think you're wrong not to go to the authorities. But I have a brother I'm not close to, so maybe I can understand how you feel. A little."

A glimmer of a smile touched his lips. "Is that a yes, then?"

"A conditional one." Her boot heels clicked on the wooden floor as she crossed to the door. "First, I need you to help me get this tree inside, without destroying the finish on these." She swept a hand over the oak boards underfoot. "If you do that, then we'll go over those notes again and see if we can get some kind of feel for your kidnapping ghost."

Chapter Two

They went to Eduardo's on the outskirts of Pittsburgh for pasta, beer and more boisterous Christmas cheer than Noel would have anticipated from a man in Jack Ransom's position. As she gave her dinner order to a waiter with a large red mustache, she reminded herself never to underestimate Jack, even in mundane areas.

Christmas rock music underscored loud voices, laughter and the occasional shriek of a cranky child. Noel swallowed a mouthful of the cold lager Jack had ordered, caught him staring and leaned forward on her elbows to smile at him. "You're surprised I like beer?"

His unexpected grin disarmed her. "You strike me as a member of the white wine set, but then I'm hardly in a position to typecast."

"Not even a little," Noel agreed. "Are you a rebel, then, or like Rudolph, a full-blown nonconformist?"

"I was born three years after *Rudolph the Red-Nosed Reindeer* aired for the first time on TV. That translates to 1967."

"You look younger," she murmured.

"I know. My father was a rebel in an age of sexual revolt, heavy drug use and a renewed interest in world peace."

"Your father was a hippie?" Noel was genuinely amazed. "Iron-fisted Jacob Ransom's son was a bell-bottomed, incense-burning, sexually liberated hippie?"

"Actually, that was more my mother's thing. My father was a Marine."

"Really? He had no interest in your grandfather's businesses?"

"None at all."

"I'm sure your grandfather did his level best to change that."

Jack's lips curved. "He tried everything except medically assisted brainwashing, and he might have gotten around to that eventually if my father hadn't been killed overseas."

Noel caught the momentary cloud in his expression and touched his hand. "I'm sorry, Jack." He'd told her earlier that his father had died before he'd turned twenty. And he'd lost his mother years before that. "It must have been a terrible blow for you and Caroline."

Noel was relieved to see the sadness vanish as Jack took a deep drink. She didn't like to see people in pain, not physically, mentally or emotionally. It was, as her colleagues took great pleasure in pointing out, one of her stranger failings.

"We got through it," Jack told her. "You'd think his dying would have brought Caroline and me closer, but it didn't."

Since there was little she could say to that, and their food had arrived courtesy of the waiter with the red mustache, Noel let the subject drop. Wrestling with her Christmas tree for the past three hours had given her an appetite, and the spaghetti smothered in rich meat sauce smelled delicious.

She waited through half the meal before returning to the subject of Jack's upbringing.

"Your grandfather had a partner in the early years, didn't he?"

Jack gave a humorless chuckle. "Scrooge and Marley," he said. "Without the redemption."

Sore spot there, Noel realized and knew she would need to tread carefully. "Ransom Price Enterprises, initially comprised of Jacob Ransom and Philip Price. I think a lot of people now wouldn't realize there ever was a Philip Price. When did he die?"

Something sparked in Jack's eyes. "Two decades ago, but trust me, Noel, there are people who'd remember him."

"In the good or bad way?"

"In the female way."

"Philip Price liked women. And yet he never married, never had children."

"He was notorious for his affairs," Jack told her. "But he did marry once. Her name was Natasha. She was right off the boat from Russia when they met." He lifted his glass but didn't drink. "Being a romantic, Philip took one look at her and decided she was the one for him. By the time he figured out that this epiphany had come from below the waist, they were married and she was busy spending his money and sleeping with any and every willing man she met." Noting Noel's expression, he shrugged and tipped his glass back. "My grandfather not included. Jacob Ransom had weightier matters on his mind in those days. And Philip was his friend."

"So you're saying your grandfather wasn't all bad."

"I'd put it at ninety-ten on the side of bad."

That meant he'd had enemies, but then Noel had already figured that much. "Your grandfather died five years ago, right?"

"Five years this Christmas Eve."

Now there was a spooky thought. She played with the crust of her garlic bread. "How long did you work with him?"

"Including most of the summers I was in college, twenty years."

"Is your sister involved in the business?"

"She likes to spend the profits." When Noel merely stared at him, he continued. "She has a head for business, but no desire for sustained hard work. She was given three companies to manage before old Jacob died. They'd have fallen into bankruptcy if he hadn't stepped in."

"If her companies were headed for bankruptcy, why did you say she had a head for business?"

The smile he didn't manage to hide reached his eyes for the first time. "Are all your conversations conducted this way, counselor?"

She opened her mouth to reply, but she stopped short when she realized she indeed had been cross-examining him. "Old habits," she admitted. "And we are trying to solve a puzzle here.

I was taught the fastest way to obtain information is to ask questions."

"In rapid-fire succession."

Her answering smile was sweet. "You don't seem to be having any trouble keeping up."

Amusement danced briefly in his eyes. "You never met my grandfather. He used to grill me about business at breakfast on Sundays after I'd just crawled in from a Saturday night party. You kept up or you never heard the end of it." He made a carry-on motion with his glass. "You were saying?"

She'd almost forgotten. He really had the most fascinating eyes. "I asked you about Caroline and her questionable business sense."

"Oh, she knows how business works, and she has a good mind. What she lacks is mental toughness."

"Meaning she couldn't stand up to your grandfather."

Jack glanced at a table where a young couple was arguing over where to spend the holidays. "Caroline started her own company with a friend after college. It involved fruit extracts and healing plants. They opened two spas called CaVa and had expanded to four before they hit their first big financial bumps. Val, Caroline's partner, bailed at the first sign of trouble. Caroline tried to turn things around, but that's not as easy as it sounds when you have a vulture circling overhead, searching for a fresh kill."

"Your grandfather took the company from her?"

"Bought her out for a fair market price, but, yeah, same thing. She grabbed the check and took off for Geneva to lick her wounds. She inherited the three companies I mentioned before, from my grandmother, but she didn't have the guts to tough out the bad times with them, either."

"You don't sound very sympathetic."

"I offered to help her in all cases, Noel. She turned me down flat."

"Were the two of you ever close?"

He glanced again at the couple beside them. "Not really. Distance was our way as a family. There was duty and a certain amount of loyalty, but not a whole lot in the way of emotion."

Noel pictured a black-and-white version of Ebenezer Scrooge's house and wondered what it would have felt like growing up in such a bleak environment. As Aunt Maddie said, money could buy warmth for the flesh, but not for the soul.

Noel smiled at the memory. When Jack arched a brow, she waved him off. "I was thinking of something my aunt would say. She's a philosopher."

He went back to his linguine, but looked up to ask, "The aunt who's a pastry chef?"

"You know her?" Why that should come as a shock, Noel wasn't sure, but she didn't like it. She lowered her lashes in suspicion. "Have you been spying on me?"

The amusement that hovered on the corners of his mouth didn't improve her mood. "Maybe a little. Does that bother you?"

She wanted to hiss at him, but professional etiquette prevented it. "I'm not a public figure, Jack."

"Meaning I am, and therefore should accept the fact that people are going to pry into my personal life, while you, being only one of this country's many fine attorneys prefer to be exempt from any form of scrutiny."

Instead of responding, Noel swirled the dregs of her beer and used a calming tactic her aunt had taught her years before. Count to ten in an unfamiliar language. As a rule, by the time she had managed that feat, most of her anger had dissipated. She opted for German this time, coupled with a single deep breath.

"You've achieved a high degree of anonymity, Jack. I respect, even admire that. But you have no right to be sneaking around, probing into the private corners of my life."

"You live with your aunt, Noel. That isn't a private corner."

"I don't like being pushed."

"Neither do I, but it happens all the time, doesn't it?"

Sustained anger was unhealthy. Noel let her vexation go and her better nature rise. "You should be nice to me, Jack Ransom. It's you who needs my help, not vice versa."

"No?" He refilled their beer glasses from the pitcher between them. "Don't forget, Noel, the kidnapper named you as his liaison, and while you might think he simply picked your name out of a hat, my instincts tell me he has a very specific reason for wanting you to be part of this."

A layer of ice coated her throat. Not so much because of what Jack had said, but because a similar thought had been drifting around in the back of her mind since she'd read the kidnapper's second note.

Propping an elbow on the table, Jack clinked his glass to hers. "To the sins of our forefathers," he toasted. "And to those more recent ones we've committed ourselves."

SHE HADN'T COMMITTED any big sins. Not really big, at any rate.

There was a split second, less than a heartbeat, when Jack was able to read the thought in her eyes. Then it was gone, and the clear, stunning blue was back in place. She was a professional. Panic was not allowed. She had a temper, but for the most part she kept her emotions in check. She wasn't anything like what he'd expected.

There was beauty on the surface, no question about it. Caroline would kill for hair like Noel's—straight, black, thick and silky. And Michael's artistic fingers would already be itching to paint her portrait. Her features were soft but cleanly sculpted, and he wouldn't mind tasting that mouth of hers sometime.

"Remembering your sins, are you, Jack?" The question was offered with enough humor to make him realize he'd probably let his own expression slip.

"There've been a few." He pinned her with a look. "But that's not the point, is it? My sister's been kidnapped, no doubt for a large sum of money. Seems straightforward enough to me. I pay, she's returned safe and sound."

"That's the promise," Noel agreed. "Whether it's kept or not is the question. Why me, specifically?" she demanded in the same breath.

He sensed she was asking herself as much as him. "I have enemies, Noel. I imagine you've made a few yourself."

"That's not an answer, Jack." She tapped a thoughtful finger against her glass. When the waiter slid the bill onto the table between them, she spared the tray a quick look, but her mind was clearly elsewhere. "Your ghost only wants me to play go-between. It's your sister's life that's in danger, not mine. Yes, okay," she amended before he could speak, "I'd be in a certain amount of danger simply by dealing with a kidnapper, but Caroline's at far greater risk than me."

"So why did he choose you?"

Her eyes shot up, and for a moment Jack was struck by the sheer loveliness of the color. Like a cobalt vase he'd seen once in a Venice art gallery.

"If you're trying to spook me, you might want to rethink your logic. I can still turn you down. Certain members of my law firm might be on retainer to various companies within your corporation, but nothing about that obliges me to help you recover your sister."

"Common ground," he said and knew full well she understood his meaning.

She released a breath. "You think it's someone we both know, or who knows both of us. I had that same feeling when I read the notes. There could be a lot more going on here than the kidnapping of your sister."

"We'll find out." Unprepared to give more than that, Jack rolled his head where a tension headache throbbed. "Do you want to get going? The food here's great, but I think there's an office Christmas party gathering steam across from us."

Through slitted eyes, he watched her look at the bill. He had no intention of letting her pay.

"Interesting," was all she said, then raised her head to regard the waiter with the red mustache as he presented them with another small black tray.

"I hope everything was satisfactory." He set the tray on the table with a flourish. "Your bill."

Jack narrowed his eyes, but it was Noel who took the paper from the first tray and read.

Dear Jack:

Are you enchanted? I didn't expect that, but I'm not really surprised. She's quite beautiful, my liaison. Her mother's Italian, if you're interested, born in Pavia, which is south of Milan.

So, are you missing your sister? Worried about her? Desperate to get her back? Probably not, but you'll go through the necessary motions because it's the right thing to do. Family's not your thing, is it, though you'd never admit that publicly. Side note: With one exception, my liaison is totally into her own family ties. Whether she'll want to get into yours is difficult to say. Maybe you should sweeten the pot, just to be on the safe side.

As for dear Caroline, she's as well as can be expected under the circumstances. Do you know she's afraid of the dark? Hates the cold? And cobwebs? Turns up her nose at day-old French bread and unbottled water? Oh well, a few less pounds won't hurt her.

Listen up, Jack. I want ten million American dollars. That's absolute and nonnegotiable. But we're going to play this game of kidnap and Ransom my way and according to my schedule. First you suffer, then you pay. (You might want to pass that on to my lovely liaison.)

You're slipping, Jack. There I was, wearing a false mustache and standing right beside the pair of you. Did you see me? If you're reading this, the answer's no. You see nothing and no one. But then that's always been your problem, hasn't it?

Now it's yours, mine and Caroline's. Kiss our liaison for me—if you dare.

The Ghost of Christmas Past

P.S. Your linguine sauce made me think of something a fisherman might have caught once upon a time in the AM. Point Stated and made, I trust.

NOEL KNEW she was going to regret reading that note to Jack, and she was right.

"This isn't a race, Jack." She'd cracked a heel when they'd left Eduardo's twenty-five minutes ago, and she'd been struggling to keep up ever since. "I got the kidnapper's clue, as well as you did. I just don't think we should be rushing headlong into his trap."

Jack's lips twitched as he cast a look at her high-heeled boots. "I wouldn't exactly call this rushing."

"Jack, it's dark, it's snowing and it's too slippery to run. I'll also repeat, it's just plain stupid. A post script like that is a trap waiting to be sprung. Point State Park, at the junction of the AM—Allegheny and Monongahela rivers. Jack." She grabbed his arm, hoping to at least slow him down. "I'm not sure this person is sane."

"He's playing games with us. That doesn't equal insanity."

She hung on, refused to let him speed up. "Kidnapping isn't a game. You read the note. Money's a secondary motive for this guy. The note came to you, but he knows enough things about my life to suggest that I'm very much involved here. And stop looking at me like I'm an employee who's irritating you." She shook his arm. "You're not thinking this through."

He stared at her for a full five seconds while snowflakes dusted his shoulders and cold wind whipped the ends of his hair.

"Was your mother born in Pavia?"

"Yes." Noel tried to keep her teeth from chattering. "She was less than a year old when her parents immigrated to the United States. It's no secret, Jack. But while several of my associates might know about it, very few of my clients would."

He glanced away, as if impatient to be off. "Information like that is easy to obtain, Noel."

"It's also easy to walk into an ambush when you're not in control of a situation." She gestured at the snow-coated trees around them and the broad expanse of open ground ahead. "Is this what he wants? Us? Here in this park? We make good targets, if that's his goal."

"If he kills me, he won't get his money."

Noel ground her teeth. "You're not the only person here, are you?"

Jack's gaze rose to the trees, standing white and eerie, like ghostly skeletons. "If he knows anything about me, it's that he won't get his money if he harms you, either."

"Well, that's a relief."

"I hate sarcasm, Noel."

"And I hate impulsiveness, especially when I'm dealing with an unknown and potentially dangerous commodity."

"Fine." With a quick, perfunctory smile, Jack set his hands on her shoulders and turned her back in the direction they'd come. "You wait in the car. I'll deal with the madman alone."

She was so tempted to leave him. However… "You can't win, Jack. You know that, don't you? Winning complex games involves doing the unexpected, not playing into your adversary's hands."

He leaned in close to whisper in her ear. "We're not playing. We're testing."

The shiver that ran through her didn't come from the wind or the snow. Since it unsettled her, Noel set the realization aside and let her gaze wander as far as it could in the winter darkness. "What are we testing for? Sanity? Credibility? Temperament? You said you don't like to be pushed. Maybe your sister's kidnapper doesn't, either."

"Then he won't get his payoff."

She sighed. "Money."

"It's his ultimate goal, it has to be. Let him play his games. In the end, he'll want the ten million."

Noel didn't turn back to face him. Instead, she continued to scan the trees. "I think you're wrong, Jack. Money isn't the bottom line with everyone."

"It is with this guy."

The words *stubborn* and *unrelenting* came to mind. However, before she could challenge him on either point, something long, sleek and fast whooshed past them. It embedded itself in a tree trunk ten feet in front of where Noel stood.

"What was—" She broke off as another projectile, this one much closer to her head, whizzed by.

She ducked automatically and dragged Jack with her. Running low, they made it to the far side of a broad oak.

"Someone's shooting arrows at us." Noel caught the hem of Jack's sweater before he could step out. "Don't be an idiot."

He didn't respond, merely studied the angle of the arrows then followed the trajectory to a stand of evergreens that stood behind a long park bench.

"He's in there."

"With weapons," she reminded him.

He spared her a brief look. "I have a gun, Noel."

She didn't doubt it. "You'd be shooting blind." She heard a thunk as another arrow hit the oak. As unnerved as she was, her temper kindled. "This guy's really bugging me."

Jack squinted into the trees. "You don't like being a target?"

"I don't like being bullied."

"Yes, you mentioned that." He braced a hand on her shoulder and, with a quick motion, reached around the trunk to grab the third arrow.

Noel spied a tube taped to the shaft. Pulling off her gloves, she began to pry it free with her fingernails. "The Ghost of

Christmas Past by day, Robin Hood by night." Freeing the tube, she shook out the contents.

"Another note?" Jack assumed. He'd gone back to staring at the trees.

Noel unrolled the paper and tried to make out the words. Light from one of the park lamps behind them made it just possible for her to see them. "It's for you, Jack," she said when she finished.

"I'm farsighted. What does it say?"

Noel leaned against his shoulder. "'Dear Jack,'" she quoted from memory as she scanned the shadows with him, "'Noel is the liaison, not you. She comes alone next time, or someone dies.'"

Chapter Three

"Noel, thank God. Are you all right?" Helen all but bowled her over as Noel limped through the door of her upstairs apartment. "Mrs. Fisker next door said she saw you leaving with some long-haired worker. Before that, she said a bunch of other men came out your front door and drove off. She didn't like the look of any of them." As she spoke, Helen steered her friend toward the sofa. "I didn't know what to think and now, suddenly, here you are, all wet and hobbling and looking as if you want to punch someone or something. What happened?"

"If I tell you, you won't believe me." Noel toed off her boot and examined the heel that had come loose. "I'm not sure I believe it myself. What are you doing here anyway? Your book club meets every Saturday night, doesn't it?"

"Not between Thanksgiving and the New Year. Besides, I forgot a brief. Why are you wet, Noel?"

Noel abandoned her damaged boot, kicked the other one off and ran her fingers through her damp hair. "Okay, I'll tell you the story, but you have to promise you'll listen, not interrupt and trust that I'm sober."

At Helen's nod, she outlined the entire bizarre evening, starting with Jack Ransom's entourage and ending with the note shot to Jack on an arrow.

As promised, her friend waited until she was done before summing up.

"Let me get this straight. You met the elusive Jack Ransom, talked kidnapping, had dinner, got threatened, got shot at, then came home hoping to carry on as before?" She tapped a finger against Noel's forehead. "Think, hon. You shouldn't be here. You should be on the phone to the FBI, and forget Jack Ransom's so-called people." She waited a beat, then leaned forward to ask, "What's he like?"

Noel fell back into the sofa cushions, linked her fingers and stretched her arms over her head to relieve her tension. "He's pigheaded."

"I mean lookswise. Is he gorgeous, or a gorgon, or somewhere in between?"

"He's not bad." Noel lost the battle with a reluctant smile. "Pretty gorgeous, actually, but not in a buff calendar-guy way. I mean, he looks really good, but he's not into hard-core bodybuilding."

"That's a point in his favor. Does he like blondes who have brains but not big bank balances?"

It felt good to laugh. "He's not your type, Helen." Noel pressed her fingertips to her eyelids and willed the last of the strain away. The fear lodged in her belly was a more difficult fix. "The kidnapper said Jack doesn't really see people, and he's probably right."

"I'm okay with just sex."

Noel thought longingly of a hot bath, a glass of wine and some soft jazz. "I imagine he's got a dozen bimbos on call at all times." She pictured Jack and shrugged. "Maybe not. He's tricky to read."

"But you're not." Helen stood. "White or red?"

"Red. In a big glass." She released a deep breath. "The kidnapper knew my mother was born in Italy."

Helen uncorked a bottle of merlot from Noel's cabinet. "Is that relevant?"

"It seems like an odd thing to put in a note. At the very least, it tells me the kidnapper's done his homework on everyone involved. All I get from this guy so far is the creepy feeling that I wouldn't want to meet him in a dark alley."

"Which, as his liaison, you could very well wind up doing."

Sipping her wine, Noel rose and went to the window. "I'll have to find a way to avoid that situation."

"And if you can't?"

"Don't be such a pessimist. There haven't been any meetings yet."

"What do you call that thing in Point State Park?"

"Jack was right about that. It was a test, but not on our part. It was an opportunity for the kidnapper to make his point. Wherever he wants me to go, I'm supposed to do it alone." Apprehension feathered along her spine. "Actually, that doesn't sound very promising, does it? It's a bit like walking into a prison cell and waiting for the door to clang shut behind you."

"You could turn him down," Helen suggested.

"I could." Noel regarded her friend over her shoulder. "But then what happens to Jack's sister?"

"I hate to sound heartless, but it isn't really your problem."

"I couldn't live with myself if she was killed simply because I refused to cooperate."

Helen shook her head. "Better you in this mess than me, hon. You know, there've been times when I've envied you, going off to Pittsburgh every Sunday night to rejoin the ranks of the swish and swanky. But I have to tell you, this isn't one of them. Notoriety can carry a hefty price tag. Speaking of which, is he paying you?"

"Jack?" Noel laughed. "No. And I can't see him paying the kidnapper, either."

"Don't tell me he's cheap."

"Not at all." She smiled a little as she thought back. "He doesn't like to be pushed. He uses the tactic, but doesn't like having it used on him. I think we're going to butt heads a lot in the next while."

Helen came over to catch her chin. "You do that, Noel. But while you're butting, remember to keep an eye on your back. I'm guessing that arrows aren't the only things this kidnapper knows how to shoot."

"YOU LIKE HER." Fastidious as always, even in a downtown deli, Michael Santos shook out a paper napkin and placed it across his lap. The suit was gone, but casual Gucci wasn't much of a step down.

"She's aggravating." Jack burned his tongue on hot coffee, winced and reached for a pickle. "She's logical, she's stubborn as hell, she dresses like you, and she smells great. But I've been having second thoughts since meeting her. She shouldn't be involved in this. It's not her burden."

"She's a lawyer. Taking on other people's burdens is her job."

"I'm not paying her to do this, Michael."

"You could offer," his friend pointed out. "Though from what you've told me and what Morris has unearthed about her, I doubt she'd accept."

"Why not?"

"Word is she got some heavy hitter cleared on an extortion charge a while back. It was a media circus. The guy was guilty as hell, the evidence against him weighty. But you know the deal— illegal search and seizure and other similar accusations cropped up during the trial. Noel was all over the prosecution. In the end, she did her job. Her partners applauded her courtroom prowess, but I gather she wasn't quite as thrilled as they were. She's been battling a conscience thing ever since. She takes on powerful, sometimes questionable, clients, wins or gets the cases against them dropped, accepts healthy checks for her services, then heads up to Winter Valley to do pro bono work so she can absolve herself of the guilt she feels for aiding and abetting the unworthy rich."

Jack hadn't known that and it brought a twinkle to his eyes. "So she's not Saint Noel. Good. Now maybe I can deal with her."

Shouldn't though, his own small voice of conscience reminded. She wasn't responsible for Caroline, or for him. "The guy knows how to shoot arrows, Michael."

"That's interesting, but you and I both took archery in school. So, I imagine, did half the other males in this country." He blew on his coffee while keeping a canny eye on his old friend. "Assuming the kidnapper's male."

It was a point, Jack conceded, though in his mind there was no question. He was dealing with a man. Women tended to use other means to finagle money out of him.

Michael looked up as his corned beef sandwich arrived. "Well stacked," he remarked and earned a chuckle from the waiter who was also the owner.

Jack came to this place often, but he never could remember the owner's name. Ernie, Arnie… Same as the sign on the deli, he supposed, but he couldn't remember that, either.

"Ham, Swiss and pepperoni," the man said to Jack. "Not one of our usual combos."

Jack took a bite, made a point of looking up. "You should add it to the menu."

The deli owner snorted. He had a mop of curly brown hair, an oversize mustache, dark eyes and dimples when he smiled, which he was doing now at a blonde in a tight skirt and high heels. It was a crooked sort of smile that had Jack glancing in the same direction.

"Someone you know?" he asked, nodding at the blonde.

"Not really. It's a guy dressed up as a woman. Calls himself Angela, but we've shortened it to Angie. Ray, my counterman, tried for a date last month. He got a bit of a shock when he found out the truth. Ray keeps busy slicing cold cuts now whenever Angie comes in."

"And this is your favorite place to eat, huh?" Michael said with a grin at Jack.

"Arnie gives good value for money," Jack replied.

"Artie," the owner corrected. "We do takeout for lunches and late nights if you're interested. The bigger the business, the better the rates."

"Talk to my senior VP about menus, Artie. He does more late nights, than me."

Michael chewed his food until the owner was back behind the counter, then he asked, "You've been introducing yourself to a few people lately, haven't you?"

"Artie was unavoidable. I tip him enough that he won't tell anyone he doesn't have to. And I had no choice with Noel."

"Who's also unlikely to mention it. She's good at her job, Jack. I checked. So did Morris. She's quick on the uptake, alert and damned smart. Martin Faber's had his own law practice since before your grandfather's partner died, and he couldn't wait to get his hands on her. Figuratively speaking, of course. He took her on and left his own son, Martin Junior, out in the cold."

With his mouth full, Jack asked, "Did you know Noel's mother is Italian?"

"I'd have guessed that by looking at her, but yes, I knew. FYI, her parents own a lodge in Vermont these days. She has three sisters, Ali and Diana, who are older, and Mara, who's younger by two years. She also has a wayward brother whom no one in the family talks about. Her father was born in Florida, her mother, as you said, in Italy. Is her Italian heritage significant for some reason?"

"It was worth a mention in the kidnapper's last note."

"Which I haven't seen yet."

"And won't until our lab guys are through with it."

"You think he left prints?" Michael sounded dubious.

Jack shrugged. "There might be something else."

"Like…?"

"That's for the experts to determine." Jack's expression darkened. "My problem is what to do with Noel."

Laughing, Michael dabbed his mouth with his napkin. "I can think of one thoroughly enjoyable thing right off. Mood light-

ing to start. A little wine, some good music, maybe paint her portrait, then a slow drift off to the bedroom."

Something in Jack's stomach curled. He didn't want to examine it too closely, because God knew he'd had a similar reaction to the woman—minus the painting part. It wasn't a
sensation he often experienced these days and as much as it intrigued him, it also irritated him. Getting involved with women
on a romantic level invariably messed up his life. He could sam-
ple and enjoy, but that was strictly physical. Emotions didn't enter into it.

"You want another cup of coffee over there?" Artie called
from the counter.

Jack shook his head. "We're good. What's my tab up to?"

"Including tonight, $396.40."

"Let me know when it hits five hundred."

"Smart man," Michael commented. "You're coming around
to the ways of true business. I have at least ten ongoing tabs in
the city."

Jack summoned a vague smile. "I don't like using credit
cards for sandwiches. This is the one and only place where I have
a running total."

"My sandwich and coffee included, I hope." Michael grinned.
"I'm flat again."

Jack took one last drink from his mug. "I warned you not to
buy that penthouse on the river."

"It was worth it. The developer came down fifty grand. Pent-
houses like this one impress, and I'm thinking about starting a
new relationship."

His sly smile brought Jack's eyes into sharp focus, and drew
a chuckle from his oldest friend. "You want to know if she's a
lawyer, so I'll simply say she might be. Remember, you snatched
Myrna Sales out from under my nose in high school. It's only
fair I should get even. Someday," he added at Jack's unpromis-
ing look. "But maybe not just yet, huh?"

Now he was irritating himself, Jack decided. Why should it matter to him if Michael wanted Noel? He sure as hell wasn't about to get mixed up with her. He set his jaw. Not in any way.

He scraped his chair back. "What time is it?"

"Ten past midnight." Noting the direction of Jack's stare, Michael shook his head. "I wouldn't do it, my friend. With the snow and wind, you couldn't get there before 2:00 a.m. You'll only tick her off, and then what'll happen to Caroline?"

Jack was undeterred. "Caroline's fate is my problem, Michael. It has nothing to do with Noel Lawson."

"And if the kidnapper thinks otherwise?"

Jack's features grew grim. "Then he'll have to revise his thinking or kiss off his ten million dollar payday."

CAROLINE RANSOM'S KIDNAPPER didn't claim to know every thought in Jack's head, but he could guess enough of them to keep things moving along at a brisk clip. You needed to do that with people like Jack. And, God help him, with Noel as well. Speed was the only thing that stood a chance of keeping them off balance. And making good on threats.

Having an ally was a plus, but usefulness was limited in this instance. Toward the end, it might actually become more of a hindrance than a help. No matter. Problems of this nature were as easily disposed of as Jack or Noel.

Not that he wanted either of them disposed of yet. No, sir. Not until they knew with whom they were dealing. And why.

A smirk twisted his lips as he gazed down at Caroline Ransom, asleep for the moment and twitching restlessly.

She wasn't as pretty as her brother, or as fortunate. Old Jacob had graduated from the old school where sons and grandsons inherited and daughters and granddaughters got trust funds. Either way, it was more than he'd ever gotten.

The smirk became a scowl. Resentment churned. He hated

Jack and despised Noel. They were going to pay for the rest of their lives.

However long he deemed that to be.

SHE WAS SITTING on the floor of her Winter Valley law office, surrounded by files and legal texts, jotting notes on a large white pad and taking the occasional poke at her laptop. Andy Williams was singing about the most wonderful time of the year while an animated Santa bumped his hips to the tune. Noel hummed along, completely immersed. Her heart didn't jolt until she spotted the worn tips of Jack's boots, and even then she kept her head down and her voice level.

"It says Office Closed on the door, Jack, and I know you can read. I saw you going over the menu at Eduardo's last night."

He crouched, released a breath. "I'm sure I mentioned how much I hate sarcasm."

She could have traded barbs with him, but to what end? Reaching up, she switched off her dancing Santa. "I have home and office telephones, you know. Fax, e-mail, cell, all the current toys. I also have work to do and, no, I don't want to go somewhere for lunch. As soon as I finish this last brief, I'm decorating my Christmas tree."

He lowered his lashes to study her. "With what?"

The question, so suspiciously asked, stirred her amusement. "Sparkling balls, garland, lights, icicles, berries from my neighbor's holly tree and some ribbons that Helen, my partner here, gave me."

"You're only in Winter Valley two days a week, Noel. Why go to all the trouble of doing up a tree when you hardly have time to enjoy it?"

She wasn't quite sure how to answer that. To buy time she set her notepad aside, checked her computer screen. Then she replied, "I suppose it's because my life in the city is so hectic. I have a condo, as I'm sure you know, but I never have time to decorate it. I do a row of fiber-optic trees and some LED lights, a few penguins, a poinsettia if one of my clients sends me one. But that's not Christmas, at least not the way I remember it." Why was she explaining this to him? "Don't you do anything festive for the holidays?"

He remained in his crouch. "I send Christmas cards."

"Your assistant does that. I mean you. What do you do, personally?"

He stared at her. "This isn't about me, Noel. I was going to drive up here last night, but as Michael nagged me into realizing, you wouldn't have appreciated a visitor at two in the morning."

"Well, I wouldn't have answered the door, that's for sure." She closed her computer, then asked him in a honeyed tone, "Would it have made a difference to you, or do you carry picklocks along with your gun?"

"Your door was open today. I only ignored the sign."

He hadn't answered the question, she noted, but didn't press. She asked more directly, "Why are you here, Jack? Did you get another note?"

"No, but when I do, I'll handle it myself."

She'd expected this. "Because Caroline's your sister and nothing to me, right?" On her knees, Noel began sliding her legal texts back onto the proper shelves. "I won't argue with you there. On a personal level, she's only a name, but then so are ninety-nine percent of my clients."

"They pay you to represent them."

"True." Standing, she dusted off her jeans and her hands. "Tell me, what makes you think you have any say in whether or not I'm involved? As difficult as this might be for you to accept, you're not the person in control here. Not of the kidnapper, not of me and not of the situation. Yes, I know." She swung her black wool coat over her shoulders and on. "You control the money the kidnapper wants. But what if you're wrong and he's out for, say, revenge only?"

Frowning, he looked up at her. "Why ask for ten million if revenge is his goal?"

"Why involve me if money is his singular motive? It's a double-sided coin, Jack. You won't win by flipping it, only by outwitting him. Or her."

He rose slowly. "Michael said that last night. I don't think it's a female."

Neither did Noel. "To be honest," she admitted, "I don't think gender's the issue. It's your attitude that needs changing."

"Look, bringing you into this was Michael's idea, not mine. I take care of my problems myself. All I'm trying to do is keep you from getting hurt."

"Thank you, but it's not your decision to make."

"I can't protect you, Noel."

"That's very thoughtful, Jack, but I don't need you to protect me. I'm a big girl, living and working in a big old world that isn't often pretty or nice. I do just fine by my own devices." She pointed at his boots. "Can you go out in the snow in those?"

"I can do anything in them."

The image that popped into her head both amused and unsettled her. Helen would definitely call him gorgeous, and Noel couldn't see herself arguing the point.

"Come on, then." She took his hand. "If you want to debate the state of your manhood, we can do it while we're gathering holly in my neighbor's garden."

His dark brows came together. Oh, yes, he was quite gorgeous, especially around the eyes and cheekbones. "I haven't eaten since last night." But when she tugged, he moved forward. "And I still don't want you involved."

"Yes, well, a man in your position should know how it works. More often than not, you don't get what you want."

"No?" For the first time that day, a smile touched his lips. When she stopped to open the door, he wrapped his fingers around her neck, tipped her head back and set his mouth on hers.

More surprised than upset, Noel held herself absolutely still. He tasted like sex, she decided, and knew that was dangerous ground for both of them right now.

Whatever his reason for doing it, she sensed he paid a price, because when he raised his head she glimpsed a measure of suspicion in his expression.

She didn't pull away, but regarded him through her lashes. "If you're trying to frighten me, Jack, it won't work. I don't scare easily."

He searched her face for a moment, then smiled, just a little, and lowered his head again. "That makes us even, because neither do I. But I do," he said as he recaptured her mouth, "usually get what I want."

Chapter Four

They spent a full hour cutting holly branches from her neighbor's tree. And they only had to climb a seven-foot fence and wade through a hip-deep drift of snow to get there. That he hadn't expected to be doing this was a minor point to Jack. He hadn't expected to kiss her, either, or enjoy the moment half as much as he had.

He had to admit, though, he'd wanted to do it since meeting her, and true to his word, he'd gotten what he wanted. The problem was, having had a taste, he wanted more.

The prickly holly leaves speared through his coat and even the waistband of his jeans. He couldn't say why he simply gritted his teeth and put up with the discomfort, although it might have had something to do with the sight of Noel bending and stretching to reach the perfect branches.

As if sensing his impatience, she hopped down, added a final sprig of berries to the mound in his arms and nodded at the back door of the dilapidated house behind them. "My neighbor, Fred Yost, lives here. He's eighty-nine years old. He has gout and a heart problem, and he just got engaged to an older woman. He left a note on my door saying he's rented his place out while he's away for the holidays."

Jack cocked his head. "His house is sinking on the north side."

"Yes, I've advised him to have the foundation shored up after the wedding. His fiancée uses a walker, and there's a definite tilt to the hardwood floors."

"Old Jacob threatened to cut Caroline out of his will when she suggested he buy a walker." Jack shifted his load, felt a leaf stab him in the stomach. "He used a mahogany stick and walked upright, even though it hurt like hell, until the day he died."

"On Christmas Eve." Rather than climb the fence again, Noel headed for the gate between the houses. "At least he didn't waste away like Jacob Marley."

"No, he watched Philip do that and swore he wouldn't die that way no matter what he was struck with."

"Philip Price." Pausing with her hand on the gate latch, she tested his name. "I can't picture him. What did he look like?"

"A Viking. I used to think of him as a modern-day Thor. He had two strokes at a young age, but that wasn't what got him in the end. It was kidney failure. A surprising number of people came to the funeral, most of them women. His ex never showed."

"Is she still alive?"

"Yeah, somewhere. She used to write Jacob and ask for money from time to time."

"Did he give it to her?"

"He made it a family event to burn her letters."

"Because she had affairs while she was married to his friend and partner."

"That'd be my guess."

"But it was fine for Philip to have affairs while he was married to her."

"Better than fine. Applauded."

She worked the stuck gate until it opened. "No offense, Jack, but your grandfather and Philip Price were Neanderthals."

"They came from a certain era."

"So did both my grandfathers and old Fred Yost. Fred mourned the loss of his wife for ten years before he ever asked another woman out."

"That's abnormal."

"Eye of the beholder, Jack." She took some of the branches from him. "Why did you kiss me?"

He'd known she would ask eventually. "I like your mouth," he admitted. Glancing sideways, he added wryly, "When it's not arguing with me."

"I argue for a living. I'm not stepping back from this. If it makes you feel better, even if I agreed with you and wanted to—which I don't—I can't see your sister's kidnapper letting me do it."

"That would be a bullying tactic, which you don't like. You could fly to Tahiti for Christmas."

"I could fly to Sugarloaf Key with my grandparents, but I'm not going to. You carry a gun. That's your thing. I kickboxed my way through college, both for fitness and for self-defense. I don't faint at the sight of blood, and my only real phobia involves big spiders that jump."

"Spiders jump?"

"They do in South America and on our own West Coast. Probably in Australia, too, but I've never been there."

"It's full of wide open spaces and insects you wouldn't recognize. I explored it for eighteen months between high school and college. I'd have stayed longer if my father hadn't died."

She forged a path to her back door. "You didn't want to be your grandfather's protégé, did you?"

"I didn't want to be my grandfather's grandson." When had his tongue gotten so loose, he wondered. "Michael would have been a better choice, but unfortunately, he wasn't blood."

"I suppose Caroline was out of the question for an old-school boy like Jacob Ransom."

"She wasn't in the running. I don't know if she wanted to be or not." He studied her from behind. "Why aren't you close to your brother?"

She smiled, but the look in her eyes told him she knew he'd changed the subject on purpose. "He's a thief. Petty, and for the usual reasons, but a thief all the same." She squared her shoulders, and he realized it was the first defensive gesture he'd seen her make. "I don't defend drug dealers, no matter how high-profile they are or what their more legitimate business concerns might be. I'm only a bit less regimented with users like my brother."

"So if I did cocaine, you'd take your holly branches, go inside and slam the door in my face?"

"If you did cocaine, Jack, you'd be too wasted to run a small business, let alone oversee an ever-expanding corporation."

"I might have good people on my payroll to do the overseeing for me."

"I'm sure you have an excellent staff, but anyone I deal with who knows you would denigrate you a great deal more if they suspected a dependency. Hold these."

She piled her branches onto his stack before he could object. He had to move his head or be clawed by a fresh batch of leaves.

He heard the doorknob rattle, but not the creak of hinges. "Jack?"

"Inside, Noel, now." A point stabbed him, and he swore. "These things are vicious."

"You better put them down."

His throat clutched a little at her tone. He dropped the sprigs and branches, met her gaze, then accepted the taped envelope she handed him.

There was no mistaking the sender or its recipient. Across the back in scrolled computer lettering were the words:

To My Lovely Liaison:
Let the game begin.

NOEL APOLOGIZED TO HELEN for leaving early and returned to the city in her car. She saw Jack driving behind her the whole way while the words of the kidnapper's message played in front of her eyes.

He hadn't said much, only that another note would be waiting for them at Schenley Park in Pittsburgh, and they'd have no trouble finding it. "Where changes occurred," he'd written, "more than twenty years ago."

Of course she'd understood his meaning. It had been directed at her. Yet as disturbing as that was, there was an even more ominous aspect for Noel.

The kidnapper had been in Winter Valley. In her yard. At her back door. A door she seldom locked or even used in the winter.

"He was watching us the whole time," she said to Jack on her car phone. "I told you I didn't think he was sane, and now I'm sure of it. It's deviant behavior to toy with people's psyches."

She hadn't meant to sound so clinical, but she was shaken and worried—and not merely about her own safety. Helen worked out of her house, and Aunt Madeleine lived there with her fifteen-year-old dog, Pepper. The big black Lab had little bark in him and even less bite since three quarters of his teeth had been pulled.

"I phoned the Winter Valley police chief before we left," she went on. "He said he'd have someone watch my place."

"You have more faith in cops than I do, Noel. Winter Valley has a very small force. I can send someone who's more committed."

The objection on her lips was a knee-jerk reaction. It almost slipped out before she caught herself. "I'll think about it, talk to Aunt Maddie." She breathed in. "Why is he sending us to the ice rink at Schenley Park?"

"Are you asking me or yourself?"

"Both and neither. I'm spooking myself, and that's bad at highway speed."

"In poor driving conditions. Slow down, Noel."

She checked her speedometer and immediately let up on the accelerator. "It doesn't mean anything," she murmured.

"He did it deliberately, but I already knew. I'm tied to this somehow." She sighed. "I used to skate in Schenley Park. My babysitter wanted to be a figure skater. She took my sisters and me there whenever she could, which was quite often because my parents were professionals and her boyfriend worked nearby. I sprained my ankle and my wrist learning how to do double toe loops." She returned to the note. "It's not a coincidence, Jack. This message was for me, unless— Does Schenley mean anything to you?"

"No. Jacob had an indoor rink built for kids. I played my junior hockey there, not at Schenley Park."

Momentarily sidetracked, Noel switched lanes. "Did your grandfather build the Winter Valley Arena?"

"He and Philip did, as a goodwill gesture to the community. It cost less than it would have if they'd undertaken the same project in Pittsburgh or New York."

They'd done what was necessary to maintain good relations with charitable organizations and, through them, with the public, Noel reflected. But philanthropy had obviously not been a priority.

Not that she had the right to pass judgment on either Jacob Ransom or Philip Price. The ability to make money was an extremely seductive thing. And giving back wasn't always at the top of a person's to-do list once he or she had been seduced.

It had taken time and more than a little family disapproval for Noel to understand and attempt to correct that flaw.

The North Side off-ramp approached. She had a good idea of where to go. As a child she'd changed from boots to skates and back under the same tree every day. The instructions would be waiting there.

And the maneuvering would begin.

Dear Jack,
Holly berries and snowdrifts? Have you gone rustic all of a sudden? It's not in your blood to care about Christmas,

so I can only assume you're extremely taken with my liaison. How lucky for you that I chose her.

Or was it luck?

Noel, come to the Carnegie Mellon University campus on Monday at 6 p.m. The sorority halls are decked for Christmas, but this time you'll be on the outside looking in. It's how more than the other half lives.

The benchmark of our lives lies in what we do with what we've learned. We don't always do enough, do we?

Ciao for now.

The Ghost of Christmas Past

NOTHING NOEL DID or tried to do could erase the kidnapper's last two notes from her head. Monday passed in a blur, which, thankfully, didn't involve any court appearances. But she had to force her thoughts into line as she met with various clients.

Martin Faber's son came to see his father, snubbed both her and their third partner, Sheila Kellman, and sailed into the big corner office unannounced.

Jack phoned her twice, Michael Santos once. Their fidgety legal counsel Morris sent three e-mails on Jack's behalf and finally used the telephone as she was clearing her desk.

"You understand what to do, I hope."

Noel found it difficult to respect lawyers who bit their fingernails down to the quick. It wasn't fair, but she couldn't help it.

She put him on speakerphone while she worked. "I memorized the note, Mr. Morris."

"And you'll come to our corporate offices after—well, after?"

"I told Jack I would."

There was a pause before he asked, "Are you frightened?"

He spoke as if he relished the idea. Moving her mouth close to the speaker, Noel countered with a silky, "Would you like to take my place, Mr. Morris?"

He coughed and, she imagined, stiffened his spine. "I wasn't the person he requested. As long as you're clear on your instructions, I'll leave you to it. I just thought I should call one last time on Mr. Ransom's behalf."

"That's kind of you" —no, it wasn't— "but I'm fine. You can tell Mr. Ransom he'll know what I know as soon as it's over." She kept her tone cool and professional. "Is there anything else?"

"Mr. Ransom has a dinner meeting tonight. It would help if you could be finished before 8:00 p.m. Good luck, Ms. Lawson."

Noel hung up then made a face at the phone, "'Good luck, Ms. Lawson.' Translation—I hope you get shot."

She shut her computer and her nerves down. Morris was an unfulfilled and spiteful man. She was more fearful than she wanted to admit, and she'd let him get to her for that reason. No one was going to be hurt on the Carnegie Mellon University campus tonight.

Again, she understood where the kidnapper wanted her to go. She'd attended Carnegie Mellon for three years after high school. She'd belonged to a sorority for two of those years. She'd lived on campus. She'd necked with a classmate on the bench outside the brightly decked halls of her sorority house. That had to be why he'd used the word benchmark in his note.

The Thanksgiving weekend had passed, but the campus grounds were snowy and sparsely populated when she arrived. The kidnapper knew all of that, just as he knew her.

So who was he, and what had she done to make him include her in his nightmarish game?

It had to involve Christmas in some way. Why else would he call himself the Ghost of Christmas Past? He wasn't a ghost, and neither was she or Jack.

"Yet," she said out loud and watched her breath disappear into the campus lights.

She remembered the paths with surprising clarity, but of course she'd loved walking around the grounds at night. Sometimes alone, sometimes not. Had she dated someone here who'd grown to hate her?

No, that was ridiculous. In her entire life, she'd only had three relationships serious enough to evoke strong feelings. None of those men would hate her. It had to be a professional grudge.

And linked to Jack. Yes, there was a connection. She and Jack had pissed someone off big-time. They must have, for matters to have reached such a state. She'd remind him of that tonight after—well, after.

Students with scarves covering half their faces drifted past in groups of two and three. One young man sent her a long look, pulled his muffler down and gave a long, low whistle, which made her feel a little better. Christmas lights twinkled in several of the high windows. Stars already winked overhead. From one of the buildings she heard Bruce Springsteen's version of "Santa Claus Is Coming to Town."

Cautiously, Noel approached the bench outside her old sorority. Her heart was racing.

She kept her eyes on the bench, searched it for an envelope. She saw footprints in the snow and several discarded fast food wrappers. Bells jingled somewhere, underscored by the tinkle of female laughter. Noel looked up at the sorority house, at the lights of the room she'd shared with Helen.

She knew even before the shadow fell over her that she'd made a mistake. She felt a swish of air; then suddenly, a gun barrel dug into her neck. She felt her right arm jerk up behind her back. A wool ski mask pressed against her cheek. The voice was a purr in her ear.

"I said alone," he whispered and gave her wrist a painful tweak. "Last warning, Noel. Next time anyone disobeys me, you die."

He shoved her into the bench. If she hadn't used her hands to break her fall, she would have stumbled face-first into the back of it. As it was, her gloved palm landed on a square of paper, tidily taped to the seat.

How had he done that?

She grabbed the note and spun in a single, quick motion. But all she saw was snow, the shadowy silhouette of campus buildings and a crisscross of empty paths.

With the envelope clutched in her fist, she pushed herself to her feet. And shouted, "Jack!"

She refused, absolutely, to let her temper snap. But she could still be furious with him.

"Are you out of your mind following me here?" She took a swat at the bench. "He had a gun, a big one. I could be dead right now, and all because you have this ridiculous idea that I need protecting."

"Watching," he corrected. He stepped out of the trees, but wisely didn't attempt to bridge the gap between them. "He couldn't have seen me. I've spent half my life being accused of sneaking up on people."

"Well, maybe this guy's part cat." Because Jack hadn't, Noel closed the distance to drill a finger into his chest. "He knew you were here. He told me if anyone disobeyed him again, he'd kill me."

Jack's expression was both somber and speculative. "He knew I'd follow you. He must have."

That was certainly possible, even likely. Noel let her head drop back and relaxed her muscles. "Fine, yes, maybe he knew. Maybe he realized you'd feel compelled to do it." Maybe the gun hadn't been loaded, but she doubted it. "The fact is, Jack, the kidnapper wants this to unfold his way, not ours." She opened the envelope as she spoke and by streetlight read the message inside. The tension returned, and her breath threatened to strangle her. "Your sister's in a lot of trouble."

He stood on the path with his hands jammed into the pockets of a jacket that was completely inadequate for the weather conditions and looked both miserable and tired.

"What does it say?"

She handed him the paper. Even a farsighted person could read the single word printed there.

POW!

Chapter Five

Noel returned to Jack's Pittsburgh office complex with him. He didn't work on the top floor, as she'd expected, but on the seventh, more than fifty stories away from the penthouse.

"Michael prefers to live and work in high places," he said by way of an explanation. "I don't."

She remembered a movie she'd seen as a child. "You don't like the idea of being trapped in a fire, do you?"

"I don't like traps of any kind."

"But you'll walk into them when it suits your purpose."

The elevator door slid open on seven, and he motioned her to the left. "If you're talking about Point State Park, I didn't and still don't believe that was a trap."

"I was referring to tonight, actually, and that was a most definite trap. I felt it snapping shut when the kidnapper stuck his gun in my throat." She ignored the exquisite fixtures and muted decor and hooked his arm to halt him. "Charging headfirst into battle with weapons blazing isn't always the best approach, Jack. I don't care what your grandfather taught you."

He didn't quite scowl, but it was close. "It works in business."

"Those people are rational. This guy is a fair distance short of that." At the stubborn expression on his face, she let her hand drop. "I give up. I don't even know why I came back with you. The Ghost didn't give us any more instructions, and he isn't likely to tonight."

"He might, but that's not why I wanted you to come. I'm meeting someone for dinner."

"Morris told me. It's seven forty-five. You're right on schedule."

"My date cancelled."

She stared at him. "She…?" Amusement began to brew. "That must have rankled. I assume this woman doesn't work for you."

"I don't date women who work for me anymore."

Meaning he had once and had probably been burned. "So, you what? Want me to sub for her?"

"It would make the situation less hostile."

"An illusion designed to lull the person you're meeting or to keep him or her from throwing a plate of food at you if he doesn't like what you say?"

A smile played on his mouth. "Both, I suppose."

Noel considered the prospect. She should be going over two important briefs tonight, but she was an early riser and her brain functioned better in the morning. Dinner with a raider sounded too intriguing to pass up. And there was always the possibility that he might kiss her again. She'd been obsessing about that a little more than necessary. It might be interesting, though definitely not smart, to find out why.

She glanced at her black pin-striped skirt suit. She had dress shoes in her car, and both the skirt and top were fashionably clingy, with or without the jacket.

Jack arched inquiring brows, and she nodded.

"All right, I will. But first," she said, smiling in a deliberately guileless fashion, "I want to know why your date cancelled."

"The man's name is Ralph Burnley. He manufactures auto glass. He has plants in Pittsburgh, Detroit, Seattle and Houston, with sales outlets in those centers as well as twenty other North American markets. That number used to be thirty-five. He's been training his nephew to take over the business, but it's not working out. The company lost twenty million dollars last year. That total will be up to thirty by the end of this fiscal year."

"So the prey's wounded, and the cat's moving in for the kill."

Jack gave his keys to the valet outside one of Pittsburgh's finest restaurants and took Noel's arm to guide her under the awning. "This is business, not life on the savanna. Do you want to talk about some of the clients you've defended?"

She let him help her with her coat. "Nice try, Jack, but our situations are far from comparable. I defend. The verdict is out of my hands. You take advantage, knowing full well you have the upper hand." She pivoted as she heard the strains of "The Coventry Carol." "I love this song on the harp." She turned back to Jack. "By the way, you clean up nicely." If you could call the dark hair that spilled over his forehead and the collar of his suit nice. Black on white gave him a roguish look, but thankfully not the aspect of a shark, or, as she tended to think of him, a hungry cat.

"I know Deirdre Burnley," she revealed as they were led through the elegant dining room by the maitre d'.

Their table was the perfect distance from the harpist and was flanked on both sides by a row of glistening white-on-white Christmas trees. All very well done, in Noel's opinion. The urban side of her appreciated it. The part that enjoyed snowball and pillow fights with her sisters would have welcomed a more confused color palette.

"How do you know Deirdre?" he asked.

"I met her through a friend of my father's, and, well, mine, too. Matthew Railback."

Jack's forehead creased. "Why does that name sound familiar?"

"He works for you, Jack. In your business equipment division."

"Sales or maintenance?"

"Sales management." At his blank expression, she shot him an exasperated look. "Tall man, dark hair, gray at the temples, mustache. Classically handsome."

Jack's eyes narrowed. "So who knew him first, you or your father?"

She shoved a discreet elbow into his ribs as Ralph Burnley stood to greet them. His wife remained seated.

Deirdre's expression was genuine, her hair a chin-length strawberry blond. At fifty-five, she hadn't gone under the knife and, as far as Noel was aware, she had no plans to do so. She had business sense and savvy, but from her body language, Noel suspected no particular affection for her husband. Which probably explained why Burnley Auto Glass was in financial distress.

Her face lit up when she spied Noel. "Oh, now, this is an unexpected pleasure!" She held out both hands. "I thought Jack was bringing Lorna."

Noel regarded Jack. "I thought he was bringing Miranda."

Jack's smile seemed a trifle forced. "Miranda cancelled, and Lorna and I haven't seen each other for two years."

Deirdre beamed. "Ah, well, she wasn't your type anyway, was she? Oh, she was smart and very lovely, but there was no zing."

Deirdre's husband, who'd been silent until then, made a dismissive sound. "We had two martinis while we were waiting for you, Jack. They seem to have gone straight to my wife's mouth. Should I know this young woman?" He inspected Noel from head to toe, made another sound that Noel took for a laugh and raised his nearly empty glass of scotch. "No, I'd remember someone like her."

Noel had encountered too many Ralph Burnleys to be offended. But Jack seemed unimpressed. She gave him a point for that and accepted the seat he held for her.

It was all banter to start with, small talk about current events, the weather and the Christmas shopping rush.

"My nephew hates the whole season," Ralph remarked. "Took off for the Cook Islands last week. Won't be back until after the New Year."

"That's our nephew's answer to a crisis," Deirdre confided

to Noel. "Whether distressed in business or in his personal life, his motto is 'Flee the scene.'" She raised her glass in a mock toast to her husband. "He learned from the best in that regard. In many regards actually, right down to his temper. Mix it with alcohol, and you've got nitro poured on dynamite."

"Are you talking about Ralph or your nephew?" Noel asked.

Deirdre shrugged. "Take your pick." She sipped her drink. "Ralph and I don't live together anymore, and I will say, he never hit me when we did. He's a ball of frustration and bluster, my hubby, but he lacks the killer instinct. You know, Jack got the tire company from him three years ago for a song."

Her curiosity piqued, Noel nudged her chair closer. "Was your husband upset?"

"It's hard to say. He gets angry over so many things. Matthew only had to give him a tiny poke in the arm when they were children to set Ralph off. You know Matt well, of course."

"Matthew Railback?" Noel glanced at Jack and Ralph, who were deep in their own conversation. "Were he and Ralph friends as children?"

"Not friends." Deirdre sampled the shrimp creation that had just been placed before her. "Brothers. Half brothers actually— different fathers, same mother. But of course Matthew's always been so charismatic, and Ralph has the charm of a cranky ape."

Stunned, Noel sat back in her chair. She'd known Matthew Railback for almost five years. She'd met his father and his mother. She'd been involved with him for six months, yet not once had he so much as hinted at a half brother named Ralph.

Ralph's voice rose. "You rape people, Jack. You wait them out. Wherever you can, you force their hands. You stole my line of tires." He sounded equal parts outraged and drunk. "If my nephew was here, he'd..."

"Take the money Jack's offering and run," Deirdre inserted. "He's a spineless young man, and you know it."

While Ralph griped on to Jack, Noel asked, "Deirdre, how many brothers does your husband have?"

"Three full brothers. One's dead—he was our nephew's father. One lives in Turkey, and the third is a charter airline pilot in Alaska." She tapped a finger on the back of Noel's hand. "Matthew hasn't seen any women for quite a while. I suspect he never really got over you, Noel. For what that's worth, coming from a woman who, once upon a time, would have sold both her husband and his auto glass company for a five-day fling with him."

"Only five days?"

"I never was as greedy as my husband, or as ambitious as Matt. Not that those traits have paid off for either of them, but you know the old cliché. You won't get if you don't try. And try and try and try."

Noel picked up on the inference but disagreed. "Matthew's done very well for himself, Deirdre. He wasn't cut out to be a CEO or even a VP."

"Failure and success are matters of perspective and degree." Deirdre kicked her husband's ankle under the table. "Keep your voice down, Ralph. This isn't the center ring."

No, it was enlightenment. But Deirdre was wrong about her and Matthew, Noel decided. They'd ended their relationship almost four years ago. Among other problems, the age gap had been unbreachable. And he'd been just a bit too easygoing for her taste. He lacked a steel spine and a fighting nature. He'd also shot birds for sport, lent her wayward brother money and had no feeling for Christmas.

Jack broke her concentration when he speared a glazed carrot from the artistic canvas that was her fourth course. "Time to wake up, Noel."

She zoned in and noticed Ralph weaving a path across the floor. "Is he leaving?"

Jack shook his head. "Men's room."

She'd gone right off planet, Noel realized. "Where's Deirdre?"

"A friend nabbed her. They're on the other side of the big Christmas tree. Did she say something to upset you?"

"Hmm? No. I was thinking about someone I used to know." She faced him, head tipped to the side. "Tell me, Jack, deep down, do you like Christmas?"

He looked as if he thought it might be a trick question. "In what way?"

"In the not-Scrooge way. In the 'I like turkey and stuffing and being with other people' way."

Humor flitted through his eyes. "Is this a hint that you want me to give you a present?"

"Like my own auto glass company?" She picked up her wine. "Do yourself a favor, Jack. Buy it from Ralph and offer Deirdre the job of CEO. Make it worth her while in a way her husband never did, and the company will turn a profit within eighteen months, maybe less."

Jack clinked his glass to hers. "You read my mind, darling," he said. And kissed her before she could drink the toast.

It was hot, hard and fast—and over before she could blink.

"Why—" She had to regroup quickly. "Why do you keep doing that?"

"You have a great mouth, Noel."

"I know a few prosecuting attorneys who'd disagree with you, but I'm flattered, I think. You really shouldn't kiss me like that in a public place. People love to gossip."

"Not about Jack Ransom. Didn't you hear the name I gave the maitre d'?"

"I was listening to the music." Which had unfortunately given way to the piano.

"I use the name Jacob when I come to restaurants. Philip Jacob."

"I take it you don't want your own name paving the way."

"Brownnosers grate after a while."

"Most people would say it depends which side you're on. Yours is hardly the unpleasant one." She thought for a minute. "Why do you suppose the name Jacob's so popular all of a sudden? I'm hearing it everywhere."

"It's my grandfather's name. And Ebenezer's dead partner. You hear his name a lot at this time of year."

"I guess so." She went over it again, then shook it off. "Not important. Are you going to buy Ralph's company?"

"He's out of money and options, so yes."

"At a fair price?"

"He'll be able to stuff several mattresses comfortably."

Her eyes danced. "So you hate sarcasm, huh?"

"What sarcasm? Ralph's known for being a mattress stuffer, or he used to be. What were you and Deirdre talking about?"

She ran her gaze over the perfectly aligned white trees. "Mutual friends. Family ties. Apparently, Matthew Railback is Ralph's half brother. I didn't know they were related until Deirdre told me tonight."

Jack's frown gave him a sulky look that Noel found surprisingly sexy. "Ralph Burnley's in his mid- to late fifties, Noel. How old is his half brother?"

"Fifty now. When we dated, forty-six, so, yes he's twenty plus years older than me. It was no one's business then and it's no one's business now, right?"

"Hmm."

"Do you want to tell me about Miranda?" she teased.

"She does photo shoots for corporate magazines. I've known her since I was five. She has a thing for Michael."

"But not vice versa?"

A vague smile appeared. "No. Anything else?"

"Lorna?"

"A one-month relationship that never quite got off the ground. We had three okay weeks in a resort in the Bahamas. When we got back and reality set in, things fizzled."

God, his love life sounded like hers. It was terrifying to hear the mirror image version and realize he might have been talking about almost every man she'd been involved with.

"I don't think I like this conversation," she decided, and took too big a drink of wine. "I'm seeing myself in you, and it's not nice."

"Two of kind, darling."

"Only in one area, Jack. I happen to like people. And Christmas."

"I—" He closed his mouth. "I don't have a problem with Christmas, but you can't expect me to participate in a lot of holiday festivities when my sister's being held for ransom."

"The payoff might or might not be the finale to this guy's game, Jack. Remember the first note you got, the one Michael showed me at my house? It said you were going to suffer for what you and your grandfather had done in the past. It also said the suffering wouldn't be easy or fast. And there was a reference to your name being on the kidnapper's wish list, with another close behind it."

He stared in solemn amazement. "Do you have a photographic memory? I don't remember all that, and I have good recall."

"I'm a quick study when I need to be." She found herself straightening his tie, and immediately withdrew her hand. "I think you were right when you said we need to start looking more closely at ourselves and the things we've done. Things that might have caused serious anger or resentment. We move in similar circles. We probably know a good number of the same people."

"Like Deirdre Burnley?"

"Yes, for example, though her head's screwed on just fine."

"How's Matthew Railback's head?"

Amusement bubbled up. "I don't think he's too fond of you."

"Why not? I don't even know him."

"Exactly. But don't you think you should? He's been with Ransom Price for twenty-five years and in an executive position for over eleven of them." The expression on Jack's face gave him away. She caught his chin again. "You don't know if you know him or not, do you? Do you?" she demanded when he didn't respond.

His eyes came up, fastened on hers. "Do you know everyone who works in your law office?"

"Of course I do."

"Multiply that number by a thousand or more, Noel, and you'll be in my league. And that total only accounts for the Pittsburgh offices of Ransom Price."

She sighed. "I don't expect you to be on a first-name basis with your mailroom staff, Jack, only with the executives." She hesitated as a man's sullen face flashed in her mind. "Martin Faber Junior," she said. "He's done work for some of your board members."

"Is that significant?"

"Maybe."

"Which means?"

"He dislikes me. His father didn't make him a partner in the firm so he struck out on his own. Last I heard, he wanted to get into corporate law. He's handled at least three divorces within your corporate infrastructure. Old Martin said that was his son's idea of greasing wheels."

Jack rubbed a tired eye. "I'll talk to Michael and to Morris. But even if Faber Junior is on retainer to us, he's unlikely to have a grudge against me."

She conceded that. "I still think those are the kinds of avenues we need to explore in order to unmask Caroline's kidnapper. And there's obviously some involvement with Christmas."

Reaching around, he straightened her jacket, which had slipped sideways on the back of her chair. "Or maybe kidnapping Caroline is someone's idea of a twisted birthday gift."

Noel raised a brow.

Again that hint of a smile crossed his mouth. "Christmas is family and friends and decorating to you, Noel, but when I was a kid, all it ever did was bring me another year closer to the time when I'd be bulldozed into the family business. My birthday's December twenty-fifth. I was born at 12:01 a.m. on Christmas Day."

Chapter Six

The week passed without another note from the kidnapper. Jack understood how alone he was familywise when he couldn't think of a single relative he could call and talk to about this.

There was Caroline's most recent ex. He'd worked for Ransom Price once, but Jack had cut him loose after the breakup. In truth, he'd only given the guy a job because Caroline had made him feel guilty.

"You hire Michael's friends to work for you," she'd complained at their Winter Valley estate last year, "but when I ask you to do one little favor for me—and it's not much of a favor, because Steve's an excellent graphic artist—you say no."

What he'd said was maybe, but Caroline seldom listened. She'd harangued him all weekend until, for the sake of spending a peaceful evening watching a Penguins–Flyers hockey game, he'd given in.

Their relationship had lasted for seven-plus months. The day they'd broken up, Jack had made a point of firing the lazy jackass personally. Five people in the advertising department had shaken his hand. One of the senior members, Hilda Ruchinsky, had sent him a platter of homemade breads and cakes.

He'd appreciated the food, and it pleased him that he still remembered her name. Of course, she'd watched out for him as a kid on several occasions when his father had been out of town and old Jacob had taken custody of him.

Kidnapping had never been far from Jacob's mind, although Jack couldn't recall a single occasion when his grandfather had insisted on watching over Caroline.

Shoving the memory aside, Jack looked up to clear his head. He found Michael perched on the corner of his desk.

"Was that a trance or a daydream?" his friend asked.

"A guilt trip mostly." Jack checked the time. "Seven-twenty already?" He ran his hands over his face. "It seems like I just got here."

"Well, you didn't, and with one notable exception, you've been sitting at this desk since 7:00 a.m. with your head buried. Annabelle told me the only thing you've said to her all day is, 'Have you gotten through to Noel Lawson yet?'"

"It was the only roadblock I kept hitting all day. I've left messages on all her phones and with her legal assistant."

"She was probably in court, Jack. Time-outs there are called at the judge's discretion, not hers." He grinned. "Anyway, she's been in touch."

Jack's head came up. "When?"

"Twenty minutes ago. You weren't at your desk—that's the exception I mentioned—so Annabelle put her through to me, as per your instructions."

Swiveling, Jack stared out the window at the building next door. It was glass and steel and concrete and reminded him of his grandfather. "What did she say?"

"She wants to see you. Play catch-up, I imagine. No," he said, raising a hand, "she didn't mention a note."

Jack slid a hand through his hair, held it briefly off his face while he regarded his desktop. "This guy has gotten personal with her in the last two notes, almost as if he was talking more to her than to me."

"He knows things about her life, that's for sure. But the knowledge could be a smoke screen."

"To make us think he has a grudge against both of us, when he really doesn't?"

"And while you're tied up in knots searching for a connection, he goes about business as planned."

"It's a thought," Jack agreed. "What did Noel say?"

"Oh, this and that. I enjoyed talking to her. She's a stimulating conversationalist."

The snarl in Jack's throat almost made it to his lips. "What kind of this and that, Michael?"

His friend grinned. "She likes Gilbert and Sullivan, for one. She was going to come here, but I figured somewhere away from the office environment was probably healthier for both of you. I suggested your favorite deli."

He was hungry, Jack realized. Had he eaten today? "Did you phone in an order while you were at it?"

"I sense Noel won't be as fond of ham, cheese and pepperoni as you are." He flicked his wrist to glance at his Rolex. "I told her seven-thirty. Leave now and you'll only be ten minutes late."

As Jack stood to search out his black wool jacket from its peg in the closet, his forehead creased. "Mike, Hilda Ruchinsky still works for us in advertising, doesn't she?"

"Are you kidding? Her coconut fudge cookies are a Friday afternoon event. I copped two before she left tonight."

"I want to talk to her."

"Not about her cookies, I presume." Michael let out a deep breath. "Caroline's ex?"

"He struck me as a vindictive little snot."

"I'll have him checked out. Where, what, who, as well as any possible connection to Noel. Hilda'd be a good source if you want the fast inside track to his mind-set when he left."

"I'll talk to her tomorrow."

"Tomorrow's Saturday, Jack," Michael patiently reminded

him. "Look, go see Noel before she decides you're not worth the wait and takes off for Winter Valley. I've got a hot date tonight, and I like to think the same could be said of you."

At the door, Jack jingled his car keys. "Noel and I aren't date material. Not separately or together."

"Cut right to the sex, then. It'll do you good. Trust me."

The ghost of a smile appeared. "I do trust you, Mike, but we're not the same. We never were."

Friendship aside, he and Michael had always been worlds apart, Jack reflected as he flipped up his collar in the empty corridor. Had been in the past, were in the present and would be in the future. Old Jacob's legacy had ensured that.

NOEL CONSIDERED LEAVING, but decided to wait another fifteen minutes. Jack might not look, dress or often act like a corporate mogul, but that was precisely what he was. Responsible and burdened. He wouldn't drop important business matters, no matter how hard his senior VP pushed him.

A man in a smeared white apron and cap clopped over. He had a scruff of three-day whiskers, slightly stooped shoulders and a Navy tattoo on his forearm. One eyelid drooped lower than the other, and his fingernails, though clean, were ragged.

His voice was surprisingly high when he asked, "You want more coffee, ma'am?"

"Love some," she said and, because he reminded her of a lost dog, smiled at him. "Do you own this place?"

"I work here." He cocked a thumb. "Behind the counter mostly, but sometimes Artie, he takes off and tells me to watch the place. So I do. He took off at the wrong time today, though. I tell him, all the pretty ones come in when he leaves." One droopy eye closed, the other lowered in suspicion. "You're a real woman, right?"

"Sometimes I feel more like a robot, but most days, yes, I'm a woman. What's your name?"

"Ray. That one over there, he's really a guy." Ray pointed to somebody behind her. However, when Noel turned to look, all she saw was the waistband of a man's pants.

"Who—Ah, Jack."

Jack motioned toward a blonde sitting alone in the corner. "He's talking about that guy."

"Comes in here all dolled up," Ray said, "sits down and writes in his stupid notebook. Then suddenly, like tonight, Artie ups and leaves, and I gotta deal with him."

"In the meantime, you can deal with us." Jack took the seat at a right angle to Noel's. "Ham, pepperoni and Swiss on pumpernickel for me. Noel?"

"Is it after eight?"

"Five to, why?"

"A toasted bagel with cream cheese," she told Ray.

"I'll bring coffee with it." Sending the blonde a final dour look, the counterman hastened off.

Jack regarded Noel. "Why eight?"

"If I've already had dinner, I don't eat after eight."

He continued to stare. "It's a woman thing, right?"

"Obviously not a thing your sister does, or would you know her habits."

"I can still bring my sister's face, and several of her habits, to mind. You've never seen her, have you?"

"No. Does she look like you?"

"She used to look like Jacob, but that changed when she hit her mid-teens. Then she wanted to look like a cross between Elle MacPherson and Julia Roberts."

"Did she make it?"

"You decide." He pulled a worn leather wallet from his back pocket, flipped it open and handed it to her.

Noel studied the image. "Actually she looks a bit like Peppermint Patty." At Jack's uncomprehending expression, she explained. "You know from Peanuts. Freckles, red hair, cute face."

"She hates that word. Puppies are cute."

"It's just a word, Jack. How would you describe your sister?"

He waited until Ray deposited their plates before he answered. "Whiny, but with reason."

"At the risk of sounding too personal, I don't sense a lot of affection, even now that she's missing." She touched his hand before he could pick up his sandwich. "You must have some feeling for her, if not now, then from the past. Or were your childhoods so completely bereft?"

She saw the resignation on his face. "We were never friends, never close. It just didn't happen, okay? Caroline didn't ask for attention, she demanded it, loudly. She used to bang her Barbie dolls over my head when she wanted something. The hitting was seldom preceded by a question."

She got the picture, and it wasn't pretty. "I suppose," she said, inspecting a crumb on her cream cheese, "it's the optimist in me that hopes you'll be closer to her when this kidnapping is resolved." If it was resolved, she thought but didn't add that.

Jack knew, though. She saw it in his eyes as he bit into his sandwich.

"Do you know Peter Greaves in legal?" Jack asked as Noel ate her bagel.

"He used to be Martin Faber's partner, didn't he?"

"Before you joined the firm."

"Quite a while before. I don't think he'd be upset with me for anything."

"What about Matthew Railback?"

She couldn't resist a small laugh. "You're really stuck on him, aren't you? It's over, Jack. We're done. We ended it almost four years ago."

"Amicably?"

"I'd say so."

"In that case, you must have done the ending."

"I did, yes, but he'd have gotten around to it. Matthew likes to take his time with things, not plunge in feetfirst."

She felt his scrutinizing gaze on her face. "How serious were you?"

The possible reasons for his question tantalized, but Noel chose not to consider them. Yet. "I thought it could work. For a while. But, for example, he was into Deep Purple, Jim Morrison and Janice Joplin and I preferred the Pretenders, Prince and Elton John."

"No Beatles?"

"I like them, Matthew doesn't. Jack, he's not behind this, whatever he might think of you. At his nastiest, he'd never be anything more than passively aggressive."

"What do you call the kidnapper's notes?"

"Psychotic. And there was nothing passive about the gun he shoved into my throat."

Guilt registered but was quickly covered as Ray approached them again. "Got a message for you," he said, looking from one to the other.

Jack glanced at the man's hand, but there was no envelope. "Where is it?"

"Came by telephone," the counter man explained. "It was a guy. He said I should tell you to come to the Ransom Price office tower over on Fifth."

Jack's brow furrowed. "Was the message for Noel or me?"

"For both of you. Jack and Noel. You're both supposed to go there."

"Did he say where in the office tower?" Noel asked.

"He told me to tell you to go in the back way and to follow the lights."

"Put the food on my tab," Jack said to Ray as they left.

The street was a mess of mud and slush and out-of-sorts drivers who'd been forced to work late on a Friday night. Noel located her keys, but Jack caught her hand before she could turn for her car. "It's better if we go together."

She agreed but noted, "This isn't right, Jack. He's diverting from his established pattern."

Jack offered no comment, not that she'd expected him to.

Noel's mind spun with possibilities. She added one more into the mix while she buckled up in the passenger seat of his BMW four-by-four. The cross-dresser from Artie's Deli stood on the street corner under filmy lamplight and watched them through a haze of cigarette smoke.

THEY ENTERED THE Ransom Price Tower by a rear service door. Jack had keys and cards that he used to access various dark corridors.

They crept along what felt like the hundredth passageway, heading toward the front of the building. Jack hadn't lied; he was good at sneaking around. He didn't make a sound when he walked, and he was wearing a pair of worn but sturdy boots.

"Stay behind me," he said and kept a firm grip on her arm.

"There." She spied a glowing green light. "That way."

They turned left. The shadows shifted, as if the darkness itself were watching them. There was a red light, then a gold one and finally a shower of soft blue.

She tapped Jack's shoulder. "Where are we?"

"Behind the ground-floor conference room. The ballroom area."

She halted. "Jack, I've been thinking..."

The rest of her sentence was drowned out when the six-inch thick door swung open, and Michael Santos appeared. Music from trombones and trumpets, drums and saxophones spilled out. There was light, laughter and a huge twenty-foot Christmas tree, decorated from lowest bough to starry top. The song was "Joy to the World" and Mannheim Steamroller couldn't have played it better. Or louder.

Shock registered on Jack's face. Before he could react further, Michael clapped him on the back, winked at Noel and ushered both of them inside.

With the exception of his senior VP, not one of the three hundred people noticed their arrival.

Noel looked up. The ceiling was a black arch studded with

red, gold and silver spotlights that resembled stars. People, obviously employees at Ransom Price, milled and mingled, chatted and sang. They were dressed in party clothes, so stunning in some cases that Noel actually sighed. She had exquisite silk creations at home, but that didn't help her out here.

Jack rounded on Michael, his features explosive. "You sent that message to Artie's?"

Michael stood his ground. "If I hadn't, would you have come? Would you even have remembered that tonight was the executives' Christmas party?"

"You put us through hell."

"I sent a verbal message. Atypical for your Christmas Ghost." Unperturbed by Jack's thundercloud expression, Michael swept an arm over the crowd. "Lighten up for a night. There's food and drinks. The band's in from New York, the champagne's fifty years old. You're paying, Jack, so you might as well enjoy it. Hang on, okay, I'll be right back."

Jack cast a slitted sideways look at Noel. "Did you know about this?"

She started to shake her head, paused, then shrugged. "I figured it out while we were sneaking through the hallways. The message was out of character for the kidnapper."

Jack's expression, somewhere between sullen and sulky, remained in place. She prodded his arm. "Come on, take Michael's advice and lighten up. Parties are for having fun. I'm guessing you don't do that very much."

"Noel!"

At the sound of her name, she glanced up. "Helen?" Astonishment rolled through her. "What are you doing here?"

"I closed up shop for the day." Her friend offered a huge grin and a hug that smothered. "Your aunt Maddie's home with Pepper and, well, Michael called and suggested I should come, so I said goodbye to *White Christmas* on DVD and hello to the city lights."

"You know Michael?" Jack put in from Noel's side.

"I phoned him right after Noel came hobbling in from Point State Park and gave him hell for accosting her like he—and you—did. He was very nice and calm, and he let me abuse him quite severely. When I finally stopped ranting, we started to talk." Her cheeks went pink. "You have a charming senior vice president, Mr. Ransom."

Noel's head was still reeling. Belatedly, she remembered her manners. "Helen, this is Jack Ransom. Jack, my best friend and associate, Helen Stowe."

"We were roommates in college," Helen explained. "I was four years older than her, yet she pulled me through law school on her coattails."

Noel began to protest, but Helen cut her off with a laugh.

"I'm kidding, hon. Honestly, I've been into the champagne. It's delicious and heady." When Jack's brow remained knit, her expression grew solicitous. "You didn't get another note, did you?"

"No. Ah…" Looking past Helen, Noel worked up a dazzling smile. "Hello, Matthew."

Jack's head snapped around. "Where?"

"Tall guy, mustache, dark, curly hair, at five o'clock," Noel said through her smile. She held out her hand, kissed Matthew on both cheeks and drew back to perform the introductions. "You remember Helen," she said. "And of course Jack."

"We've met." Matthew's light blue eyes carried a perpetual twinkle.

While the men shook hands, Helen sidled over to whisper, "Jack's hot, Noel, in a scruffy vagabond sort of way."

"He has an aura," Noel admitted. And, although it really shouldn't have, it shone a great deal stronger than Matthew's. Then again, that might have had something to do with the fact that her gaze kept wandering to Jack's mouth. It was expressive and sexy, and she'd been fantasizing about kissing it, and him, since he'd arrived at the deli.

Michael, who'd disappeared moments before, returned. To Noel's amazement, he slid an arm around Helen's waist. "Dance?" he asked. Blushing, Helen handed her champagne to Noel.

"Only one life to live, right?" she murmured as she left.

Noel took a big drink from the glass. Disinclined to interrupt whatever conversation Jack and Matthew were having, she surveyed the crowd of executive partygoers.

Exotic scents drifted past. Cinnamon and spice wove their way into the mix. A female soloist sang "Have Yourself a Merry Little Christmas" at a tempo conducive to slow dancing. She spotted Helen and Michael again and marveled at the twists and turns fate occasionally took.

Her eyes were traveling up the sparkling tree when Matthew's arm wrapped itself around her shoulders and squeezed.

"I've missed you," he said in her ear.

She made no attempt to free herself despite Jack's dark look. "Time's passed, Matthew. A lot's happened since we split up."

"My point exactly."

"I went for dinner with Jack on Monday night. Deirdre Burnley was there."

His light blue eyes perused the dance floor before coming to rest on her face. "I heard about that. Another company sucked into the corporate melting pot."

Six feet away, Jack remarked, "Burnley doesn't have to sell to me. He can dissolve the business."

Noel slipped out from under Matthew's arm. "Jack has some good ideas for Burnley Auto Glass." At least, she hoped he did. "Takeovers aren't necessarily deals struck with the devil, Matthew."

Matthew's teeth flashed. "You never met Jacob Ransom. Or Philip Price, for that matter. The devil had nothing on those two, and I wouldn't think he has much on Jack here, either. No disrespect intended," he said, but his smile had a glittering edge.

Not good, Noel reflected. She gravitated to Jack's side and set her mouth close to his ear. "Wanna dance, boss man?"

His mouth turned down, his brows came together. "Here?"

"Well, there is music, and lots of people are doing it. And it'll get us out of an uncomfortable situation."

For an answer, he shed his jacket, tossed it onto an empty chair, polished off her champagne and handed the glass to Matthew. "Excuse us."

The dance was slow, very close and there were many couples enjoying it. The word *mistake* flitted through Noel's mind as Jack drew her against him. Still, life was all about taking chances. Or so Aunt Maddie insisted. She let her body relax into him.

"What did you think of Matthew?" Noel asked. She kept her eyes on his when he answered.

"He seems more like a serial adventurer than business management material."

"He likes to climb mountains. He wants to assault Everest before he turns fifty-five."

"He'll be lucky to make base camp."

"You don't like him."

"Too much polish, Noel. I'm not big on egos."

"Michael's polished," she pointed out.

"It comes naturally to him." He caught her gaze. "You really shouldn't look at me like that."

"I know." He smelled like soap and warm skin. She wanted to kiss him. "Did I mention that I find your mouth quite fascinating."

His lips quirked. "That's my line, isn't it?" His eyes shifted direction for a second. "Your ex is watching us."

"The operative word being *ex*. He didn't control me when we were involved. He certainly doesn't now."

Jack dropped his gaze to her lips. With an inviting smile, Noel fisted his hair.

This time when he kissed her, it was hot, hard and very thorough. He tasted like champagne, and he really did know how to kiss. Every thought in Noel's head simply melted away. She slid both hands into his hair and reminded herself to breathe. His tongue was doing incredible things to her mouth, so much so that she almost forgot where they were.

Her hands moved from his hair to his chest and down. She only caught herself because one of the dancers bumped her elbow.

They broke apart, and for an instant stopped dead on the floor. Noel struggled to get air into her lungs and realized Jack was doing the same. This wasn't what she'd expected at all.

"Damn," Jack said, then, as someone jostled him, took her hand and resumed the dance. "That wasn't supposed to happen."

Noel still wasn't entirely sure what had happened, so she settled for keeping silent and letting her mind clear.

Matthew had never kissed her like that. No one had. Tipping her head back a little, she eyed him in mild suspicion. "Who taught you to kiss so well, Jack?"

"I was going to ask you that question." He touched his forehead to hers. "Do you want to stop?"

Amusement asserted itself. "Kissing or dancing?"

He half smiled. "What do you think?"

It didn't matter in the end. The slow song ended, and a more up-tempo one took its place.

People were finally beginning to notice Jack. Noel watched him as they headed toward the long bank of buffet tables. Men called out to welcome him. So did women. One woman in her sixties, with gray-brown hair and a poinsettia fastened to her waist, rushed over to plant a kiss on his cheek.

"Good Lord, you're the last person I expected to see."

"Hilda." He didn't appear the least bit uncomfortable. "I forgot you might be here."

"Thought I wouldn't be into this kind of party? Sixty-eight's not dead. And if you mention the word *retirement,* I'll clip you a good one. Who's your lady friend? I'm Hilda Ruchinsky," she said before Jack could reply. "I used to bandage his knees when he fell off his skateboard in the underground parking lot. Never told old Jacob about that, and I don't expect he noticed." She fanned her heated face with her hand. "Have we met before, dear?" she asked Noel.

Noel searched her memory. "I'm not sure. Do you have a sister named Gerta?"

"That's it." Hilda snapped her fingers. "You represented her when she got divorced. Oh, that was a few years ago. You were fresh out of law school, but I could tell you knew up from down. You remember Gerta, Jack. She was married to Harry Dexter in Accounting."

"Harry Dexter?"

"He accused old Jacob and her of having an affair, or, well, he thought it. He would never have gone up and actually accused the old man of anything. Harry and Gerta lost their son in September. He worked in one of our steel factories."

"Did he die on the job?" Noel asked.

"No, it was lung cancer."

"Related to smoking?"

"Actually, no. He didn't smoke. Naturally, that got Harry going. He started pestering Michael when the boy was diagnosed. Harry figured Jacob and Jack didn't monitor the emissions within their factories like they should. Oh, it's all bunk, but if you knew Harry, you'd understand his reasoning. He'll probably show up here tonight, if only to consume his allotment of food and drink. Gerta's doing fine, by the way. She's devastated by the loss of her son, but otherwise happily remarried and living in South Dakota."

"Harry Dexter." Jack continued to mull over the man's name.

Chuckling, Hilda patted his arm. "Like his granddad when it comes to names and faces, but not like him at all in the ways that count. I'll point Harry out to you if I see him. And, Noel, you make sure this one stays for at least another hour, you hear me? That's a whole hour, Jack."

"Hilda, wait." Jack forestalled her when she would have left. "I need some information about Steve Crookshank, Caroline's ex."

Hilda folded her arms. "He's an idiot, and we're well shot of him. That's the best information I can give you."

"How did he react after I fired him?"

"Let's just say he called you a few ugly names. Most of them under his breath."

"Do you know if he's still in Pittsburgh?"

"No idea. I imagine so. His family's here, aren't they? And I wouldn't put it past him to try and patch things up with Caroline." She held up a warning finger. "A whole hour, now, Jack. Promise me."

"Yeah, sure." His smile was distracted. "An hour."

Noel waited for ten seconds before she nudged his arm. "Are you still on Earth, Jack? Harry Dexter and Steve Crookshank. Both men sound antagonistic toward you. The question is, is either of them kidnapper material?"

"Steve's a definite candidate. Harry Dexter's…" He gave his head a faint shake. "He's a blank."

The aroma of pasta sauces, cheese, cold cuts, quiche and sausage rolls reached her. Turning Jack, she steered him toward the tables. "I'm going to break my no-food-after-eight rule just this once. On the way, I'll give you my take on Mr. Harry Dexter."

"He sounds like a jackass."

"He's more of a sniveling pest. Still waters, though, Jack. Your numbers man was on the verge of being discharged from the military once. There were strong allegations of improper conduct while on active duty. There was no court martial, probably because the evidence against him was illegally obtained, but in the end, and undoubtedly under pressure, he resigned his post at the age of twenty-six."

"Nothing as simple as a drunk and disorderly, I assume."

"More like theft from the quarters of two senior officers. His wife told me about it during the divorce case. I'm not against second chances, and maybe this guy's cleaned up his act, but his wife said that while they were married, he seemed to be able to acquire a lot of possessions they couldn't afford. I threatened to challenge him on that point in court if he didn't give her the settlement we were after, and it was a hefty one. He hadn't exactly been a model husband and father."

"You made him pay?"

"Big-time."

"What was his reaction?"

"He called me a bitch and said he'd love nothing better than to see me burn in hell."

Chapter Seven

"I can't believe he's really the fearsome Jack Ransom." It was nearing midnight when Helen nabbed Noel and propelled her behind the Christmas tree. "He looks so ordinary."

Noel glanced at Jack, who was eating a sandwich with Michael in the corner. "I wouldn't say ordinary, Helen. Just not what you might expect."

"Oh, I don't mean he's not good-looking and hot. It's just he doesn't have the look so many men in his position do. Matthew has it, and so did that other guy you used to go out with."

"Roberto Turano."

"Yeah, him. I always thought he'd make a great runway model for Valentino."

"So did he. Speaking of the executive look," Noel said, grinning, "what's the deal with you and Michael Santos?"

"I told you. We talked. We clicked. He invited. I came."

"Are you still clicking?"

"So far." Helen pressed her palms together. "You're not upset because I closed the office early, are you?"

"Of course I'm not upset."

"But you're not sure about me and Michael."

"I don't want you to get hurt. All I know about Michael Santos is that he and Jack have been friends since grade school, he dresses well, and he likes to work in high places."

"Uh-huh. So what do you know about Jack? Does he kiss as well as it appears he does?"

Noel winced. "Saw that, huh?"

"Oh, yeah. Saw and envied. I said he was hot. I wasn't lying."

The party showed no signs of winding down, but Noel had been up since six, and the long day was beginning to take its toll.

"Just be careful, okay?" she said and patted Helen's arm. "Have you seen my jacket anywhere?"

"It's on that chair near the back door. I locked your purse up with mine. I'll get it for you."

Noel couldn't resist giving Jack's neck as tickle as she passed behind him. "I'm leaving now, Mr. Ransom. I promised Hilda an hour. It's been over three. You're on your own."

Jack took one last bite of his sandwich and handed it to Michael.

Michael gave the remnants to a passing waiter, brushed the crumbs from his fingers and helped Noel locate her jacket.

"This looks right," he said as he removed one from under a large layer of wraps that had been shed by other women throughout the evening. "Ralph Lauren's good on you, Noel."

Jack found her coat and, as a series of seasonal lasers and strobe lights flashed around them, helped her into it.

The party was shifting into tech mode. Normally, Noel would have enjoyed the club atmosphere, but a long day had given her a headache, and to complicate matters, Matthew kept popping up at her elbow every fifteen minutes.

"Here's your purse," Helen announced. "And a piece of fruit-cake for luck."

She pushed the cake into Noel's hand, then slid the purse onto her shoulder. Michael rearranged the collar of her coat. Jack put on his jacket and frowned at them. "She's not a doll that needs dressing. Go back to the party and have a good time."

"We will." Helen hugged her friend. "Get him to kiss you again," she whispered.

It was a tempting idea, but the timing was wrong, and the laser lights were making her dizzy.

Cold air helped. In fact, it hit her like a slap to the cheeks. The traffic downtown had dwindled to a reasonable level. Jack seemed lost in thought, and Noel decided to leave him there for now. She'd been weighing the possibility that Harry Dexter was the kidnapper since Hilda had brought his name up.

She hadn't exaggerated when she'd told Jack that Harry relished the idea of seeing her burn in hell. But he'd been stinging from a nasty divorce and looking to vent his hostility on someone. She'd been convenient and, from his embittered point of view, deserving. What she wondered was, had he meant any of it?

The sidewalks were coated with half-frozen snow mixed with sand, salt and grime. In an absent gesture, Jack took her hand, holding tight as they walked toward his truck.

"You have an underground parking spot, don't you?" she asked him.

"Yeah. I use it sometimes. Most days, I just pull in wherever there's an opening."

"You don't quite possess the VIP mindset," she remarked. "Why is that?"

He thought for a minute. "I guess I don't like the trappings of extreme wealth."

"Like the fact that it makes you a target for kidnapping? Or worse?"

His mouth tipped up at the corners. "I'm not fond of traveling with an entourage. Last Saturday was an exception. I don't make many of those." He swept his gaze down the sparsely trafficked street. "If you're interested, Noel, your friend Matthew isn't as harmless as you think."

"I never said he was harmless. Easygoing and lacking a steel spine in business, but he also wields a mean rifle, and he can outpace anyone I know in the woods."

"He hates me."

"Resents might be a better word, but I noticed that."

"He wants you back."

"He knows that's not going to happen."

"Knowing and accepting can be worlds apart to some people. I want to have him checked out."

He kept his eyes on her face when he spoke, as if he expected her to object. When she didn't, he lowered his lashes in apparent scrutiny. "Are you always so logical?"

Noel sighed. She couldn't help it. "Not remotely. When the cat I'd had for twenty years got sick, I slept with her on the sofa in my parents' sunroom for two weeks because it was the only place she seemed comfortable. I was in my second year of law school. The cat's name was Mocha, and I got her for my first birthday. It took two of my sisters, both parents, my grandmother and an aunt to convince me that the kindest thing I could do was to have her put down. When I finally saw reason, I had her cremated. I keep her ashes on a shelf in my Winter Valley home."

Jack stared for a minute, then gave his head a small shake. "Mocha was a lucky cat. I had a dog once, but only for nine months."

"Do I want to hear this story?"

"He didn't die. I saw old Jacob kick him one day, so I told my father about it. He said I should keep the dog out of sight. I tried but he got out and Jacob kicked him again."

"I don't mean to sound disrespectful, but I think I'd have probably kicked old Jacob."

"I was ten and not overly big for my age. I gave the dog to Michael and his family. He lived to be almost sixteen."

Of the numerous thoughts that had been running through Noel's head that night, Michael Santos's name was high on the list. While they waited for the crosswalk sign to change, she said, "If I ask you a touchy question about Michael, will you promise not to get angry?"

"He doesn't resent me." Jack faced her, brows arched. "Was that the question?"

"Yes, and since you knew I was going to ask it, the idea must have crossed your mind at some point during all of this."

"It hasn't crossed my mind, Noel, since the day I met him."

"Is he that good a friend?"

"Yeah." Jack gripped her hand more firmly as they crossed the intersection. "He is."

The car came out of nowhere, or rather the headlights did. Noel heard a large engine to her right but didn't given it much thought. Until the vehicle squealed its tires and headed straight for them.

"Jack—"

"I see it."

The instinctive thing to do would have been to dart forward, in the same direction they'd been going. So Noel did the opposite. She tugged on Jack's hand and pulled him backward.

"He's veering right," she shouted.

Jack didn't hesitate. Keeping her ahead of him, he ran back the way they'd come. The vehicle swerved, skidded and squealed its tires again. Fishtailing wildly, it bumped over the curb, forcing them up against a concrete wall.

Noel hissed in a breath. Jack swore. The mammoth black truck stopped mere inches away from them.

Exhaust swirled around Noel's head. She was half-afraid to breathe. Seconds ticked by. Five. Ten. Fifteen.

"Where's your gun?" she whispered to Jack.

"In my truck." Jack squinted into the superbright lights. "If you hurt her, you won't get your money," he called out to the driver.

It was a chivalrous gesture that Noel appreciated despite her terror. Ten more seconds ticked by. The engine growled.

Noel's eyes stung. "What's he doing?"

"Enjoying himself."

She caught the snarl in his voice, and, grabbing his wrist, held on tight. "Don't challenge him, Jack. If he's playing games, winning will be paramount. He wants to make sure we're frightened."

"En route to being really pissed off."

The big engine revved again. Exhaust from the tailpipe blew up and over them. Noel coughed but saw nothing except clouds of white in the glare of the headlights.

The driver gave the accelerator one last punch, then threw the truck in reverse and peeled to the far side of the street, roaring off in a blast of white.

Noel didn't want to move. She slid her free hand up to check her heart. It was beating—about three times faster than normal.

When she glanced at Jack, she saw him staring after the truck with a determined look on his face.

She couldn't quite match him this time. Bullies didn't frighten her. But the prospect of being squashed like a bug against a concrete wall wasn't one she relished.

"He could have killed us." She fought to steady her breathing. "I think he really wanted to."

"So do I." Jack's arm was around her shoulders. She didn't know when he'd put it there, but it felt good. Her mind began to function. "It was black," she noted, "and it sounded like a four-by-four, like your truck."

Jack nodded.

"It might have belonged to the kidnapper, but it could have been stolen."

"It was stolen."

"How…" Noel's head pivoted sharply at his tone. "Was it yours? Are you sure?"

"Sure enough. I have a personalized license plate on that truck. It says RAIDER. I caught the first two letters as he took off."

"But your truck's alarmed. A dozen gadgets flashed and beeped after we got out." She closed her eyes as it occurred to her. "You have an extra set of keys, don't you?"

"My assistant keeps a set locked in her desk. Michael has one in his office, and I have another at home."

Noel said nothing to that. Would Harry Dexter be up to the challenge of infiltration? She hadn't noticed him at the party, and

Hilda hadn't pointed him out. But they hadn't seen Hilda after the first half hour.

What about Caroline's ex-boyfriend, the one Hilda had derided? Could he have broken into Jack's home? Noel tapped Jack's hand. "What was Caroline's ex's name?" As she spoke, her eyes fell on something lying on the wet sidewalk in front of her. "Jack."

"Steve Crookshank," he said, then followed her gaze. "Hell." Crouching, he regarded the envelope. Wrapped in plastic, it had his name clearly printed on the back.

Noel crouched beside him. 'I'll say it again." Lifting her head, she gazed into the darkness of the near empty street. "This isn't strictly about money. Our ghost is a madman."

Dear Jack:
Are you scared? Jumping at shadows? Losing sleep? Wondering about people you thought you could trust? Searching for ones you think you can't?

Are you suffering yet?

I doubt it. But you will. I promise, you will.

Noel has a lovely luster about her, doesn't she? Her hair makes me think of a beautiful black pearl the way it shines in the moonlight. Do you still have that black pearl you found in the Caribbean, Noel? Such a lucky child. Sunday's Child, born under a Lucky Star at 10 p.m. But maybe that Luck's gone sour now. You'll be sad and lonely at 95, Noel, a dusty Juliet with no Romeo to serenade you. Such a sorrowful Christmas Present.

I'd be more direct, but you don't deserve it after the episode at the university.

I send this gift as a token to you, Jack.

Enjoy.
The Ghost of Christmas Past

A LOCK OF CAROLINE'S hair. The madman had snipped off a piece of his sister's hair and taped it to the bottom of his note.

Noel called it an intimidation tactic. Jack just called it sick. But he wasn't prepared to bring in the authorities. Not until every one of his alternatives was exhausted.

Ransom Price owned a large pharmaceutical company. It had an extensive lab in Atlanta and two smaller ones in Cleveland and San Francisco. When he contacted them early Saturday morning, they gave him nothing, because, as the technician in charge told him, there was nothing to give. No fingerprints, no trace of saliva, hair or skin for DNA testing and not a single outstanding feature connected with the paper or the print.

"It's twenty-pound white copy paper done on an IBM printer," Jack told Noel when he arrived at her Pittsburgh condo Saturday afternoon. "And any office, department or drug store carries the envelopes."

Snow clung to his boots and the frayed cuffs of his jeans. He would have stomped it off except he was held in place by a dalmatian that had to weigh a good one hundred and thirty pounds.

"You're dripping on my limestone tiles, Jack," Noel observed.

She had her hair piled loosely on her head, and she was wearing black sweats with a tight blue T-shirt. Her feet were bare, and he thought he glimpsed a silver ankle chain.

He returned his attention to the dog when it shoved its nose into his fly. "Friend of yours?" he asked as he tried to maneuver the animal to the side.

Noel smiled. "Her name's GiGi. It's a nickname. She's really a Gibson Girl. She belongs to my sister. She and her husband needed a dog sitter. They received a last-minute invitation to a lodge party in the Poconos, and the owners of the lodge have Dobermans." Setting her hands on either side of the dalmatian's jaw, she put her face up close and kissed the air between them. "You're just a big suck deep down, aren't you, sweetheart? And those Dobermans are mean old things." Giving GiGi's ears a playful scratch, she turned her attention to Jack. "You're still dripping."

"How can you keep a full-grown dalmatian in an eight-hundred-square-foot loft?"

"We go for walks in the park, and she has her chew toys." She patted the dog's rump and sent her clattering across the tile floor. "We've done this many times, GiGi and me. And it's nine hundred and twenty square feet of prime real estate."

His smile, though vague, was telling.

Going to her knees, she batted at his snowy cuffs. "You own this building, too, huh?"

"Among others."

"Then that would make you ultimately responsible for any and all repair work."

"There are half a hundred sales people, developers and contractors between this place and me, Noel."

"I prefer going straight to the top. It saves time. The bathroom sinks don't drain properly, the storage closets were never painted inside, and the hot water tank leaks. This condo's exactly fifteen months old, and I'm the first and only owner. Builders warranty's in effect, pal, and I'm not the only one with a gripe." But her eyes were sparkling when she stood. "So what's the deal? Have you decided to call in the feds?"

"When hell freezes, I'll consider it. Ask me why another time. Have you thought about the last note?"

"For most of a long and sleepless night." Because he made no move to do so, she unbuttoned his jacket. "Give me this, lose the boots and I'll make us some coffee."

Jack looked around. She had a scattering of plants that resembled palms, big leafy things in even bigger ceramic pots and others with large red flowers. The ceiling was old wood and worn brick, and it shot up thirty feet. Pipes crisscrossed it from wall to wall, and a set of ladder stairs led to a small upper level. Otherwise, the place was open, spacious and decorated with extreme good taste.

He watched as GiGi curled up next to a large fireplace on the north wall.

Behind a long black counter Noel poured water into a sleek stainless pot and set it in an equally sleek coffeemaker. Resting her forearms on the counter, she leaned forward. "I think the note might be relatively straightforward. The ghost talked about Sunday's child, which I am, but I wasn't born at 10:00 p.m., so I assume that's the time I'm supposed to be there."

"Be where?" Although the sofa tempted him, Jack found Noel more of a lure. "There's no place I could find called the Lucky Star."

"I know. But if we assume he wants me to go somewhere on Sunday at 10:00 p.m., then he might also have been referring to my birth sign, which is Gemini."

"That's a constellation."

"That's a technicality. There's a Gemini Theatre in Winter Valley. It was closed down three years ago because it desperately needs work."

Jack knew of the theatre and its problem. "The foundation's crumbling."

"To say nothing of the interior walls. And there's serious rot in the floors. It was a beautiful place in its day. My aunt Maddie said she went there as a little girl to watch weekend matinees, not because the shows were great, but because the seats were real red velvet and there were carvings all over the ceilings and balconies. So far, no one's stepped forward with an offer to fund a reconstruction project."

Jack rested his arms on the opposite side of the counter and faced her at close range. "Is that a plea for money, counselor, or just a sentimental tug at my heartstrings?"

"It was a statement of fact that you can take any way you like. My point is, there's a good chance the kidnapper was referring to the Gemini Theatre in his note. It's my birth sign, so possibly my Lucky Star. It's abandoned, therefore dusty. And it has a balcony, thus the reference to Juliet. The seats—I phoned Aunt Maddie to make sure—are numbered from one to three hundred, front to back, and he mentioned the number ninety-five."

Jack let his gaze stray to her mouth, unpainted but full and soft. "You thought of all that last night?"

"Early this morning." She pushed off with the barest hint of a smile. "In the shower."

He didn't need to picture that. Not if he wanted to keep his mind on track. He forced himself to think. It was Saturday afternoon just after four. Ten o'clock Sunday night was thirty hours away.

The smell of coffee brought his mind back. Noel handed him a steaming mug. "I'm guessing you like it black, but I have cream, milk and sugar."

"Black's good. Thanks."

She led the way into the living room. "Did you at least report your truck stolen?"

"Not yet, no."

She swung around, almost causing him to spill his coffee. "Jack, that's a customized BMW SUV he stole. I know quality when I see it. You might be able to afford a fleet of the things, but it was still stolen. For all you know, it's sitting on the side of the road somewhere waiting to be stolen again. The kidnapper won't have any more use for it. It would only be a liability for him."

He tried for patience, set his coffee on a low table and his hands on her shoulders. "Look, Noel, we're talking about cops here. One thing invariably leads to another. I tell them my truck's missing, and they ask questions, and more questions. I told you before, my family's had dealings with both the police and the FBI in the past. Their intention might have been to help, but it didn't work out that way. I'm not going to get into it with you now, just believe me when I tell you I really don't want them involved in this, okay?"

She narrowed her eyes at him. He expected her to ask why anyway. It was only natural, after all. But to his surprise, she simply said, "Okay, I'll let it go. But you have to know, Jack, at some point the authorities are going to find out about Caroline. She must have friends who'll notice her absence, friends who won't necessarily contact you before they report her missing."

"Her female friends won't hesitate to call me. Most of her male friends wouldn't dare."

"Wouldn't dare call you or the police?"

"Either one. Steve Crookshank might be a jackass, but he's also the most upstanding man Caroline's ever been involved with."

"All right, fine, you win. No police. But no Steve Crookshank, either. I don't know him, Jack. He couldn't possibly have anything against me. I do have two other theories, though, if you're interested.'"

Oh, he was interested, but not in theories or even, at the moment, in Steven Crookshank. He slid a hand up her neck to her jaw. With his thumb, he grazed her bottom lip. "You've got to stop looking at me like that, Noel. My family started out in steel, but I'm not made of it."

"I'm glad to hear that." She curled her fingers around his wrist. "Because neither am I."

There was nothing to stop him, Jack thought, except his conscience, and he'd been told he had little enough of that. So when he kissed her, he didn't intend for it to end there. Didn't see how it could.

He wanted a good, long taste of her this time, needed it to satisfy the hunger that had been growing inside him since he'd met her.

She moved seductively against him, and he responded. His breath threatened to choke him. Blood pounded in his ears. Had this happened to him before? Did he care?

He found her mouth and explored it quite thoroughly with his tongue. He pictured the sofa and Noel on it while he pulled off her clothes and released her hair.

Well, he could do the last thing right now. A gentle tug on the clip that held it in place, and the full, silky length of it spilled down over his hands.

Somewhere, in the very distant background he heard GiGi yawn. Then she barked. Then she growled.

It was Noel who drew away just far enough to ask, "What is it, girl?"

GiGi barked again, short and sharp. Noel let out a breath. "You better not be barking at birds."

"She isn't." Jack was facing the bank of windows. He saw it first. There was scaffolding and a man dressed in black standing on it. He was holding a stubby, gray object in his right hand.

Chapter Eight

Noel didn't know if it was from relief or amusement, but she couldn't seem to stop chuckling. "A window washer." She gave Jack a hug from behind. "Stop scowling at everyone on the street and remember the look on that poor boy's face when you rushed across the room toward him. He dropped his squeegee and almost vaulted over the edge of the scaffolding. He looked more befuddled than that Looney Tunes dog does when Foghorn Leghorn puts a pot over his head and bangs a spoon against it while he's sleeping."

That got a brief smile out of him, but within seconds the crease had formed between his eyes again. "He said he worked for the building. You said he didn't."

"I said he wasn't our regular window washer. He explained that, Jack. He's subbing because our regular guy's got the flu. And GiGi's not to blame, because she was only doing what dogs do when they spot strangers." She rubbed GiGi's ears while the dalmatian pulled on her leash.

The dog had already had her park outing that morning. Now they were walking through the southside hills, enjoying the crisp, cold air of early evening and looking for a place to satisfy Jack's craving for gnocchi.

Noel would have made it for him if she hadn't thought exercise and fresh air might improve his mood. And his outlook. How could anyone be out of sorts with so much color and light and so many delicious food scents wafting around them?

"I have a friend from Eastern Europe," she told him as they passed a Polish bakery. "Her mother makes these incredible stewed plums wrapped in dough and smothered in a sauce made of honey, cinnamon and cloves."

"I want gnocchi."

What he wanted was to be testy and irritable.

"I was making conversation, Jack. We're walking through the ethnic neighborhoods. Fixating on one food dish is a complete waste."

"I don't have a wide ranging palate."

"You ate that squiggly fish course Monday night that Deirdre and I could hardly even look at."

"Eating it doesn't mean I liked it."

She took a deep breath, started to count, then aborted halfway. "Why are you being so disagreeable? Is it because of Caroline?"

"We're being jerked around." He sidestepped a heavyset woman carrying an armload of gifts and baked goods. "It's getting to me. I'm starting to jump at shadows."

"Like substitute window washers." She gave GiGi extra leash. "Let it go, Jack. Mistakes happen. The guy'll recover, and the whole story will change to his advantage when he tells it to his buddies. Why don't I tell you the theories I mentioned earlier?

"I've been drawing mental pictures of the kidnapper, trying to get inside his head based on what little we know about him. What I keep visualizing instead is the movie *The Three Faces of Eve.*"

"You think he has multiple personalities?"

"Or we're dealing with multiple people. Two, to be specific. Someone who has a grudge against you and another who wants to punish me."

His expression told her he was weighing the possibility. "Like Steve Crookshank and Matthew Railback working together?"

She bit back a retort. "Like that, yes, but not them in particular. FYI, Jack, Matthew wasn't my most intense relationship."

"He thought he was."

"Well, he's wrong. Before Matthew, I was with Roberto for seven months. For almost a week, I actually considered marrying him."

"A week, huh? Tops me. Where is he now?"

"Last I heard, Tuscany. His brother founded the VSE—short for Vince's Sleep Easy—motel and restaurant chain, which, by the way, you and your grandfather bought and sold to two large hotel chains, one national, one international."

"I remember the deal, the brother and your ex."

"Roberto."

"He looked like a model."

"He was."

"The brother came to us, Noel."

"His name was Vince."

"Okay, Vince. Look." He turned to her. "I know you think I'm a heartless bastard who can't even be bothered to remember the names of the people whose livelihoods he's destroyed, but all I do is take advantage of situations that are created or exist long before I arrive on the scene. You like your house in Winter Valley, don't you?"

"I love it, but—"

"No buts. I know, you paid good money for it." Although he stared straight at her, for the life of her she couldn't read his face. "What if the previous owners had desperately needed to sell, for money, health or some other reason? Would you have offered top dollar, or, realizing the circumstances, gone for the jugular? People can say what they like when they're not involved, but in the end most of them would cut the best deal they could and not give a damn about any voice of conscience."

She stared back at him. "You're awfully quick to justify your actions, Jack. I wasn't going to argue with you. I understand completely what it is to capitalize on someone's misfortune, but I think you're wrong about people. There are some—not you or me, maybe—but some people out there who wouldn't take advantage of others."

"They're fools."

"No, they're good people, not just decent but good deep down inside. Sometimes I wish I could be like them."

"Do you know even one of them?"

"My aunt Maddie's late husband. He was totally selfless. He didn't have a greedy bone in his body."

"And he's dead."

"Yes, well, there are those who would say he's in a better place, but I'm not getting into that with you right now. We were talking about Roberto."

"Your most intense relationship." He schooled his features, but she sensed an interest when he asked, "Why did it end?"

"We had different goals that we were both in the process of pursuing at that time in our lives."

"I don't suppose Vince's losing the motel and restaurant chain improved things between you."

"No, it didn't. Down, GiGi." She shortened the dog's lead before the animal could plant her paws on an elderly man with a cane. "I know all about brotherly love, but my feeling is that there was nothing Roberto could do. Vince was his own worst enemy. He did drugs and apparently dealt them, as well. I don't know if that had any bearing on his financial downfall, but I'd guess it played a part."

Jack pushed his hands into his jacket pockets. "Am I going to come out the villain at the end of this?"

"There was no villain, only unpleasant circumstances."

"More than your breakup?"

"Way more. My older sister and I fell out for a while over Roberto's brother."

"She wanted him?"

"No, they were friends. She knew him at school. When Vince was arrested, both Ali, my sister, and Roberto asked me to defend him. I wouldn't do it because I knew about the drug deals, and I told you before, I won't defend dealers no matter who they are."

"Fair enough. Didn't your sister agree?"

"Vince pleaded with Ali and Roberto to talk to me. Ali really believed I should take the case, but I wanted in with Martin Faber, and he had a full docket waiting for me. She said I was being selfish and accused me of turning my back on my friends. Roberto made a similar accusation."

"I thought you'd considered marrying this guy. What's his last name?"

"Turano, and I had thought about it, but that was before you and your grandfather entered the picture, and Martin Faber offered me a position with the promise of a partnership." She sighed. "I'm human, Jack. I wanted to be on the fast track to success. Roberto and I were pretty much done, and my brother was having his own legal problems. I wasn't about to defend someone who might very well have sold my brother the drugs that landed him in jail. After a few months, Ali and I talked it out, and she was okay about my decision. The difference between us is that she's a doctor and she was doing her E.R. residency at the time. You can't make judgments in life and death situations. A dealer comes in shot, you work to save his life. Anyway, we're fine now." Her eyes widened. "Are those cream puffs in that bakery?"

Jack peered into the frosted glass front of the neighboring shop. "Super-sized. Do you want one? It's—" he squinted at the wall clock inside "—6:12."

She caught his wrist and held it up. "Why don't you wear a watch?"

"I used to." He checked his wallet for cash.

"I can pay, Jack."

"My treat. You buy the gnocchi. It's easier to let everyone

around me worry about time and appointments. I'm seldom late, either way."

She believed him, and watched as he went inside to purchase the pastries. GiGi whined at her side, prompting Noel to give her several long strokes. Her mind wandered back in time as she did. She hadn't seen, heard or really thought about Roberto for over five years.

Did he hate her? She hadn't gotten that impression from him, but she'd been so focused on her career that she might have missed something.

"He probably hates you, though," she murmured when Jack returned with a white box tied up with string.

"Are we talking about your intense ex?"

"Roberto and Vince were close."

"Not close enough to be partners."

"Roberto wasn't interested in running a business. He wanted to hit the runways in Europe before he got too old." She shook the memory aside, handed Jack GiGi's leash and untied the string. "Anyway, we're light years off topic. I said the ghost could be two people. Roberto's only one. So's Matthew."

"You've defended some powerful people, Noel. Powerful people often have powerful enemies. There could be strong animosity against you for cases you've won where the defendants were less than worthy of the verdict they received."

"In other words, I've gotten some badass people off the hook. I do practice a certain amount of discretion with the clients I accept, Jack."

"Ditto with the companies I take over. We're still talking about the prospect of a lot of people on my side hooking up with a substantial number on yours. I like the single-person theory better."

So did Noel.

Cream puff in hand, she and Jack let GiGi lead them forward. "My second idea involved your grandfather's partner, Philip Price. He was a self-confessed ladies' man. He had affairs."

"So did his wife."

"Ah, but if she'd had children with other men, she'd have known about it. The same can't necessarily be said of Philip."

Jack stopped, knit his brow. "You think Philip might have a child somewhere that he didn't acknowledge?"

"Or possibly even know about. But if that child was unstable, if he knew about Philip, and he was old enough to do something nasty with his resentment, well, you can figure the rest."

"Why not come forward?"

Noel let GiGi lick some of the cream from her fingers. "It's possible he did. He could have spoken to your grandfather, Jack. Or written to him. And had his letters burned in the same way Philip's ex-wife's were."

"A kid." Jack rubbed his forehead. "Jesus, I hadn't thought about that. Hell, old Jacob might have done the same thing, sired a child no one knew about."

"We could also be bashing them unfairly," Noel acknowledged with a smile. "Sticking them with kids that might or might not exist, then compounding that by turning the alleged offspring into maniacal kidnappers. I was tired when I came up with that theory. It's probably way out in left field."

Jack looked at her. "I played left field in college, Noel. I caught the fly ball in the bottom of the ninth inning in the 3-2 game that gave us the intercollegiate championship. We need to start doing background checks on Philip and Jacob. Now."

IT WAS COLD and a little damp. It didn't matter how many fires he lit because the central heating system didn't work.

Tired of listening to Caroline Ransom's complaints, he climbed up to what he called his dark room.

It had a single bed and fifty or more bad paintings leaned up against the wall. He especially liked the old remnant of signboard that said Coffee Shop. It was nailed cockeyed above the window. There was a little TV in here, and a VCR. He had a box full of tapes to play in it. He had his memories, too. And a huge store of anger to warm him.

Jack had estates, condos and a megacorporation. Noel had a house, a condo and a thriving career. He had nothing he wanted, no matter how many people told him he had it all. Or at least a lot more than most.

His fingers crawled along the mattress to the scrapbook he'd been working on for years. He had pictures of them separately on the pages inside. He'd pasted an image of them together in his mind.

But he really liked a different mental snapshot best. The clear-as-glass new climax shot where one of them was dead and the other had to live with the knowledge that he'd killed her.

Whoever said revenge and Christmas didn't mix?

NOEL LEFT FOR WINTER VALLEY early Sunday morning. She wanted, needed, time alone. She'd negated Jack's suggestion that she wait so they could drive up together.

He had a business meeting at 9:00 a.m. Who knew, by the time she unlocked her front door, he might be in possession of the bank that held the mortgage on her house.

"It's big business, GiGi. I get a headache thinking about all the dips and dodges involved." She parked in the driveway, then opened the door so the dog could hop out.

But to rush into unfamiliar territory wasn't GiGi's way, so Noel unloaded the trunk and left her to her cautious inspection of the snow.

Her next-door neighbor, Mrs. Fisker, waved from the porch she was sweeping and called, "Did you hear, Noel? Old Fred's gone to Connecticut for Christmas."

"He left me a note," Noel called back.

"I've got cookies for you, dear. I'll fetch them before you go inside."

"Come on, GiGi," Noel encouraged the skeptical dog. "Come

and meet the nice neighbor. She bakes raisin cookies twice the size of your paw."

At the fence, Mrs. Fisker clucked her tongue. "Helen dashed out of here on Friday like she'd been shot from a cannon. I saw the Closed sign on your front door. When you didn't come back, I started wondering about that awful gang of men I saw last week, and I got worried. But I said to myself, now those girls can take care of themselves. Probably got a whole lot more sense than old Fred. Marrying at his age. Can you believe it? Not that I'm not happy for him, but what if she wants to live in Connecticut? He'll sell his house, and who knows who we'll get for a new neighbor. He's got a renter there now, you know. Oh, but then you would know, wouldn't you, since you and that man with the long hair went into Fred's yard to gather holly. Is he a nice young man?"

Noel simply waited until the old woman ran out of breath. "He's very nice, actually. The renter wasn't upset with us, was he?"

"I haven't met them, not him or her, though I've seen them three or four times coming and going." She lowered her voice. "But the real problem is the rumor I heard about two people right across our street who are wanting to sell. There's another three doors down as well. If you add Fred's name to the list, that would make four, and you know what that means." She gave an emphatic nod. "Condominiums."

Noel struggled not to laugh. "I really don't think—"

"Oh, I know you won't sell, and neither will I. It's just that strangers are already coming in more and more. Not boarders like I take in, or that man who lives in Mr. Riley's attic rooms."

"Someone lives in Mr. Riley's attic?" Noel interrupted

"Well, the lights go on and off, and Mr. Riley's been in Wichita for the past month. Riley's an odd one though. Could be he set a timer to make it seem like he's home when he isn't. What did you say your young man's name was?"

The road to juicy gossip was a winding one, Noel reflected.

"Jack," she said. "He works in Pittsburgh. Mrs. Fisker, do you know the Gemini Theatre on Broad Street?"

"I saw *Casablanca* there as a girl. It's all boarded up now. Not safe, they say. I rested my feet on Errol Flynn first time I went inside."

As astute as she usually was, Noel couldn't quite make sense of the old woman's statement.

"Errol Flynn?" she repeated.

"On the floor." Mrs. Fisher pointed at her boots. "In the theatre. In front of the seats. Have you never looked?"

"I haven't been to the Gemini."

"Well, there are stars on the floor. Hollywood stars, like at Grauman's Theatre. In front of each seat on a square of tile there's a star. Then around the star, there's a famous name. Inside's the initials. I stepped on Errol whenever I could. He was fifty-seven. Tyrone was a hundred and three. Cary Grant was eighty-six."

Noel rested her arms on the fence. Now, finally, clarity. "Who was seat ninety-five, Mrs. Fisker, do you know?"

The old woman chuckled. "As a matter of fact, I do. All the nineties were local celebrities, including the man who owned the theatre. He was ninety-nine. They were the best seats in the house, the nineties."

"And ninety-five was?"

"Tillman. Ronald Tillman. He reported the news and weather on the local radio station. Your aunt Maddie'd remember him. He did just fine for himself over all. Came out with a line of barbecue sauces. Took them to Pittsburgh and Philly, then went national. I imagine his kids have been living fat off those smelly sauces ever since." She offered a heaping platter over the fence. "Here's your cookies, dear. Spiced up with a nip of brandy." Her husband shouted to her from the bedroom window, but she ignored him and pressed a hand to her chest. "Ronald Tillman. Goodness. I haven't thought of him in years. I wonder if he's still alive?"

Chapter Nine

Michael entered instructions into his handheld computer as rapidly as Jack fired them.

"Got it," he said when Jack finished. "Check out Philip Price's liaisons. A tall order, I'm afraid, but I'll get a team onto it. Ditto, Jacob. Put someone on locating your truck. Search for any and all links between you and Noel. Also tricky and time-consuming, but I'll do my best. Look into the backgrounds of Matthew Railback, Roberto and Vince Turano, Steve Crookshank and Harry Dexter." He finished up with a flourish. "Anything else?"

Pacing in his office, Jack massaged his neck with the fingers of both hands. "Keys," he recalled. "Which of my extra sets is missing?"

"Already determined." Michael hit a few more buttons, then set his computer aside. "It's the one from Annabelle's desk." He held up a finger, forestalling Jack's reaction. "I spoke to her this morning. She has no idea how. But come on, Jack, it could happen. Annabelle leaves her desk for five minutes. Someone's watching, waiting for her to go. He slips in and out."

"There was a fire alarm a few days ago," Jack recalled. "Smoke in one of the utility storage rooms on seven."

"I remember it. The fire department came and cleared the floor. The smoke created a certain amount of confusion. Someone could have gotten past security and into Annabelle's desk."

"What about the security disks?"

"I'll run them. But a pro would know, Jack. He'd hide his face in a way that wouldn't look obvious."

"Or pay someone on the inside to do his dirty work."

"Or that."

"We never got the guy who delivered the first notes, did we?"

"Everything's normal on disk. I ran them myself."

"What about deliveries?"

"Everyone was checked out and passed by the guards."

At the window, Jack turned his head to regard his friend. "Where's Talberg?"

"Where he's supposed to be at 2:15 p.m. on Sunday. Relax, Jack," Michael advised. He slipped his computer into its case and double-checked his watch. "We'll get Caroline back without any damage to you, her or Noel."

Jack ignored the twinge of guilt in his stomach and changed the subject. "Is Noel's friend here?"

"In my office. I thought I'd drive her home if we finished up before dinner."

"You can stay at the house tonight if you want." Jack glanced in the direction of the penthouse office, gnawed his inner cheek. "She's Noel's best friend," he mused aloud.

"You want to talk to her?"

"For a minute."

"Yeah, I know how your minutes work." But Michael used his cell to call upstairs.

While he talked, Jack circled a room that suddenly felt too small, too hot and too restrictive. He'd been a rebel once, a hell-raiser with an attitude. Girls had lined up to date the bad boy with money. Jessica Verdon had stripped naked on their first date before he'd even tried to kiss her.

He'd dug in his heels over conformity, hadn't wanted to follow in old Jacob's footsteps. He'd shouted at the old man to let Michael run the business. He might even have tossed out Caroline's name, he couldn't remember now. He sure as hell hadn't wanted to do it.

But he had. His father had died and Jack, who'd been running wild for a lot of years, knew exactly how it would be. Jacob would lay down the law. His grandson would conform, and that was that.

"You won part of the battle, old man." Jack regarded his black jeans that were worn through at the knees, his battered boots and a blue sweater that had seen better days. "But not all of it."

"She's coming down," Michael told him. "You want coffee?"

Still adrift in his memories, Jack offered a faint smile. "Thanks." He ran a hand through his hair. "You know, Jacob never approved of my style."

"You were family," Michael said. "You were smart. It was enough."

"If you think that, you didn't know Jacob Ransom."

"He'd have liked Noel."

"He'd have loved her. And argued with her at every turn." Another vague smile. "He'd have been in heaven."

"So where are you?"

Jack wasn't prepared to answer that just yet, and didn't have to because he heard Helen call, "Hello? Are you in here, Michael?"

She paused when she spied Jack, but plastered a smile on her face, regardless. "I feel like I'm about to take the witness stand."

Jack leaned against the windowsill. "I only want to ask if you know of anyone who might bear a deep grudge against Noel."

"Ah." She took the seat and the coffee Michael offered. "Clients or associates?"

"Or former lovers."

"Well, hmm. You know Matthew."

"We met."

"And didn't like," Michael put in with a grin.

It broke the tension and made Helen laugh. "He's nice, really. He didn't care for the idea of you and Noel possibly being together, that's all."

"So he's the jealous type."

"A bit possessive, but not as green-eyed as you might think."

"What about Roberto Turano?"

Her smile widened. "Gorgeous. Tall, brown hair, black eyes. But you don't care about that, do you? He was a good guy, into his family like Noel, so they got along well that way. Their careers didn't mesh, that was the biggest problem for them. His brother was a bit of a rat, but then so's hers."

"Was there anyone else?"

"Damian Lowe, but she wasn't as involved with him."

"Was he before or after Railback?"

"After. Two years ago, actually. They flared, then faded."

"What does he do?"

"He's a lawyer. His father owned Lowe's Jewelers. He sold off, and—"

"Sold off?" Jack looked to Michael for confirmation, but his friend merely spread his fingers. "I can't recall dealing with anyone called Lowe, though we did buy and break up a national jewelry chain a year or so before Jacob passed away."

"Lowe's hasn't been called Lowe's for ten years or more," Helen said. "I only mentioned the business because Damian used to give very expensive gifts."

Jack frowned. "To Noel?"

"She looks good in diamonds. He sent her a couple of bracelets, some earrings, and he got his father to make a ring for her with a black pearl she had."

Jack's frown deepened. "The kidnapper mentioned a pearl she found in the Caribbean."

"It was in Martinique. We went there one winter for our college break."

"You and her?"

"And her sister Diana." Helen glanced at Michael, then back at Jack. "Listen, I understand you're concerned about her—I am, too—but I thought you wanted to know about clients and associates who might resent her, not about her love life or the crazy vacations we took as undergrads."

He wanted to know everything, Jack realized in a moment of sudden revelation. He wanted to be with her now.

Drinking the coffee Michael had given him, he forced himself to relax against the sill. "You're right. I need names, Helen, of anyone who might be vindictive enough to want to hurt her."

Helen shivered and looked to Michael again. "I can only think of one person vicious enough to want revenge. His name's Kurt deRosa. He's a dealer in black market goods, everything from drugs to weapons to sex. When his wife was murdered, his closest associate was accused. Noel defended the associate and got him off. Kurt waylaid her in the corridor outside the courtroom. He got right in her face and swore he'd find a way to make her pay for what she'd done."

IN ALL THE TIME she'd owned her house in Winter Valley, Noel had never once felt uneasy being alone inside it. Until today.

It was a backlash from everything that had happened over the past week. She knew that, understood it, but couldn't seem to shake the eerie sensation that a pair of eyes were watching her wherever she went.

She had lunch with Aunt Maddie, but her aunt left for the city immediately afterward. Still, there were two large dogs downstairs, and she had her cell phone clipped to the belt loop of her jeans.

To take her mind off things, she watched Boris Karloff's Grinch slink through Who houses on TV. She decorated her Christmas tree, finally, watered it and ate three of Mrs. Fisker's delicious spice cookies.

She thought about Jack more than she should and continued to think about him even though she had a copy of the kidnapper's note in her hand with the number ninety-five circled and the name Ronald Tillman written with a question mark in the margin. She was just being jittery thinking someone was spying on her.

She was being totally reckless dwelling on Jack.

They were comrades of a sort, tossed together into a difficult situation that left no room for fantasy and even less for romance. She didn't want a romance, anyway. They always screwed up, and although she wasn't sure why that happened, she sensed it had to do with her unswerving desire to be the best defense attorney on the planet.

Her sisters, all three of them, told her she set unattainable goals in her life, and to be the best lawyer ever was absurd. To be the best she possibly could should be enough. Unless she wanted to die alone, unhappy and childless.

Like Scrooge would have, she reflected, if he hadn't mended his ways.

With a rare sound of frustration, she got a Coke out of the fridge, plunked herself down on the sofa and repeated the name Ronald Tillman until she could no longer get her tongue around the sounds.

The name meant nothing to her. Was he alive? A computer check told her nothing, except that he no longer lived in Pennsylvania.

Bright lights winked behind her. She finished her Coke, adjusted the top star on her tree and took a long look out the window at the street.

All of her neighbors' lights were on. Five or six cars were parked at the curb. Mrs. Fisker's cat was heading home from wherever he'd been, and darkness was beginning to settle.

She hadn't heard from Jack. Why?

It didn't matter. He wasn't supposed to go with her to the Gemini in any case. Assuming she was right about the location.

She walked around the living room, stretched her cramped lower back muscles. Jack had enemies. So did she. But how many madmen numbered among them?

She rubbed her arms, considered throwing a sweater over her

T-shirt or starting a fire. While she debated, GiGi and Pepper nosed their way in from the stairwell and barked.

Noel let her hands fall. "I should have had sex with him yesterday."

When GiGi nuzzled her leg, Noel ruffled her ears. "He has such an arresting face." She crouched to rub Pepper's stomach. "I mean, you could look at him all day long and not be bored. But he's eccentric, and I'm not. We're different in a lot of ways and alike in a lot of others. But where we're alike is where the problems lie, so nothing could come of it. It would just be sex. Okay, great sex, but nothing that would last." She breathed out. "Nothing ever lasts."

Restless, she left the dogs and returned to the window. None of the cars had moved. There was no one on the street, and still the skin on the back of her neck prickled.

"Walk," she said in a flash of inspiration. "Come on, guys. We'll do the whole block, up and down, then stop and see if Helen's back yet."

That was another concern. Helen and Michael. Maybe they were good together now, but for how long? What kind of a man was the private Michael Santos?

Holding her gloves between her teeth, Noel swung her coat over her shoulders. "Let's go, Pepper," she urged the older dog. "We'll walk slow." She opened the door. "I know you can't— Damn!"

Her heart leaped into her throat and stayed there, racing.

"What?" Jack looked over his shoulder. Then he smiled. "Did I startle you?"

Noel pressed the heel of her hand to her chest. "Would it startle you to open the door when you thought you were alone and find someone standing less than a foot in front of you?"

"I'll take that as a yes." He regarded the leashes in her hand. "Are we walking dogs again?"

"Well, I want to walk. I'm not sure about them." Both dogs barked, then hunkered down to play. "You're wearing your worried crease, Jack. Do you have news I don't want to hear?"

"Kurt deRosa," he said.

Her heart gave a sizable thump. "He's in Cannes. He lives there."

"Lives there, yes. But he's not there now. Michael and I checked with U.S. Customs and Immigration. Kurt deRosa returned to the United States via JFK six weeks ago."

"IT'S BEEN ALMOST three years since that case was tried." Because the dogs seemed disinclined to walk, and Noel needed something to do, she dragged out a ladder and got Jack to help her with her inside window lights. "Red bulb, green bulb, blue bulb, repeated. Lose the yellow," she told him. "Kurt deRosa was a strike hard and strike fast person. He wouldn't wait three years to have his revenge."

From the fourth rung, Jack regarded her. "You know that for a fact, do you?"

"That's what his associate, one Salvatore 'Squeaky' Bandero, told me when I got him acquitted for the murder of deRosa's wife. Besides, by all accounts deRosa's remarried and happy."

"People like that are never happy."

Noel handed him the light string. "Do you know Kurt deRosa?"

"Not personally, but I've heard the name. He owns a few legitimate businesses."

"Any that you've taken over?"

"Not that I'm aware of. We're looking into it."

Noel was proud of the fact that her hands didn't shake as she continued to replace the colored bulbs. "I can't let people like Kurt deRosa get to me, Jack. If I do, I won't be able to do my job effectively. He said what he said, and I braced for the worst. But nothing materialized." She swept her gaze over the street below. "He's not out there watching me."

Someone was, though. She felt it as surely as if there were ants crawling on her skin.

"Tell me what your neighbor said about Ronald Tillman," Jack suggested from above.

"He's seat number ninety-five at the Gemini. She said he concocted a line of barbecue sauces and eventually went national with them. She thinks he sold the business several years ago." Smiling, she handed up another light string. "Ring any bells for you?"

"No more than Lowe's Jewelers."

So he'd talked to Helen.

"Damian and I weren't a big deal."

"He gave you jewelry."

"He gave everyone he knew gifts of one sort or another. Lowe's changed its name several years ago. You could have bought it out and not realized it." She lowered herself into a cross-legged position beside the tree and regarded his rather nice butt from the floor. "Are you sure Michael doesn't feel any animosity toward you?"

Jack let his head fall back. She imagined he was fighting for patience. "Michael's where he wants to be. Believe it or not, he doesn't want to be responsible for making big decisions. Let's just leave it at that and get back on track."

Noel conceded. "Well, what I know, Jack, is that I think I'm supposed to go and stand on Tillman's star at the Gemini Theatre in about one hour's time. If I'm wrong in my assumption…" She pushed the lights from her lap, stood and regarded the unchanged street below. "Let's just hope I'm not wrong."

Jack kept his eyes on her face as he descended the ladder. "Squeaky Bandero's dead, Noel."

The invisible ants scurried up her spine to her neck. "I heard about it."

"He was shot in a downtown parking lot fifteen months ago. DeRosa was a suspect, but he was never arrested."

"His wife-to-be alibied him. I was told, Jack."

"He waited almost two years to do it." Jack cupped his hands around her neck, let his thumbs caress the vulnerable area of her throat. "That's striking hard but not especially fast."

Wariness slipped in. "Is that your way of saying you want to follow me again?"

Whatever response Noel expected, it wasn't to be caught by a hard, searing kiss that sent her head spinning and had her thoughts slamming into each other.

Fear and uncertainty became a hunger that seemed to spring out of nowhere. She pressed herself into him, wrapped her arms around his neck and pulled him, if possible, even tighter against her.

She felt his arousal. He wanted her. She moved her hips, heard his throaty approval.

She didn't want reason to intrude. He'd caught her unprepared and she loved it. So few men, or maybe none at all, had ever broken her stride.

Until Jack.

"Time, Jack." She broke away to gasp the words. "We—I have to be at the theatre. For your sister."

Breathing heavily, he closed his eyes, laid his forehead on hers. "It's too dangerous, Noel."

"No, it's not." For some reason, she felt certain of that. "This is another move in the kidnapper's game. I'm not saying there's no danger," she added before he could protest. "I simply think he has a game in mind that he wants to play out. And that's definitely not Kurt deRosa's style."

Jack had a stubborn look on his face. Noel had seen it before. She ran her fingers through his hair until his head came up. "You can't come, okay? You have to say it, Jack, because I know what you're thinking. He knew you followed me last time. He'll know if you do it again."

A full ten seconds passed before he spoke. "I'll stay well back." His fingers tightened on her neck, and his thumb grazed her lips. "Keep your cell phone activated. Promise."

She nodded.

He kissed her again, more gently than before. She closed her eyes, then opened them again, wide. The tendrils of fear that had been twining in her stomach suddenly climbed up into her throat. It was terror she felt now, full-blown and out of control.

And only a small part of it had to do with Caroline Ransom's kidnapper.

NOEL KEPT HER MIND on her destination and every unconnected thought locked tightly away.

The Gemini stood amid a row of derelict buildings behind the town center. The architecture was exquisite, even from the outside, or it would have been in its heyday. At present, both the theatre and its neighbors appeared as lifeless as old skeletons.

Snow crunched underfoot as she made her way across the street to the entrance. The door resisted but opened with a solid effort.

Taking a deep breath, Noel walked on. She passed through a lobby lit only by the beam of her flashlight, on a carpet riddled with holes chewed out by rodents and dust so thick she could see it puffing with each step she took.

Cherubs and angels with harps and halos followed her progress. Her heart beat like a drum, her palms were damp, her eyes in constant motion. Adrenaline pumped through her the way it did before a big trial. She'd learned to use it over the years rather than fight it.

This wasn't, she reminded herself, the way Kurt deRosa operated. Yes, the man was a cold-blooded killer, but he wasn't insane.

Because thoughts like that didn't help, she locked them away with the others and concentrated on locating the entrance to the main seating area.

The Balcony sign was faded but legible. It stood crooked on a red carpeted staircase that curved to the upper level.

Not there, she decided when she spotted the plaque that indicated seats two hundred to three hundred.

The ceiling grew steeper as she passed through a large set of double doors. Aunt Maddie had said it rose to form a dome. It had carved moldings and a crystal chandelier that boasted at least a hundred arms.

Noel shone her light around. The chandelier was gone, but the carvings remained intact. Blank white eyes trailed her along the main aisle while strains of music started up in her head.

She halted, raised her eyes, moved the light more cautiously. The music wasn't in her head. It was tinny but real. It came from somewhere ahead of her and to the right.

She kept going. He wouldn't hurt her. He didn't want that. Not yet.

She heard a squeak and swung the flashlight toward it, but there was nothing except dust on the carpet and the dull sheen of starry tiles on the floor.

She counted rows and at the same time listened to the music. There were no vocals, but she recognized the tune.

"'Santa Baby,'" she said in a soft voice. Oh, yes, she got the message, loud and clear. Karaoke in the Caribbean during Christmas break. She and Helen had had a little too much to drink. Helen had gotten up on stage and done "Sleigh Ride" while she'd done this song. Noel flinched at the memory. She might have done it twice.

She brushed her fingers against the cell phone in her coat pocket for reassurance.

"Noel."

His voice swirled around her, as if coming from a synthesized echo chamber. Or the throat of a ghost.

When he didn't speak again, she continued walking. The row began at ninety. The floor had a star with a name she didn't recognize. At number ninety-five, she stopped and stared.

The star was there, swept clean as the ones around it were not. In the center were the initials RT and surrounding it the name Ronald Tillman.

Could this really be about barbecue sauce?

"Noel." The voice spoke again.

She spied an envelope taped to seat ninety-five and glanced up at the balcony. The kidnapper had made a reference to it in his last note. But it might only have been a clue to get her to this theater.

"Pick up the envelope, Noel."

The words seemed to feather along her spine to the point where her shoulders twitched. It was as if he'd stroked a cold finger over her skin.

The envelope had Jack's name written on it. Why always his name when so much of the note was directed at her?

You couldn't apply logic to insanity, Noel reminded herself and slid the envelope into her coat pocket.

"Read it, Noel."

Her head snapped up. His voice sounded much closer, although it still seemed to come from all around her. The tinny music, she realized, didn't. She spied a grubby little cassette recorder under one of the seats, but made no move to pick it up.

The sensations that crawled through her made her want to bolt. She stayed put, removed the envelope and pulled out the note.

The light was bad, dim and shadowy, but the print was legible—and not what she'd expected.

"A poem," she whispered, then froze when the voice reached her without benefit of speakers or synthetic devices.

"There are many sides to my personality, Noel."

He was behind her, directly behind her, no more than three or four seats away.

"If you try to look, I'll kill you," he warned in what struck her as a slight Spanish accent.

"Why the games?" she managed to ask.

"Because you and Jack love to play them."

"We don't—"

"You play with people's lives, both of you, and with no more concern for the consequences of your actions than a cat has when it torments a mouse."

He'd shifted from a Spanish accent to a British one midsentence. They were both fakes, and so was the timbre of his voice. He was pitching it lower than it would have been naturally.

The trick worked, however. If she knew him, and she must, she didn't recognize the sound of his voice.

"Is Caroline safe?" she asked.

A chuckle, then, "Of course she is. Oh, but then I have to say that, don't I, to keep the game going? A very stupid question, Noel, unworthy of your talents."

Now the accent was French. The music ended but began again, the same song. He moved closer, began to hum. She thought she felt his breath stir her hair.

Her muscles screamed, they were so rigid. Her chest felt constricted. It was what he wanted, she knew that. To make her feel trapped and helpless. Terrified.

"Are we going to stand here all night?" she asked in her softest voice.

"I could handle it."

He was speaking into her ear. She could smell him—cologne and soap beneath a layer of sweat.

"Am I driving you crazy, Noel? Scaring you? Do you want to run like I've heard you can?"

She pressed her lips together and stopped herself from asking the obvious question. Of course he knew about her. But was the knowledge personal or gleaned from other sources? She really couldn't tell.

"Why so many notes?" she wanted to know.

"I like notes. I like watching you and Jack squirm. I enjoy imagining him a mile from here, twisting himself in knots because he's helpless to do anything." A gloved finger stroked her neck from jaw to collarbone. "I could slit your throat, and he'd be powerless to stop me."

She hoped she didn't sound as breathless as she felt. "So this isn't about money?"

He merely chuckled. "I like money, too, Noel. But if a person can have it all, why shouldn't he take it?" His hands moved to her hair. With exaggerated care, he pulled it away from her face and secured it with... She didn't know what.

"A moment, cherie. Do you speak French?"

"No."

"Does your mama?"

"No."

"Does she speak Italian?"

Could this be Kurt deRosa? "We both do."

"I don't. Or any other language. Pity. Ah, well, enough of this chitchat. I'm enchanted by you, of course, but a businessperson at heart. Shall I give you a clue?"

"About your identity?" Noel hesitated. "Why?"

The hand, still wrapped around her hair, gave a painful tug. "Because I want you to know, to figure it out, to understand. Then I want the money."

She didn't believe him. "What about Caroline?"

Humor entered his tone. "If I were Jack, I wouldn't want her back, but if I'm satisfied, he'll have her. As for you—" he kissed her neck "—my plans are somewhat different." He drew back, released her hair. "As for the clue I promised, you've already been given a very good one."

"In the poem?"

"Read it again," he suggested. "But that wasn't what I meant. Initially, dear Noel, initially, I had in mind a plan whereby I would kidnap you and Jack and hold you captive, as if in a filthy prison cell, until you died. But then you'd have been directly underfoot. Are you getting this, Noel? Because you'll want to relate it to Jack verbatim. I'll tell you a secret if it helps." She steeled herself as he grazed her ear with his mouth. "Robert Tillman's dead. His daughter, the only one of his offspring still alive, has two children. One's in prison where I predict he'll die. The other is scrambling to make a life for himself. The sauce thing went belly up when the American palate altered. We like Southwest and Mexican flavor now. Savvy, Noel?"

"I'll have to think about it."

"Starlight, star bright. Brightest star within your sight. Say it fast, say it right. You'll know to whom you owe your plight."

He was easing away. Noel breathed out carefully while she listened to his receding movements.

The envelope slipped from her fingers. She bent to pick it up. As she did, she glanced behind her. There was no one and only a dusty mess on the floor tiles where he'd walked.

Except, she realized as she took a closer look at the long trail, he'd shuffled rather than walked. He'd moved without a sound.

Like the ghost he professed to be.

Chapter Ten

Dear Jack,
I offer you a Christmas poem:
Red Touch green,
Jack Ransom's mean.
Red Touch gray,
Another day.
(In Hell)
Red Touch red
Jack Ransom's dead.
Red Touch I,
It's time to die.
Catchy, yes? Meaningful, yes? Harmless? No! I'll be in touch.
Oh, Merry Christmas, Noel.
The Ghost of Christmas Past.

"He tied her hair back with a scarf she says he could only have taken from her purse at our Christmas party. He was at the party, Michael."

"Lots of people were there. Lots more could have snuck in."

"He touched her." Jack's features were stony as he faced his friend across the small deli table. "With his mouth."

"Yes, you told me," Michael said again. "Twenty times or more. He's crazy, Jack. I think we're all agreed on that. The poem he wrote was childlike, and as far as I can tell, nonsensical, although I'm sure it has meaning to him. The scarf was calculated. It says he could be anyone, anywhere, watching her. But what he said to her after was just a jumble of words."

"There's something in them." Of that Jack was certain. "She managed to get the cassette out of the machine he used."

"There were no prints on it, and the tape's ancient. He probably bought it at a thrift store."

"No background sounds?"

"Nothing."

"I still think it'll come down to money in the end. Thanks." Jack didn't look up as his sandwich was served.

"Where's the pretty lady?"

Michael sat back and grinned at their server. "You've met Noel?"

"You bet. I'm Ray." The counterman smiled, revealing a gap between a pair of crooked front teeth. "She's real pretty. Not like that one."

Jack's eyes wandered through the five or six occupied tables to the blond cross-dresser in the corner. He was scribbling something on a large notepad.

"We have a late-night order to fill, Ray," the owner called out. "Coffee?" he asked Jack and Michael.

"Double sugar," Michael returned, still grinning. "You bring me to the nicest places, Jack."

"I like the food."

"Yes, I've figured that out. Thank you," he said to the owner. "Artie, right?"

The man nodded. "Ray wants you to bring your pretty companion back for dinner one night soon." His eyes glinted. "Myself, I wouldn't do it. Despite his ratty appearance, our Ray's quite the ladies' man."

Jack found himself studying the blonde. "Does that guy come in here every night?"

"Pretty much. Orders coffee and a bagel, no butter, then sits and picks at it for an hour or more while he writes." Artie moved a slim shoulder. "I don't mind. He tips well enough to cover the use of the table. Freaks Ray out a little, but I'm the one who usually deals with him."

Jack regarded the blonde. "Maybe I should talk to him."

"He'll run."

Jack looked up at Artie, then shoved his chair back anyway. The blonde's head rose in a flash. When he realized Jack's intent, he grabbed his notepad, his bag and his coat and darted out the door.

"Told you," Artie said from behind. "He's a bit spooky. I'd call the cops but he never does anything to report."

"He left you ten bucks." Jack stared after him. "You're sure he's a guy?"

"I know a guy when I see one. And I saw Angie in the john. Women's clothes and wig aside, his sex isn't a question."

Michael backhanded Jack's arm. "Let it go, man. You've got bigger problems then paranoid cross-dressers."

"Yeah." But the hasty exit made him wonder. "Wrap up the sandwich, and make the coffee to go," he told Artie.

"Look, don't let some weirdo drive you out of here." Artie plucked the ten-dollar bill from the table and stuffed it in the pocket of his white shirt. "He won't be back tonight."

But Jack's mind was made up. "We've got work to do. Computer work," he said to Michael.

"At midnight?" Artie motioned to Ray to bag the food.

Resigned, Michael buttoned his coat. "There are no clocks in Jack's world." As he drew on his gloves, he asked, "Why now, out of the blue?"

"I got a look at that blonde's face."

"So did I. He needs lessons in proper makeup application."

"Yeah." Jack looked back at his friend. "And he has the same crooked nose as Philip Price."

"PHILIP PRICE'S NOSE. Yes, I get it, Jack." Noel's desk was piled with files and printouts. "Look, I'm really swamped right now, and I have to be in court at two."

"I have a meeting at three," he responded. "I wasn't suggesting we go through Philip's old papers right now. I was thinking about tonight."

"Where are his papers?" Noel waved at her paralegal, then motioned to the grinding fax machine. "In Pittsburgh or Winter Valley?"

"Winter Valley. He owned the house next to ours."

"I've seen those houses, Jack. My entire building has less square footage than the ground floor. But I might catch a break today. This particular judge prefers his sessions to be short. We're told he likes *Monday Night Football* and a scotch to kick-start the evening. I could be back in my office by five."

"I'll pick you up."

"I'll—" She removed the handset from her ear at the click on the other end. Jack had hung up on her. She turned to her waiting paralegal. "This is why no-strings sex is better than a relationship. As soon as you get to know them, men think it's perfectly fine to be rude."

"From what I've heard about Jack Ransom, rude is one of his better qualities." He set the faxes on her desk. "Are you thinking of having sex with him?"

"Nice try, Danny, but it was only an observation. Take this to Martin for me, okay?" She scratched a message on a blank pad and initialed it. "Tell him it's important."

"Glad to do it, because…" He drew the word out with a grimace. "I have to inform you that Martin Faber Junior is waiting outside. He says—and I'll paraphrase to be polite—he's going to nail your lovely butt to the wall in court next week. When he's done, if he plays his cards right, he'll be hanging his shingle on your corner office door by the twenty-fifth. Merry Christmas, Noel."

"YOU WANTED to see me?"

Harry Dexter was out of his element and nervous because of it. Jack had decided to use Michael's penthouse office for precisely that reason. He'd changed his clothes and considered shaving, but that would be going too far to set a scene.

"Sit down, Harry." He didn't rise from behind Michael's massive desk, but instead tapped his knuckles on the blotter.

Harry was larger than Jack had anticipated, a good six-two with broad shoulders, a bald spot that shone and speckled brown and gray hair with which he endeavored to cover the spreading spot. He wore black framed glasses, had a prominent Adam's apple and a slow way of talking that made him seem a bit dim-witted.

He had all his wits, however. Jack had ascertained that from his co-workers, from Hilda and from Noel who'd advised him not to underestimate the man.

"Is there a problem?" Harry asked.

"Could be." Jack ran a considering finger over his upper lip. "Tell me what you know about Noel Lawson."

"She's a lawyer. High-profile. Puts scum back in the boardroom, or so I'm told."

"She represented your ex-wife in your divorce."

Harry's mouth opened, then clicked shut. "Are you— Is she going to be joining us here at Ransom Price?"

"Would you have a problem with that?"

"Not at all."

Jack dropped his hand. "I heard your son passed away a while ago," he said. "I'm sorry."

"Thank you."

"You blame my grandfather and me for his death, don't you?"

Harry's shoulders squared. "I felt then and still do that some of your factories are not up to scratch where certain safety issues are concerned."

"In actual fact," Jack countered, "our factories exceed the current government safety standards." Jacob had been rigorous in that area. "Do you know Winter Valley?" At Harry's nod, he continued, "What about the Gemini Theatre?"

Harry's lips compressed. "I've never heard of it."

"So you weren't there last night."

The man's eyes went cold. "No."

"Could you prove that if, say, the police were to ask you the same question?"

Harry didn't flinch. "I was home last night, Mr. Ransom, with my dog and my TV. I live alone, as you would of course know since you're aware of my divorce."

"And Noel's part in it."

"Yes."

"Are you upset with Ms. Lawson for the role she played?"

"She used unfair tactics to gain an uncalled-for settlement."

"At one point in your life, you were on the verge of being discharged from the military. Instead, you resigned. There were allegations of theft. We only discovered this recently, Harry. Noel learned about it during the divorce hearing."

"Ms. Lawson made other allegations that had nothing to do with my stint in the navy. Rather than have her drag my name and reputation through the mud, I gave in and accepted the conditions of divorce that she set down."

"If none of what she alleged was true, why didn't you challenge her?"

"Are you accusing me of theft?" Harry's knuckles had gone white.

Jack picked up a pen, tapped it lightly on the desktop. "I'm asking questions, Harry, not making accusations."

"It sounds like I'm being accused." He shot forward, a snake ready to strike. "Did Ms. Lawson see my name on a personnel sheet and put you up to this?"

"Actually, I asked her about you at the Christmas party. That's when I discovered you'd threatened her."

"Those were words, Mr. Ransom, uttered in the throes of defeat. I make a decent wage, yet I live in a one-bedroom condo."

"In a fashionable area of Pittsburgh."

"I didn't say I was suffering, but I'd have a great deal more financial security if Noel Lawson hadn't coerced me into signing away my life and two-thirds of my savings during the settlement dispute."

"Did you meet with her out of court?"

"I chose not to."

"Why?"

"Because—" His face, already red, grew redder. "My reasons are my own. It wouldn't have made a difference. My belief is that judges tend to rule in favor of the wife in cases like mine."

"So Noel might actually have saved you money in the end."

"She saved me nothing, and neither did you or your grandfather. I've lost a son, a wife and a great deal of money. If I seem bitter because of that, I have a right to be. Is there anything else, sir?"

Jack stared at him for several long seconds. Harry stared back but the flush was fading from his face as his spate of temper drained away.

"Will you be asking me to resign?" he wanted to know.

"Have you committed any crimes against Ransom Price?"

Harry's Adam's apple bobbed, prompting Jack's brows to elevate. "I do my job. There haven't been any complaints."

"Well, then." Jack stood. "Thanks for your time, Harry. My assistant will see you to the elevator."

He waited until the door swished shut before saying, "What do you think?"

Michael emerged from the conference room attached to his office. "I think we might want to do a little sniffing around."

"He's cooking the books."

"Not big-time, he isn't. But I agree. I'll get someone on him."

"It's clear he dislikes Noel."

"And you." Michael played with his pinkie ring. "To change the subject, Helen suggested you might want to watch Matthew Railback, after all."

Jack headed for the door. He wanted to be in his office, in his regular work clothes. "Why him in particular?"

"She called it intuition. She says Noel would describe him as having a passive-aggressive personality. But Helen's been giving it some thought, and she thinks he might have changed. Something about seven-year cycles and male menopause. Whatever the reason, I saw the way Railback looked at Noel at the party. I'd say he wants her back."

"And he's threatening her life to make that happen?"

Michael shifted his gaze to the window. "He's been under the care of a psychiatrist for close to two years. Not a psychologist, Jack, a psychiatrist. That suggests deep emotional problems to me."

It did to Jack, as well. "Anything else?"

"Apparently, he shot a man in Maine thirty years ago. It was hushed up very well. One of the other people in the hunting party took the blame, but I gather it was Railback who did the deed. It's the usual story. They thought the victim was a deer."

"And?"

"We're working on a connection, a possible motive for Railback wanting the victim taken out. So far there's nothing. But I agree with Helen on this one, Jack. Keep an eye on the guy."

In the doorway, Jack worked up a smile. "And don't go deer hunting with him in Maine."

UNFORTUNATELY, THE JUDGE didn't like *Monday Night Football* as much as Noel and her associates had hoped. Her court session ran very late. The last witness for the prosecution had a fainting spell, then tried to pass it off as a heart attack. It was after eight by the time she returned to her office.

With the exception of Martin Faber, the entire floor was empty. Noel tried for the fifth time to reach Jack, but she got no answer and finally gave up.

"Noel!"

Two feet inside her office door, she swung around. "Matthew." She forced a smile. "What are you doing here?"

"I need to talk to you."

She let him come in, motioned to a leather armchair. "About Jack?"

He gave a short laugh. "How did you know?"

"You don't like him, and I was with him at the Christmas party." She shed her jacket. "What's that in your hand?"

He shook the box. "Chocolates. They were on your secretary's desk. Your name's on the label."

"You can open them if you want to."

"You know me and my sweet tooth all too well, I'm afraid."

She also recognized the charm he was turning on for her benefit. "Jack and I are business associates, Matthew, and that's exactly all you need to know."

"He wants you, Noel."

She faced him from behind her desk. "I'm not going to do this with you, okay? We had a relationship. It ended. I'm sorry, but we're done."

With deliberate, almost velvety movements, he undid the ribbon and paper. "They're Belgian, your favorite. You don't seem overly sorry."

"I was at the time. Right now, I'm tired—of work and games."

"Jack has his grandfather in him. You shouldn't discount that, darling."

She hated when he called her darling. "Jack's his own person, Matthew. If you bothered to know him, you'd realize that."

"If *I* bothered to know *him?* He's a Ransom. You can't get anywhere near him."

"Have you tried?"

"What, go into his office and say, 'Hey Jack, let's do lunch'?"

"Maybe he'd surprise you, and say yes."

Matthew selected two chocolates and sampled the first. "Mocha creme. Excellent flavor. Noel, I didn't come here to argue with you." The charm returned full force. "I was hoping we could have dinner."

"Sorry. I have other plans."

His mustache twitched sideways, a sure sign he was displeased. "With Jack Ransom?"

"That's my business. Have another chocolate, Matthew, then let yourself out."

His very handsome face didn't look quite so handsome when the color rose in it. But he smiled and acknowledged her with a nod. "Obviously, I can't force you. But I'd watch myself where Jack Ransom's concerned. You know the saying."

"The apple doesn't fall far from the tree?"

He held up forbearing hands. "It's your funeral, sweetheart."

"Mmm. Matthew?" She watched him pocket two more chocolates. "What brand of cologne do you use?"

"It's a blend of three."

It figured. "Which three?"

His eyes gleamed. "That's for me to know and you to sniff out. Ciao, Noel."

"Hey—" Jack came through the door just as Matthew was preparing to leave. He looked the man up and down, then glanced at Noel. "Am I interrupting?"

Jack wore jeans so faded they were white in some places, a dark leather jacket with a khaki shirt underneath and the Pirates cap he'd worn when she'd first seen him. Noel had a strong urge to jump him.

"Matthew's leaving," she said. She dropped two more chocolates in his pocket. "The express elevator will take you straight to the first floor."

"Mr. Ransom."

"Mr. Railback." Jack's eyes trailed him through the outer office to a second bank of doors. Then, with hands in his pockets, he swung casually on his heel to face Noel.

"Are you going to tell me to back off?"

"That depends on what you plan to say."

"Why, when, what?"

She pulled the clip from her hair and let it fall around her shoulders. "He invited me for dinner, then he warned me about you. I don't sense he's madly in love with me. I'm guessing it's more a case of not having ended our relationship his way, which probably makes it an ego thing. He wears cologne, Jack. So did the kidnapper."

"So do lots of men." Jack came in, studied the open box of chocolates. "These are expensive. A gift from Railback?"

"He found them on my secretary's desk. Clients drop off gifts from time to time."

He caught her hand, stroked a thumb over her inner wrist. "Like diamond bracelets, for example?"

She shook the chain. "Yes, like that. This one didn't come from Damian Lowe. The last present he gave me was a sable coat. I gave it back. I'm too much of an animal lover to wear real fur."

He moved closer. "It's too late to drive north." His face was inches from hers when he asked, "Have you had dinner?"

"No, but I warn you, Jack, I'm in the mood for hot and spicy, not pepperoni on pumpernickel."

"I can handle that." He still had his fingers curled around her wrist. When he tugged her closer, she came. She let him kiss her, felt the quick rush of heat, but drew back.

"Hot and spicy food," she said quite clearly.

"I'm hungry, too, darling. Dessert can wait."

Coming from him, the endearment didn't bother her at all.

Jack rooted through the chocolates while Noel retrieved her jacket and purse. He bit into one. "Brandy," he said, then caught her gaze. "I hear Railback likes to shoot deer. Among other species."

Surprise stopped Noel halfway through changing her shoes. "He shot a person?"

"You didn't know?"

"Of course not. When?"

"Over thirty years ago. In Maine. The guy's name was Gordon Avery. He's a medical doctor."

Something dull and heavy landed in Noel's stomach. "He's also," she said without inflection, "one of my father's best friends."

Chapter Eleven

He took her to a small Greek restaurant. It had six cozy dining rooms that held three tables each and sat above a Greek grocery store. It was dark, smelled of garlic and rosemary, and the owner and his wife cooked and served. There were Christmas trees decorated with colored balls and soft Christmas music played on Greek instruments.

Over dinner, they talked about everything except ransom notes, blondes with crooked noses and ex-lovers. It surprised Jack that Noel liked old movies and even more that she knew and understood a number of sports. She was a Bruins fan, but he forgave her for that and ordered another bottle of wine.

He shouldn't have, he realized. He had a blinding headache and the souvlaki he'd chosen wasn't sitting well in his stomach. Still, she enchanted him enough that he overcame his discomfort and tasted the chardonnay in his glass.

"Favorite Bogart film."

She considered and drank. "*African Queen.* You?"

"*Key Largo.* I figured you'd go for *Casablanca.*"

"I loved Katherine Hepburn as Rosie. I enjoy watching people transform. Sixties sitcom."

"*The Dick Van Dyke Show.*"

"I bet you liked Alan Brady best. Mine's *That Girl.*"

Jack worked on a tension knot at the back of his neck. "Are you a wannabe actress, Noel?"

"No, I'm already what I wanna be." She leaned forward on her elbows, smiled and made him want to forget about the diners at the other two tables. "What would you have been, Jack, if you could have chosen?"

"A rock musician."

"Now that's a shock. Do you play?"

"Guitar and a little piano."

"Sing?"

"Not a note."

Her smile faded. "It's not much of a segue, but we probably should talk about the kidnapper's note, and what he said to me in the theatre."

The people at the next table began to laugh. The Christmas music took on an East Indian quality.

"It didn't make sense, you know, and yet I got the feeling he intended it to. He said he'd give me a clue, that he already had— and he wasn't talking about his latest note. He told me that initially—and he repeated the word—he planned to kidnap both of us and hold us in a filthy prison cell until we died. But we'd be underfoot then. He asked if I understood because I'd want to tell you about it word for word."

"Are you?"

"Pretty much verbatim—which was his word."

He regarded her somewhat blurred features. "What about the 'starlight, star bright' thing?"

"'Brightest star within your sight. Say it fast, say it right. You'll know to whom you owe your plight.'"

"Say what fast and right?"

She shook her head, studied him. "Are you all right, Jack? You look a little pale."

"How can you tell in this light?" The people beside them

laughed again, and the sound of it set his teeth on edge. "Is any of this related to the Gemini Theatre?"

"I wondered about that. We should probably go back there in daylight."

The music, the laugher and even Noel's voice became a buzz in Jack's head.

"Jack?" He felt her hands on his face, lifting his head, noted the concern in her voice. He hadn't heard much of that growing up with Jacob and Caroline.

A layer of fog wanted to settle over his brain. He shook it away. "What are you doing?"

"Checking your eyes."

She had his head trapped, so he looked straight at her. "They're brown."

"They're hazy." She pushed the hair from his forehead. "How do you feel?"

"My head hurts."

"So does my hand. You're crushing the bones, Jack."

He pried his fingers free, hadn't realized he'd grabbed her. "I think I need to get out of here."

He paid the bill but he wasn't about to drive. "The engine's got power," he said and dug the keys from his jeans pocket.

It was a sleek black Jaguar, the sports model. It had been Jacob's final purchase. Jack drove it from time to time to keep it in running order. He'd have sold it except it ran fast, and some days when he needed it most, it took him away from his life for a while.

"Come on, hotshot, let's get you home to bed."

His smile felt as fuzzy as his eyesight. "I love a woman who lays it on the line."

"I love a man with a Jag." She slammed the door, then slid into the driver's seat and started the engine. "Did you have anything to drink before you came to my office?"

"Coffee and bottled water." The haze became a rolling black mass. He closed his eyes and fought it.

If she spoke to him again, he didn't hear her. Didn't hear the engine, the traffic or the stereo. But his grandfather's voice came through loud and clear.

"Never let them see weakness, Jack. Remember that. If you've got a problem, hide it, or better yet kick its bony ass out of your life."

Other sounds started out low and grew to a deafening din. Through it streaked words and phrases uttered by Jacob, Philip and a number of federal officers.

Colored lights, hundreds of them, flashed and winked and sparkled. Angry shouts erupted. Jack was a teenager. He wanted to be out doing teenage things. Cruising, necking, drinking beer.

The images skewed. It was almost Christmas, almost his birthday. Didn't feel like a birthday. Cops and FBI agents swarmed everywhere, like a plague of locusts. Jacob kept shouting at him. His grandmother chuckled. Then she screamed. All the lights turned red. And dripped blood.

The FBI had done her more harm than good. He remembered thinking that. He hadn't known what Jacob had been thinking. No one had. His grandmother was gone. Jacob grew more distant. Colder. Harder.

Kidnapping had been the only thing Jack had ever seen the old man fear. Then it had happened, not to Jack as he'd expected, but to his wife.

Philip had died days after Jack's grandmother. Natural causes, they said. But Jack knew he'd drunk himself to death, a man with full-blown diabetes who'd ignored it and wound up with kidney failure.

Then his father had died overseas, making three people gone within months. Jacob had stuck his claws into Jack and held fast. Caroline had sulked and whined and lashed out at her brother. As if he'd wanted to be the old man's successor.

His thoughts took a twist. Michael's face swam in. The nerd had become an urban sophisticate.

Michael had grown up in chaos. Three generations of Santoses had lived in one crowded house. Michael and his older brother had slept in the attic. His four sisters and two other brothers had alternated their living quarters. His grandparents had managed in a small suite in the basement. God knew where his parents had slept.

How was it there'd always been room for one more? Jack couldn't count the nights he'd spent at Michael's place. He'd only had Michael over to his house a handful of times—which was a handful more then anyone else.

Guests tended to feel uncomfortable at the Ransom mansion. Caroline could be brash and unfeeling. Angered, she threw things at anyone in range, at Jack more often than not. He'd hated being home. No wonder he'd taken off with Michael for California that summer in college.

But you couldn't run away from Jacob Ransom for long. And you couldn't pass your inherited responsibility to anyone else. Not while the old man was alive.

So why hadn't he done it after Jacob died, just tossed the whole complicated mess into Michael's capable hands?

"It's in your blood, boy," Jacob used to thunder at him. "I amassed a fortune. It's up to you to build on it. Life's all about money."

A sinister black fog rolled in, obscuring the face in Jack's head. Then suddenly the blackness vanished, and there was color. And light. And a dazzling display of Christmas trees. And Noel.

Why was she called Noel when she hadn't been born at Christmas?

Her voice reached him through the fog in his mind. "It was my great-grandmother's name. Maria Noel deMori…" He heard her sigh. "You know, looking back, I'm not sure what I saw in Matthew."

How had they gotten from great-grandmothers to Matthew Railback? Was he asking her these questions, he wondered, or imagining both them and her answers? Once again, her voice seemed to float into his head.

"Matthew hunted. I knew that. He didn't do it while we were together. I thought I'd made him understand, but I heard he went back to it. Why would anyone want to shoot Bambi?"

Had Railback been aiming at Bambi?

"It must have been a deer. I can't believe he meant to hurt Gordon Avery. I couldn't be that wrong about someone, could I?"

Anyone could be wrong about another person. How had her father felt about her relationship with one of his friends?

"Ah, well, Matthew and my father weren't exactly what you'd call friends. They had acquaintances in common. My dad didn't like it, but don't forget, he's been my dad my whole life. I think he figured if he stayed out of it, the relationship would end on its own. He was right. They always end."

Some faster than others, but, yes, they always did. What was the deal again with Roberto Turano?

"Just another ex. He lives in Tuscany now."

But he'd returned to the United States recently, hadn't he?

"That was Kurt deRosa."

Jack's head hurt. He didn't want to dream anymore, if that's what he was doing. Kissing Noel was more enjoyable, more explosive. He never got this emotionally involved when he kissed a woman. Sex with Noel might be an annihilation.

He felt her lips on his cheek. "Right now, sex would kill you, Jack."

Maybe it was time to die.

Behind that thought, a man's synthesized voice roared: "Jack!"

Jack's eyes popped open. He shot upright with a shout, felt the lump of pure terror lodged deep in his throat.

He smashed his head against something, swore and fought off a surge of pain and nausea.

"What the hell did I hit?"

"Me." Noel's hands probed his face, tipped his head back. "You have a very hard, thick skull, Jack. Are you awake?"

"If a minor concussion qualifies, then, yes. Where am I?" He squinted around a small sparsely furnished bedroom. His room. "You brought me home?"

"Is that what this is?"

"I live here when I'm in Pittsburgh. The family estate's in Winter Valley. How did we end up here?

She continued to check him out, running her fingers through his hair, pressing them to his cheek. "You gave me this address while you were throwing up on the side of the road."

He grimaced. "I was hoping I imagined that. What time is it?"

"Five o'clock in the morning."

He fell back onto the mattress. "I feel awful."

"I kind of figured that. Are you sure you only drank the wine we had with dinner?"

"Only that." His head was spinning. So was his stomach. "Don't ask about food, okay?"

"As far as ptomaine goes, I don't have to. I sampled everything on your plate and vice versa." The bed sank beside him. Slipping a hand under his neck, she lifted his head. He felt smooth glass against his lips. "Come on, drink this. It usually helps."

He didn't like ginger ale, but he took a long sip to please her.

It was difficult to make his mouth work properly, but he got out a vague, "Is someone using a jackhammer outside?"

"No, only in your head." She ran a light hand over his cheek. "Can I call a doctor for you? I know you don't want to go to the hospital, but a doctor would be a good idea."

He cracked his eyes open in suspicion. "How do you know I don't like hospitals?"

"You told me several times."

"Did we talk about Railback?"

"Him and other people." For some reason, her worried tone made him feel better. "This really seems like food poisoning to me. One of my sisters had it. She went through much the same thing as you."

"Did she live?"

"Lived, and sued." She played with his hair, an act that momentarily mesmerized him. "What else did you eat yesterday? Did you stop by Artie's Deli before you came to my office?"

"I had lunch with Michael in my office." He made it onto his elbows. "I have a meeting at nine."

"Jack, I could blow on you and you'd fall back onto that mattress. Let Michael do the meeting."

"Can't. We're closing in on a deal for a winery." His stomach pitched. "Did I really give you this address?" He never did that. Not ever.

"You said it three times. I was a bit surprised when you told me you lived on the North Side, but looking around this place, I'd say it suits you."

"You and Michael are the only people who know about it."

"Yes, I sensed that. You made me promise not to repeat what you'd said to anyone. Where do you get your—" she stopped for a beat, knit her brow and took on a faraway look.

"What is it?"

"I'm not sure. I need to call my secretary." She looked around the room. When she found her purse, she pulled out her cell phone and dialed. At 5:00 a.m., Jack didn't even want to think about what the conversation would entail. He tuned out—or tried to—until she ended the call.

"The chocolates," he said. He'd already promised himself he'd never touch another one. "You don't know who left them."

"My secretary says they weren't on her desk when she left. But they were there when I got back from court. So was Matthew."

"You play P.I. while I shower," Jack said and levered himself off his elbows to a sitting position. "Am I up?"

"Halfway." She sat down beside him. "Why don't you just stay home today and let this pass?"

"I want a shower, Noel."

"You'll fall flat on your face and drown in half an inch of water."

He managed a smile and a quick look at her face. "Yeah, well, I wouldn't say no to company."

"We'd both end up on the floor."

"That's the whole point."

Laughing, she ruffled his hair. "You have a healthy mind, Ransom, but your body's a bit of a question mark right now."

"Say that to me in the shower, Noel."

"I plan to." She spoke into his ear and made him shiver. "Ask me another time, okay?"

He would, he decided. He absolutely would.

She massaged the back of his neck. "If you're not out of the bathroom in thirty minutes, I'm calling your doctor. Deal?"

"I'll be out."

He had to lean on her to get across the room. Even so, it took forever. The floor was cold, and his feet were bare. "Call Railback first. See how he's feeling."

"Anyone who can eat the things he says he's eaten in the woods must have dealt with ptomaine poisoning at some point in his life."

"I'll bet he has," Jack agreed. "But in this case, is he dealing with the effects of it, or was it his deal to make sure someone else got poisoned?"

ALTHOUGH NOEL HATED to leave him, she borrowed Jack's Jaguar and drove to her office. The building was dead silent, the streets virtually empty. She bypassed the security station and went straight to her floor via the elevator in the parking lot.

This was familiar ground, she reminded herself as she was transported noiselessly upward. It was nothing like the Gemini. There was no one here to slide a finger across her throat, or kiss her cheek, or whisper in her ear.

A shudder ran through her. She'd had nightmares about that

encounter. Even last night, catnapping in the chair next to Jack's bed, she'd dreamed about it. In each case, when she'd turned around, it had been a shackled ghost she'd seen. Presumably Jacob Marley's ghost, tortured as the story said, yet terrifying in a way Marley's spirit hadn't been.

In her version, the spirit had red eyes, teeth like a steel trap, and he wore a black coat. By the end of her dream, he'd had a mustache.

She regarded the stainless steel elevator walls. She was alone in a place she knew. So why did she feel again as if someone was watching her?

She had to concentrate. She couldn't give in to a case of jitters. Jack had been poisoned, it was the only explanation. The restaurant food had been fine because she was fine. The source could only be the chocolates.

She tried Matthew's private number for the third time in forty minutes. She got his voice mail. He was a light sleeper, and he didn't turn his phone off at night. He wasn't home.

Or he couldn't answer.

"I'm not going to overreact," she promised herself as the doors swished open. Maybe Matthew was in the shower, too.

The image wasn't as tantalizing as the one she envisioned of Jack, the one she couldn't stop imagining of Jack. The one she needed to get out of her head before it developed into more than an enticing image.

Low lights showed the way along the corridors. As she passed Martin Faber's office, Noel recalled the message her paralegal had relayed to her from Martin Junior. It had ended with him wishing her a Merry Christmas, just like the kidnapper had done in his last note.

She really didn't need to add Junior's name to the list, but there might be some as yet unknown reason for him to resent Jack. They were of a similar age. Maybe they'd gone to school together. Or Jack might have turned him down for a legal job at Ransom Price.

Or maybe Martin simply disliked her.

Noel let herself into her office. A cemetery would be noisier at five-thirty on a Tuesday morning. She should leave music playing at night.

She checked her secretary's desk, glanced over her shoulder, then went through to her private office. Even her computer was silent.

"Don't do this," she said out loud. "You're not in an abandoned theatre. This is an office you worked your butt off through law school to obtain." Her eyes landed on the desk. Her breath stalled in her throat. This was also an office someone had been inside since she'd left last night.

The box of chocolates was gone.

Chapter Twelve

Jack got through the morning on autopilot—aided by seltzer, Tylenol and ginger ale. Noel had been right—the soda helped, but it didn't chase the fog from his brain or make his limbs feel any less heavy.

He closed the deal on the winery, which was good. And at lunchtime, Artie brought over a ham and mozzarella on white from the deli.

"Your VP called and said you weren't your usual self today and maybe I could think of an easily digestible alternative to pepperoni on pumpernickel. This should do the trick." He grinned. "I also brought some blackberry tonic that Ray's mother concocted. Ray swears by it. His mother's ninety-eight, so who am I to argue? Better than hair of the dog, she says."

Jack eyed the purply black liquid with suspicion. "Yeah, well, the dog isn't exactly my problem."

Artie's eyes twinkled. "You didn't go on a bender?"

"Only a chocolate one."

"Try it anyway." The deli owner popped the top and gave it to him. "Couldn't hurt."

Jack waited for an hour after Artie left before sampling the contents of the bottle. It tasted like berries, burnt rubber and rust—and to his amazement, it cleared his head. Must be nice for Ray to have a mother who was a modern-day alchemist.

His own grandmother had been Navajo. She'd made jewelry, not on the level of Damian Lowe's family, but she'd crafted a ring for him once. She'd also done matching stud earrings for him and Michael.

That was a thousand years ago, when he'd been foolish enough to believe he might actually escape from his grandfather's clutches. Then his grandmother had been kidnapped, and the whole world had altered by half a beat.

Annabelle, his sixty-two-year-old assistant, poked her head in the door. "Noel Lawson called while you were in the meeting, Mr. Ransom. She has two court appearances today. She won't be free until at least six, but she needs to talk to you, so she'll try your cell between sessions. She hopes you're feeling better. Also, Mr. Santos is here with a stack of documents for you to initial." She ticked off several other items on her fingers. "Ralph Burnley wants to come and see you this afternoon. He sounded peeved. And I have a dentist's appointment at two, so Sophie's filling in for a few hours if that's okay."

Jack assimilated what he could, summoned a smile and took another swig of Ray's mother's tonic. "Have fun," he said, "and send Michael in."

The documents stacked up six inches thick. Jack managed a frustrated sigh, and motioned to a second desk on the far wall.

"You look like hell," Michael observed as he set the stack down. "Why don't you knock off? I'll deal with Burnley."

"He's pissed about the lowball offer."

"It's not that low, and we're not proposing to break the company up, so most of his staff will keep their jobs."

"He doesn't care squat for his employees." Jack rested his head against the chair back. "See if you can get hold of Deirdre Burnley before Ralph shows up. I have a proposition for her."

"And I have news for you. The cops found your truck."

"Not good. Did you talk to them?"

"Twice in the last hour. I told them you hadn't been using it, so you didn't realize it had been stolen."

"And when they stopped laughing?"

"I said you'd decided to handle the matter yourself. It'll be in the compound this afternoon. You can pick it up late tomorrow, unless you want to file a report."

Jack took another drink. "I dreamed about my grandmother's death last night."

"That was a nightmare."

His gaze landed on the pile of documents. "The same thing could happen to Caroline."

"We've got people working on the notes, Jack, two dozen of them at last count. We're searching for illegitimate heirs on both sides of the Ransom Price coin. I even went to Artie's and tried to corner the blond drag queen, but he wasn't there." He paused, then added a quiet, "Caroline's stronger than you think. She'll tough it out until you get her back."

"That's what everyone said about my grandmother. She came back in a box."

"Right before Christmas. I remember. This really isn't your time of year, is it?"

"It's got its downside." Jack checked his cell phone, made sure it was charged, then he leaned back and closed his eyes. "Do me a favor, send Morris to Artie's and see if he can catch up with the blonde."

"No problem." Michael gave his cuffs a tug.

Jack opened his eyes part way. "Something else?"

"I'm not sure. Apparently, a couple of people in the office equipment division were talking about Matthew Railback. They said they saw him in a quiet restaurant last week with an attractive woman. Bear in mind, Jack, this is gossip, and it went through the mill before it got to me. But the rumor is, it wasn't a business meeting. There was a lot of under-the-table knee-squeezing going on."

"And?"

"The woman in question was Deirdre Burnley."

NOEL WAS ACCUSTOMED to amassing great numbers of details and storing them in her head. But the list in this case felt endless.

She met Jack at Artie's for a midafternoon coffee break. He drank water, she noticed, and looked, if possible, even more pale than he had that morning. But she gave him credit for fortitude and did her best to take his mind off his head and stomach.

"So you're saying you think Deirdre and Matthew might be working together on the kidnapping?" she asked.

"You told me she wanted to have a fling with him. Maybe she was jealous of your relationship."

"Jack, if they were squeezing knees last week, she has no reason to be jealous."

"She does if she thinks he still wants you, which I think he does and so does Helen."

"But I don't want him."

Jack tipped his water bottle back and drank. "Doesn't matter. You'd still be in her way."

"This is becoming ridiculously complicated. We've got Matthew and Deirdre getting friendly, a blond cross-dresser with a crooked nose like your late grandfather's late partner, a pissed-off accountant who might be cooking your books, an ex-boyfriend of Caroline's who can't be linked to me yet, a hostile lawyer who resents me but doesn't appear to be connected to you, a wounded man who was supposed to be a deer, possibly poisoned chocolates, weird notes, poems and clues we can't decipher. You write that down on paper, plus the dozen other things I'm sure I've missed, and it adds up to what?"

"A cesspool."

"Which we're in and struggling to climb out of while at the same time doing our jobs and telling ourselves not to get freaked."

Jack's lips twitched at the corners. "You don't look, act or sound freaked, Noel."

"Maybe I'm a wannabe actress after all." She gave Ray the counterman a little wave. He immediately brought the coffee-pot over.

"You working alone?" Jack asked.

"Nah, I got a man in the back." He offered Noel a gap-toothed smile. "Artie had to run out for gherkins and beets." He refilled her mug. "You be sure to see me before you leave. I'll give you a coupon for free coffee."

"That would be nice, thanks." Noel noted Jack's scowl and turned her smile of amusement to Ray. "Has your cross-dressing blonde been in lately?"

"Not since he ran out when you—" Ray beamed at Jack "—tried to talk to him. He comes in here again, I'll call and maybe you can chase him out for good. Someone said he's a poet, but I have another *P* word to describe him. Begging your pardon, Noel."

"I've heard lots of *P* words, Ray. Here's my cell number." She scribbled it on the back of a business card. "Let me know if he comes in again, okay?"

Flustered and flushed, Ray scuttled off. Noel took in Jack's lingering scowl. "Problem?" she asked in her most innocent voice.

"You were flirting with him."

"Give the guy a break, Jack. He lives with his mother and a molting parrot. He has a thirteen-inch TV with a dial, and the only woman he's dated in the past year was ten years older than him and going bald."

"Artie says Ray's a ladies' man."

"In his dreams."

"How do you know so much about the guy?"

"He told me while you were in the bathroom."

"It could have been a line."

"If that's the case, I suggest he try rejigging it. Guys who live with their moms and own frizzled birds aren't much of a turn-on."

Jack took a long look into his glass. "Did you live with Railback?"

Reaching out, she ran a finger along his cheekbone. "Did you live with Lorna?"

"No."

"Miranda?"

"No."

When he caught her hand, laughter sparkled in her eyes. "God, we're a dull pair. Either that or neurotically private. My answer's no, too. I didn't live with Matthew."

"What about Turano?"

She released a breath. "Almost, but not quite. We had common problems."

"Such as?"

"Closet space, for one. We both liked clothes. And you can stop grinning. Some men actually care about what they wear. Helen says Michael has three overflowing closets in his condo."

"And that's after the purge."

"Worst of the *P* words," she said with a glance at the wall clock. "Look, I have to get back. I'm due in court. I've been trying to reach Matthew, but so far he's not answering, not at home or work." She let him play with her fingers. "Do you want to drive up to Winter Valley tonight or wait another day?"

"Let's see what time we're both off. I have three meetings this afternoon." When she angled her head to study him, his brow creased. "What?"

"Nothing important. I'm developing a theory about you, that's all."

Releasing her hand, he helped her with her chair and coat. "It's starting to snow."

"I noticed." She pushed through the door. "If Matthew's gone backpacking, or, God forbid, hunting, maybe the weather will cut his time short."

"Or maybe he's curled in the fetal position on his bathroom floor."

"Sadist. He isn't. I called his neighbor. She has a key. He's not home. Go deal with Ralph, Jack. And keep drinking Ray's tonic."

Because it felt right, and also because he still had very little color in those exquisite cheeks, Noel kissed him. She was surprised when he pulled her close and held her there just a little longer than necessary. She felt his instant arousal, felt the heat deep in her belly and hitched back a startled breath. "Wow."

"Yeah." He wouldn't let her slip away, so they stood on a crowded sidewalk while he moved his hips against hers. "You sure you want to go to court?"

Right now, she wasn't even sure why she was going to court. "You're messing up my concentration, Jack." When he kissed her again, she swore she heard bells jingling in her head.

Someone tapped her arm. "You're ringing, dear." An old woman gave her an encouraging smile when she looked around. "Your purse. It's ringing."

"My— Oh." Noel broke away and reached for her cell. "Thank you," she said, then answered, "Noel Lawson."

It was a brief call, difficult to hear on a crowded sidewalk. Jack eased her out of the pedestrian flow and over to where a street corner Santa stood with his bell and plastic pot. She saw Jack put money inside, but her mind was already zinging.

When the call ended, she took him farther along the brick wall. "That was Matthew's neighbor. The doorman told her that Matthew went to the hospital last night. He has ptomaine poisoning."

"IF HE ATE THE CHOCOLATES, Noel, and obviously the poison was in the chocolates, then Matthew can't have known about it. Ergo, it's unlikely he's your Christmas ghost."

Helen's logic was impeccable, as always. And Noel wasn't buying a word of it.

"Jack thinks he ate just enough of them to make himself sick."

"How many is enough?" Helen asked over an increasingly static-filled line. "How many did Jack have?"

"Two. I gave Matthew two or three and he took several out of the box himself, but I only remember seeing him eat part of one."

"So my original intuition about him could still be right."

"Could be. I'll give his doctor a little legal push and see if I can find out how bad Matthew really was when he came in."

"How bad was Jack?"

"He talked in his sleep."

"Anything interesting?"

Noel took care with her response. "He mentioned certain family members. I think he went through a lot of stuff in his late teens."

"We all did."

Not like this, they hadn't. "I might be coming up there," Noel regarded her watch. It was 6:45 p.m. already, and she hadn't finished her paperwork yet. "Tomorrow night." She held out her hand for the folders Danny was bringing in. "Hang on a sec."

"There's this, too." From his back pocket, her paralegal produced an envelope. "It appeared on my desk five minutes ago, while I was in Mr. Faber's office."

Noel stared at the printing, which simply said: Jack and Noel.

"Thanks, Danny." She turned it over with icy fingers.

"Noel?" Helen sounded worried. "What's wrong? Why have you gone silent?"

Noel counted to ten by twos, in English, then opened it. And swore.

"What?" Helen demanded. "Is it another note?"

"You could say that." When her temper threatened to rise, Noel reined it in, breathed and read the message. It said:

MERRY CHRISTMAS.
HA, HA, HA!

Chapter Thirteen

He'd been laughing at them all along. Now he was mocking them outright. It cost Noel a great deal of effort not to let anger rule logic. She suspected it cost Jack a great deal more.

They needed to revisit the Gemini Theatre in Winter Valley. They also had to go through Philip Price's effects, although Noel put that further down the list than their theatrical encore.

"If the kidnapper wants us to know who he is, then there must be something either inside the theatre or in what he said to me there, or both."

Even a day later, Jack was still paying the price for eating the tainted chocolates. Noel had talked to Matthew's doctor early that morning. Matthew had been more fortunate. The stomach pump had pretty much taken care of the poison in his system.

Because Jack didn't feel like driving, Noel took the wheel of his Jaguar and pointed it north. Snow had been falling off and on since yesterday afternoon. It was more on, she noted, than off at this point. The highway remained bare, but the landscape already wore a thick coat of white.

"You're still determined not to give Matthew a break, aren't you?" she said with a knowing look at Jack.

He had his eyes closed and his head back. "A smart person who wanted to divert suspicion might consider it worth the consequences to eat one of the bad chocolates, then have himself rushed to the hospital to get rid of it. No big deal for him in the face of ten million dollars and a healthy dose of revenge."

Noel found his point difficult to refute, so she didn't try. Instead, she said, "There's an aspect of this that's been bothering me lately."

"Caroline?"

She hadn't expected him to read her mind quite so easily. "I feel like we're forgetting about her."

Jack's eyes opened, but he directed his gaze at the road. "I haven't forgotten her, Noel. The guilt's there, I just prefer not to dwell on it." Still staring forward, he asked, "How much did I tell you about my grandmother the other night?"

"Enough that I understand why you want the police and more particularly the FBI left out of this. She was kidnapped and killed."

"While my grandfather was out of town and Caroline and I were staying with her. Except I was at a party, and Caroline hid in a closet. She stayed there until I got home."

"How old was she?"

"Almost sixteen."

Noel was incredulous. "And she hid in a closet, didn't call anyone?"

"Not a soul. By the time I got back, they were long gone. The feds showed up, Jacob rushed home. Philip even checked himself out of the hospital where he was being treated for serious kidney problems."

"Was there a ransom note?"

"Yeah, but we were advised to do nothing, let the FBI handle the matter. I have no idea why Jacob went along with that, unless it was because the kidnappers managed to tap into his deepest and possibly only fear. Agents tracked the guys—there were three of them—to a fleabag hotel and tried to squeeze them out. It didn't work."

"Rats in a corner?"

"Exactly. They shot my grandmother, then started shooting everything in sight in order to escape. Two of them were killed on the spot. The third made it to the roof, slipped and fell to his death. It was ten days before Christmas."

"Was that the same year Philip Price died?"

"He didn't bother going back to the hospital, just went home and faded away in his bed."

"His bed in the house we're going to search?"

"The very same." A hint of a smile crossed Jack's lips. "He had bed curtains in his room."

"So we'll be recreating *A Christmas Carol* before the visit of the three spirits."

"Or before Scrooge's dream." He closed his eyes. "It depends on your interpretation, doesn't it?"

Beneath the cynical remark, Noel sensed a weary sadness. She stopped pressing and let him sleep until they reached Winter Valley.

By some miracle, they'd managed to get away before five-thirty. Although darkness had fallen, it was still early enough for them to go to the theatre and take a look inside.

To relive her nightmare, she reflected as she pulled on the brake.

She couldn't resist leaning over and brushing her lips across Jack's cheek. "We're here, Romeo."

He didn't open his eyes. "Can we do a balcony scene while we're at it?" Before she could reply, he turned his mouth to hers and took her teasing kiss a whole lot deeper.

They should have gone to Philip's house first, was all Noel could think, and even that much was a feat. Her pulse throbbed and she became aware of an aching need deep inside. Not a good or smart thing to feel right now.

She pulled free just far enough to say, "Your timing's as off as your color."

He merely grinned and rubbed his nose against hers. "My color's fine. You wanna go to Philip's place first?" he asked as his hand slid along her collarbone to her breast.

Right to Philip's curtained bed, she thought with a sigh.

But the theatre loomed beside her, taunting her. No matter how she felt, she had to go in again. Now, before she lost her nerve. She stopped his hand. "Think about Caroline, Jack, not me."

He stared at her, let out his breath, then reached for the door. "I'm going to make a point of never opposing you in court."

"Smart man."

She really didn't want to do this. Even early in the evening, the street was deserted, the buildings cold and lifeless.

He took her hand, squinted through the thickening snow. "The front door's cracked open."

"Lovely." Her footsteps slowed.

"Noel, the kidnapper would have to have followed us to know we're here."

She glanced over her shoulder at the shadowy street. "I get the feeling I'm being followed quite a lot lately."

Jack kept a firm grip on her hand. "That would be nerves."

"Not a believer in anything remotely metaphysical, huh?"

"Like Christmas ghosts, epiphanies and ESP?"

"I was thinking slightly smaller scale."

"He can't be everywhere, Noel."

She narrowed her eyes, but in profile and obscured by blowing snow and weak light, she couldn't read his features.

"Red Touch green." Jack recalled the first line of the kidnapper's written poem. "Two caps and one lower case."

"Sounds like a clue, doesn't it? Jack…" She tugged on his hand with both of hers.

He stopped, rested his free arm on her shoulder and looked right into her eyes. "Do you want to wait in the car?"

"That's not the problem."

"What, then?"

She dug in with her fingers. "There's an envelope taped to the door."

To be opened after you leave the theatre.

Follow your instructions, Jack and Noel.

You know what will happen if you don't.

JACK SNATCHED the envelope free and stuffed it in his pocket. "This guy's really pissing me off. You ready?"

"As I'll ever be." She made a sweeping circle of the street. Despite the lack of light, he saw the telltale glint in her eyes. "I hate manipulators."

One of many things he loved—liked—about her.

"Are you all right?"

"What?" He frowned. "Why?"

"You stuttered a bit just then."

Had he made that comment aloud?

His mind was still stuttering big-time. There was no chance to examine why as he ran his gaze around the darkened lobby.

They both carried flashlights, and Noel knew the location of seat number ninety-five. Jack glimpsed white angels, red velvet seats and elaborate moldings. The curtain still hung over the big screen, but it did so in deep black tatters. It would have resembled a funeral shroud in better days. Hardly an uplifting thought.

Noel angled her beam downward. Most of the names on the tiled floor were illegible. The clearest was Ronald Tillman's and it was circled with a slash of red.

Jack crouched, drawing Noel down with him. "Was this paint here before?"

She shook her head, then raised it.

"What?"

"The skin on my neck's prickling."

"It's drafty in here."

"Or someone's watching us."

"Noel…"

"Yes, I know, you don't believe. I was thinking maybe we should look at the note."

"He told us to open it after we leave the theatre."

"I only want to see the envelope." She dipped a hand into his pocket and pulled it out. Felt it. "It's damp and wrinkled. I think it's been taped to the door for a while. He must have guessed we'd come back. He probably wanted us to." She considered for a minute. "You don't suppose he's holding Caroline here, do you?"

Jack made a thorough sweep of the room. There was the backstage area and the projection booth, maybe the manager's office. "I doubt it, but I'll have it searched tomorrow just in case."

Noel removed a digital camera from her bag and began to snap pictures.

"What do you make of the red circle?" he asked.

"It looks violent." She lowered the camera. "Have you run a background check on Ronald Tillman?"

"He's dead."

"Yes, the kidnapper mentioned that. He also told me Tillman had a daughter and that she had two kids. Two boys, he said. One's in prison where he'll probably die. The other's doing his best to make a life for himself."

"Okay, now we have a discrepancy, because so far there's no record of Ronald Tillman having any living children or grandchildren."

Noel rested her shoulder against one of the chair backs. "This is so bizarre." She traced the circled star with her finger. "And so convenient. I don't think Ronald Tillman's a major player here."

"What, then?"

"If I knew that, Jack, I'd have this mystery half solved. The red circle surrounds the star. It cuts right through Tillman's name in places."

"Red Touch red," Jack recalled and indicated the surrounding floor. "The tiles are a deep red color."

"Right. That's it." Noel stood, returned the camera to her bag. "We need to get out of here. 'Red Touch red,'" she quoted. "'Jack Ransom's dead.'"

"He won't—"

"Get his money if he kills you. Fine, Jack. But I don't want to push the point. Let's go to Philip's house, read the note and think this whole thing through where it's warm and dry." She paused for a moment. "It is warm and dry there, right?"

"We'll see, won't we?"

Jack made sure she walked in front of him when they left. The kidnapper struck him as a person who'd love nothing better than to shove a knife in someone's back.

Wind moaned through invisible cracks, and the joists creaked with every fresh gust. It was a full-blown blizzard by the time they reached the car. Jack didn't think, just shoved Noel inside and let himself be blown in after her.

"Do you want me to drive?" he asked.

She gave the theatre one last uncertain look and him a droll one as she fired the engine. "I grew up in the Northeast. I took my road test in the winter."

She stopped talking and looked in the rearview mirror, just long enough to have him swiveling his head. "You see something?"

"A car." But it crawled past without stopping.

Another pair of headlights approached from behind. Jack turned, peered through the snow at the vehicle. And only had a split second to yank Noel down and dive on top of her before the rear windshield exploded.

SHE HEARD the glass shatter. Another blast and the front windshield was blown away. She felt Jack's weight on top of her and didn't move. As long as he believed he was holding her down, he wouldn't be in the line of fire. High-powered fire from the sound of it, possibly a magnum.

Her heart thudded against her ribs. After the shots came a tense silence. Jack raised his head. She gave him one second, then pulled him back down by the front of his shirt.

An engine roared. Jack had gotten his truck back, so it couldn't be his vehicle this time. Could it?

Noel wriggled out from under him but stayed low. "What did you see?"

"An SUV. American make. I need to get a better look at it."

She shoved the keys in the ignition. "We need to get away from here."

"We can't outrun him in the snow, not even in a Jag."

She gave her wrist a flick and the engine caught. "We only have to make it to a more trafficked area. He isn't likely to shoot up Main Street."

"Wasn't it you who used the word *insanity*?"

She shoved a large chunk of tempered glass from the floor console. "I think he's crazy, but I'm also certain he doesn't want to be caught. Yet."

Jack risked another glance. "He's just sitting there." Then he swore and yanked her down again.

Another deafening blast rocked the car. The truck revved, peeled back and swung out around them. His final shot put a large hole in the driver's side window.

White-hot fury blended with Noel's terror. She used it to push herself upright. "When we find out who this guy is, I'm going to blast everything around him and let him know how it feels to have a maniac—" She spotted the smear of red on Jack's arm and her anger dissolved. "He shot you!"

"Grazed." Jack cut off her attempt to tear at his jacket. "It can wait. Just go."

A portion of the driver's side of the windshield remained intact. Even so, driving was next to impossible. It took more than twenty minutes to travel the two-mile distance to her house. Keeping a clamp on her emotions, Noel got the damaged car into the garage and Jack in through the back door.

There was a lot of blood. Too much. She grabbed a clean towel, bandages and a roll of gauze from the downstairs powder room, then wrapped the towel around his arm. He didn't complain or say much of anything as they climbed the stairs to her apartment.

"Do you have the camera?" he asked once they were across the threshold.

"In my bag." She tugged off his jacket, shed her coat and ripped open the sleeve of his shirt. Seeing the wound up close lifted fifty pounds of weight from her shoulders. "It *is* a graze. It's deep, though. You might need stitches."

"You think that's gonna happen, huh?"

Not really, but his mildly humorous tone brought a smile to her lips. "You're supposed to be indignant, Jack. You know, fists clenched, ready to knock the guy's head off."

"I am, and I will, as soon as we figure—" His brow furrowed. "What are you doing?"

"Getting rid of your shirt. I can't apply a proper bandage with a bloody sleeve in the way."

"Don't you feel faint?"

"Why, do you?"

"Caroline screams if someone nicks their finger."

She planted him on the sofa, handed him the bandages and gauze. "I hate to seem insensitive, but your sister sounds like a bad-tempered wuss."

"And you're wondering why you're risking your life to help me save hers."

"I need antiseptic," she said and started for the bathroom. "Actually," she called back, "I'm more interested in how the kidnapper's reacting to her, or if she's altered her behavior accordingly."

"It's unlikely."

When she reached the bathroom, Noel took a look at herself in the mirror. It amazed her how a person could go from court-room-polished to wild and windblown in such a short time.

She searched out the antiseptic and returned to the living room. Except that Jack was no longer sitting on the sofa. He was in the adjacent area she'd screened off for her home office, and he had her camera with him.

For a moment, she leaned against one of the tall support columns and allowed herself the pleasure of watching him. His sleek, catlike body stirred her senses and made her feel slightly short of breath. Her imagination fueled the feeling.

Sex with Jack would be incredible. She knew that instinctively. But how would she feel afterward? How long would the sensation last? Would he fade from her life the way Roberto had, or pine for her the way he and Helen insisted Matthew was doing?

The last thought amused her. Jack wouldn't pine for anyone. And he certainly wouldn't fade away. More likely, she'd be the one who'd end up hurt. And she definitely didn't need that. What she'd felt, or thought she'd felt, the other day had to be wrong. She couldn't love him. The panic that had reached out and grabbed her by the throat had been an overreaction.

She hoped.

Shaking the thoughts away, she noted, "Your bandage is makeshift at best, Jack." Although he'd wrapped and tied the gauze quite well, considering. She pushed off from the column. "Wounded people are supposed to act wounded and let other people clean them up and say it'll feel better tomorrow."

Jack sent her a heart-stopping look over his shoulder. "Nice people kiss wounds and make them better."

"I can be nice people."

He started the printer, then started toward her. "That's not the rumor, Noel. Both Michael and Morris informed me that you got a building contractor so badly flustered on the witness stand yesterday that the prosecution was forced to declare him a hostile witness."

"It was his crew's negligence, not my clients', that caused a portion of a department store roof to collapse. Three people were killed, Jack. My clients might not be the most popular people in the city or the very best developers, but they followed the rules and the building codes to the letter. You take shortcuts, make substitutions, accept payoffs, you risk getting your ass kicked in court. What are you doing?"

"Risking getting my ass kicked, I imagine."

What he was really doing was drawing the hem of her red V-necked sweater from the waistband of her skirt.

"You dress very sexy for a lawyer, Noel." He kept his eyes on her face and his hands moving. "Ever since I met you, I've been toying with the idea of committing a crime so I could get you to defend me."

She swatted at his left hand, held up the tube of antiseptic. "You're a crime in progress, Jack. And you're risking infection by not letting me clean that graze for you."

"A poor bandaging job isn't against the law."

Having him this close felt as if it should be against many laws. But she didn't object when he set the tube aside. On the contrary, she ran a finger along the plane of his cheek. "Did your grandmother have this same bone structure?"

"I don't want to talk about my grandmother."

Neither did Noel. In fact, she didn't want to talk at all. Which struck her as odd since they'd just finished having the windows of their vehicle blown out by a lunatic. The same lunatic who'd almost put a bullet in Jack's arm.

"Don't you think…" she began, but he stopped her with his mouth. Cut off her protest, her thoughts and two thirds of the oxygen flow to her brain. Enough cells remained active that she remembered not to bump his bad arm, but everything else became a blur.

He explored her mouth slowly with his tongue, drew out sensation after sensation as he deepened the kiss. Blood thrummed in her veins. In her mind she saw it flowing thick and red.

It wasn't a feeling she'd experienced before. Sex was enjoyable, exciting, heady, but it wasn't intoxicating. She already felt drunk with Jack, and he was only kissing her.

But she could meet any challenge. She'd kiss him back and let him know how a good drunk really felt. Trapping his face in her hands, she angled her lips over his and plunged in.

She wanted to knock him off his feet. Instead, he swept her off hers and, with his mouth still doing wicked things to hers, carried her to the sofa.

His eyes gleamed dark brown by the light of the Christmas tree. When he laid her down, she arched up into him, marveling at the fact that her arms were bare and her sweater had somehow disappeared.

"Slick move, Jack," she congratulated.

"Nice black lace," he said, and, with a smile, lowered his head to the base of her throat. He found the pulse that raced there. "You're so cool and collected on the surface, Noel." He slid his lips and tongue along the curve of her breast and brought a shiver to her hot skin. "I want to see you lose control. I want to hear you scream."

She took that as another challenge and fisted his hair in her hands. "I don't scream easily," she warned, but the shudder that rocked her when his mouth closed over her nipple tore a gasp from her throat. "Oh, to hell with it," she muttered and gave up trying to control anything.

It wasn't sweet and tender between them. She didn't want it to be. Her blood ran as hot and fast as his. She heard the throb of it in her veins, felt it pounding in her ears, in her head, through her entire body.

She didn't think, simply went with her instincts and her cravings. She unzipped his jeans and let her hands explore.

Oh, yes, he was aroused. He wanted her. His breathing matched hers. His hands tangled in her hair, his mouth fed on her breast. And she was building toward a scream. Or a full and devastating eruption.

She'd been touched before. She'd had sex, but nothing compared to this. There was something more here. Something important.

He took her up until every thought in her head was colored a vivid red. Her mind bubbled and churned. She wanted to crawl inside him, right into his skin so she could feel everything he did.

She loved the taste of him. She kissed his face, his throat, his shoulders. She wanted to touch every inch of his body, to memorize the lines and angles, to savor each and every sensation that rocketed through her.

But it was all happening so fast. There were too many sparks shooting around inside her, urging her to take him in, surround him, absorb him if she could.

Her feelings both fascinated and intrigued her. As her hands raced over his smoothly muscled back, she told herself to breathe. But how could she do that when he seemed bent on holding her under and drowning her?

She gasped as his tongue slid along her belly, then lower to the place she wanted him most. She arched up off the cushions and bucked when he finally reached her most sensitive spot. She heard the scream of release in her mind. If it was only in her mind…

He was making her crazy, and he knew it. What he didn't know was that now it was her turn to send him over the edge.

She rolled with him when he shifted to recapture her lips. He hit the floor first, but didn't seem to notice. Wresting her mouth free, Noel rose up and straddled him.

His eyes had gone black in the filtered light of snow and tree. Noel let her hair fall around her face, then around his as she lowered her mouth to his. She took him in her hand, and, drawing herself upright, took him inside her.

The sound he made was an explosion from his throat. Noel set her hands on either side of his ribs and started the rhythm. He matched it and then some. He let her have her way even as he had his.

It was exhilarating and just a little reckless. His name was on her lips again as they pushed each other to the peak and over.

Her head fell back. Her breathing was heavy and erratic. She felt his hands circle her waist as he brought her down on top of him. Then he flipped her beneath him and covered her body with his.

She couldn't believe she had more to give, but she did. This time when lust and longing spiked through her, she went with it, until she felt herself flowing down the other side as if on a warm and lazy waterfall.

"Jack," she breathed against his throat. "That was incredible."

He made a sound like a strangled groan and turned his face into her hair.

Her eyes closed. Her racing heart began to slow. Her mind drifted. It had been amazing, she reflected in a daze. It was what she'd always thought sex should be but never quite had been.

A thread of thought weaved its way through her head. She acknowledged it from a distance, but didn't expect it to suddenly reach out and clutch at her heart.

Her eyes opened even as her breath stalled. It hadn't been just sex, she realized with a jolt, not this time. This time, for the first time, she'd actually made love with a man.

JACK WAS TOO EXHAUSTED to think about anything. Noel had blown him away, and he had no idea how to get back to where he'd been. He wasn't sure he wanted to.

He didn't know who'd been more astonished when she'd cried his name. Her, because she hadn't expected to, or him, because something strange and truly wonderful had happened between them at that moment.

Sex was sex. He'd been there many times before. But this had been different. It had gone deeper. It had melted a layer of ice he hadn't realized he had buried inside him.

He should roll away from her, that was what he always did. Rolled off and out. Created separation. Even when he believed he was in a relationship, he did that. So why was he determined to hold on this time? To keep her close and simply inhale the scent of her skin and hair?

Noel stroked his back with her fingertips. "If you were a gentleman, Jack, you'd give me some room to breathe."

"If I was a gentleman, we'd be lying in a proper bed right now." But he took her with him as he rolled onto his side. "You screamed, you know."

"Obviously you've never been around when a big spider jumps out at me. I spoke your name very loudly."

He ran a hand over her belly. "You screamed, Noel. Any louder and your neighbors would have called the police."

Her hair fell over his chest as her head came up. There was humor and something else in her eyes when she looked down at him. "You think a lot of yourself, Jack. You couldn't get so much as a whisper out of me again if you tried."

He grinned. "Oh, I think I could manage a sound or two." His fingers circled her navel before straying lower. "I'm always up for a challenge, darling."

"Uh-huh." Freeing herself, she twisted around until she was on top of him. "In that case, you'll have to rise to the occasion very, very fast." And she crushed her mouth to his.

THEY HADN'T OPENED the envelope. He'd have been livid about that if he hadn't thought it through, hadn't crept into the theatre behind them and seen them together.

Now he had things to think about other than being upset.

He'd planned and replanned. His ally had made suggestions, and he'd listened. He always listened. Then went ahead and did exactly as he pleased.

This was his game, after all. He made the rules, he could break them. He could change the plan again and again. And he didn't have to tell anyone about it.

He let the SUV coast to a halt in the deepening snow. He set the beat-up cassette deck on the seat and stuck the tape inside. He propped the note on the dash. With a penknife, he scribed a message in the leather seat. As he closed the door, he popped a chocolate into his mouth. Torment was so enjoyable.

Chapter Fourteen

Noel woke slowly. She felt like a contented cat. When had she fallen asleep? She looked at Jack beside her, then at the duvet covering them. When had they come to bed and, more to the point, how on earth had they gotten here?

A laugh escaped. It didn't matter right now, any of it. Stretching, she pressed a kiss to the hair that had fallen across Jack's face. He slept soundly and with no fuss. She could get used to this. But she absolutely couldn't afford to.

Relationships didn't work for her. Okay, they'd made love last night. That was now. Tomorrow or next month might be a very different story.

Slipping from bed, she stepped over an empty bottle of burgundy on the floor. Now that she remembered quite well. Jack had opened it around midnight, after she'd cooked him a feast of pasta with white wine and herbed cheese sauce. That bottle would be around somewhere as well, along with a hundred dirty dishes she'd barely have time to load into the dishwasher before they left.

She pulled on her red terry robe, crossed barefoot to the window, then simply stopped dead and stared.

"Don't you ever get tired, Noel?" Jack's voice was a sleepy mumble from the bed. He hadn't bothered to lift his face out of the pillow. "What time is it?"

"Four in the morning."

His sound of disgust brought a smile to her lips, but it was short-lived. "There's a foot of snow out there, Jack, and it's still falling."

He raised his head, "Does that mean we're stuck?"

"I prefer the word detained. And the answer is, we can't be. I have to be in court at two."

"I'm meeting a group of developers at eleven."

Noel suspected his grumpy tone had more to do with being forced to wake up than with their situation. Last night, he'd wanted to stay in Winter Valley through Christmas. Of course, he hadn't eaten much all day, and they'd been into the wine by then.

Resting a shoulder against the window pane, she teased, "Maybe Michael can send up a pair of snowmobiles."

"Yeah, on the back of a plow."

"You're such a pessimist. Two of my neighbors down the street own four-by-fours that are the equivalent of monster trucks. For fifty bucks, we should be able to get into the city by sometime Friday."

"Except that today's Thursday."

"I know." Pushing off, she started for the bed. Halfway there, she stopped and spun. She crept back to peer out the lower pane. "Jack…"

"I'm only moving if you come back to bed."

"There's a big SUV outside."

His head came up. It took a minute for him to understand her statement. Then he tossed off the covers.

"It's a dark color—maybe green—and there's something scratched on the side."

He bent over top of her, tried to make out the letters. "I can't read it."

"I think it says PRISONS KILL, JACK AND NOEL." She straightened, shivered, and stepped closer to Jack for warmth. "Except he's put an *X* through the word *PRISONS*. "

JACK DID CARRY a gun. He gave it to Noel while he examined the SUV from every conceivable angle. Noel spied Mrs. Fisker at her living room window in a robe and hairnet and tucked the weapon inside her jacket.

"Early riser," she said to Jack and waved at the old woman. "It isn't even dawn yet."

"When I'm retired, I'm not getting up before eleven," Jack said as he passed her.

He checked out the undercarriage and tires as much as he could, given that there was more than twelve inches of snow around them.

Noel kept a firm grip on the gun. "I feel like an arcade duck standing out here. Are the doors locked?"

"Passenger side's open." The worry crease appeared between Jack's eyes. "We should have read the note from the theatre before we came out."

They should have read it as soon as they'd left the theatre. Not that that would have been possible with the kidnapper shooting at them.

Noel took the crumpled envelope he handed her, opened the flap and removed the contents. "It's a picture, a photo, similar to the ones we took yesterday of Robert Tillman's star. He's filled in most of the star with a red marker, except for Tillman's name and initials." A frustrated breath steamed out. "Maybe Mr. Tillman did have grandchildren, and they changed their names."

"We can work on that angle."

"What about the truck? He must want us to look inside."

With his hand on the door handle, he asked her, "Ready?"

"No, but do it."

Although she braced, nothing jumped out when he opened the door. Noel wasn't sure why she'd thought something might. Maybe everything was just starting to feel more imminent. The kidnapper wanted them to play his game, and they weren't doing what he wanted fast enough for him.

When Jack didn't move, Noel set her head beside his. "A cassette recorder," she murmured. "It looks like the same one he used on me at the theatre. Another note on the dash and—" Her gaze shifted to the seat. "God, he's carved something into the upholstery."

Jack fixated on the letters. "'LOVE THY NEIGHBOR,'" he read. "Looks like he did it with a dull knife."

"Does it matter?"

"It will to Michael."

Noel's heart lurched. "This is Michael's Navigator?"

Jack removed the tape recorder and envelope from inside. "Michael wanted a truck for winter driving." He traded Noel the tape machine for his gun. "I was with him when he bought it last year."

"I DON'T THINK Michael's the kidnapper, Jack. I never did." When he continued to sit and brood, Noel sighed and perched on the ottoman at his feet. "Look, I asked if he resented you because it was a logical question. A reasonable one. Anyone would ask it."

"Any lawyer would."

"I am a lawyer, and a good one, a thorough one. Michael's your friend, not mine, but I get positive vibes from him. I figure if he resented you, he'd just say so and trust your friendship to rectify the situation."

Jack ran his fingers over his lips, stared at her long and hard. "Why steal his truck?"

"That's easy." She patted his leg. "To make you doubt. To do a number on your head. Games, Jack. That's what this guy's all about right now. He won't do it forever, but for the moment, he's using pictures and poems, notes and laughter to push us along his board."

"'Love thy neighbor.'" Jack's frown deepened. "He sounds like a religious fanatic."

"Or an old hippie, unwilling to give up the crusade." But she didn't really believe he was either. "Do you want to call Michael, or should we do the cassette and note first?"

"Let's go with the cassette."

He looked so miserable that Noel wanted to hug him, but she knew that sometimes comforting gestures weren't the best approach. She pressed the Play button.

"You're making this far too complicated," a Scottish-accented voice drawled. "It's Christmastime. Family time, yes? Oh, except for you, Jack. So sorry." He switched to Spanish. "I had a family once. I don't now. I bet you're in the right neighborhood with your guesses as to my identity, but I have to say, with all your enemies, plucking one person from the lot is an onerous task.

"I'll tell you this much, Jack. We've seen each other since the Christmas party. In fact, as you undoubtedly know, I was at your party." The voice dropped to a seductive level. "I've also seen you, yes, I have, since last night." Now it became a doglike snarl. "Read the note!"

Dear Jack,

Feeling better? I certainly am. Didn't your grandfather tell you too much chocolate wasn't good for you? He told you plenty of other things, and you listened, didn't you? You took up where he left off and built yourself a miniempire. Too bad empires crumble.

You're going to have a bad Christmas, Jack, one way or another. As for Noel, hers can go either way at this point. And Caroline? Well, she can be an aggravating woman, can't she? Would I be doing you a favor, I wonder, if I didn't return her to you?

In the meantime, consider this:

It was a Capital Offense in its initial stage. Now it's something more familiar.

Clue over. Both of you, listen up. Come to the Valley Motel off the highway at 8 p.m. I've booked a room in Noel's name. Go inside and look out the window.

Don't you hate it when a fun game draws to its conclusion? Unless you're winning, of course.

Merry Christmas, Noel. Not so much for you, JR.

The Ghost of Christmas Past.

"HOW ON EARTH did you get back?" Helen was incredulous when Noel phoned her from Pittsburgh. "And in under five hours, to boot. I've been listening to the road reports. Everything on wheels is sliding off the highways and into the drifts."

"We used Michael's SUV." In her office Noel removed the pen from her mouth and tucked it behind her ear. She had an hour until her court appearance, and she still needed to consult with both her associate and her client. She took files from the cabinets as she moved around her office, then set the printer in motion. "It was a nightmare, Helen."

"The drive, or your time in Winter Valley?"

"Both." But not all, no, definitely not. "Jack'll talk to Michael, see when he last drove his truck."

"He hasn't used it since I've been seeing him," Helen defended quickly. "Noel…" She paused. "You don't think—do you?"

Noel was adamant. "No, I don't. Michael's not a part of this. He's a victim, like Jack. If someone was watching him closely, his keys would have been easy enough to obtain. He keeps extra sets in various places."

"His office, for one."

"Jack's looking into it."

"I like him, Noel."

"I sensed that. Look, I have to go. After my court session, I've got a meeting with Martin Faber. And Jack and I are supposed to be at the Valley Motel by eight o'clock tonight."

"You're crazy," Helen declared. "If you don't get killed on the drive there, you certainly could at this motel. Slashing seats, painting messages on stolen vehicles—your ghost's getting edgier by the day. What scares me is that when he falls, he's going to take you and Jack with him."

Noel scribbled notes in the margins of her printouts. "I can't stand by and let Jack's sister die." She almost added, "the way his grandmother did," but she knew Jack wouldn't appreciate that, so she substituted, "Could you live with yourself if you thought you'd caused someone's death?"

"No." Helen seemed preoccupied for a moment. "I guess I forgot about Caroline. I mean, that there's a person who's being held somewhere. Michael's still working on connections between you and Jack."

"There are a few."

"A few score and then some. Go to court, hon. But call me before you leave for the motel and again when you get home tonight. Are you coming here, or staying in the city?"

"Depends whether or not I can clear tomorrow's calendar. Matthew's fine, by the way."

"And the chocolates in question are still missing. Michael told me. I'd check out your ex's office desk if I were you. He keeps trophies, right?"

"Not that I ever saw."

"Look, I have some free time today, Noel. Do you want me to see what I can dig up on your exes—Damian, Matthew and Roberto? Michael's already got people working the Kurt deRosa angle."

"This isn't deRosa's style," Noel reminded her. "It's calculated and methodical. The kidnapper's taken time to plan his game and execute the moves."

"So it's not like when you and I play chess." Helen's laugh was forced. Her voice tightened. "I'm so scared for you, Noel. Who do you know that could be this driven?"

Noel collected her files and documents. "No one with the persona he's presented to me."

"Think details," Helen suggested. "Think about anyone who might resent you, from former lovers to clients to business associates. Highlight small, incongruent things about their behavior. Oh, and get whoever's in the lobby of this motel to go into that room tonight ahead of you."

Noel recalled the torn leather seats in Michael's SUV, Jack's arm, the notes and, most particularly, the kidnapper's finger where it had stroked her skin at the theatre.

"We'll watch our backs," she promised, then looked up as her paralegal came in. "What is it, Danny?"

"Ralph Burnley's on two. We told him you were due in court, but he's insistent. He's also drunk."

"Lovely." Noel gave him a perfunctory smile. "Gotta go," she said to Helen. "I'll call you later." She waited a beat, before switching lines. "Hello, Mr. Burnley. This is Noel. How can I help you?"

"BURNLEY ACCUSED YOU of destroying his marriage?" Jack alternated his gaze between the icy road and the rearview mirror. "Was he drunk?"

"Totally. He called me the final nail in the coffin of his marriage. I gather he's heard the rumor about Deirdre and Matthew in a quiet restaurant doing the hand-to-knee thing under the table."

Jack slid her a sideways look.

Noel smiled. "I know. You're going to tell me that I was smart to have ditched Matthew because he has no respect for the sanctity of marriage or relationships and therefore would have wound up hurting me eventually."

"He would have."

"I'm not with him, Jack, remember? Besides, we're talking about Ralph Burnley—although there isn't a whole lot of what he said to me that made sense. For the most part, he rambled on about how, if I hadn't broken it off with Matthew, his wife would have put her sexual fantasies to bed long ago, where in time they would have died."

"Did he use the word *died*?"

"More than once. Then he said something even more frightening."

Jack looked over. She saw concern and, beneath it, ready anger stamped on his features. "Did he threaten you?"

"Not directly, no. He said where he comes from, a town called Stottville in upstate New York, a neighbor doesn't screw a neighbor."

Jack frowned. "What's he talking about?"

Noel turned up the heater to chase the chill from under her skin. "Apparently Ralph keeps a condo in the city, to use on those nights when he can't make it to the suburbs. His condo's in the building next to mine." She recalled the slashed leather seats in Michael's SUV. "'Love thy neighbor,' Jack."

"GOT CABLE," the desk clerk at the Valley Motel informed them above the howling wind. "Got instant coffee and kettles. Got a restaurant attached to the lobby. Truckers use it, mostly. Got clean sheets. Got showers but no tubs."

Noel heard about a third of what he said. Walking, even under a canopy, was difficult, noisy and cold.

"Got a Christmas tree out by the motel sign," the man went on. "We like to think it draws people in." He unlocked the door to room nine and led the way inside.

"Thank you." Jack smiled and handed him money. "How late's the restaurant open?"

"Oh, ten, eleven o'clock. Midnight, sometimes, if the traffic warrants it. Not much activity out there tonight. You folks were lucky to get this far."

Noel glanced at the bed. It was a double with a plaid spread— and an envelope. She pocketed it before the clerk turned.

"Power could go. We've had problems since yesterday. Fingers crossed."

"We're not that picky," Jack said as he ushered the man out. "Thanks again."

When he closed the door, Noel held up the envelope. "Doesn't make me want to sleep in this bed knowing a ghost got here first."

"Head games," Jack reminded her. "What time is it?"

"Seven-forty." She looked out the window but saw nothing except blowing snow. "I guess he wants us to read the note before we see whatever show he has in store for us."

"Maybe he's planning to ram the wall of our room with another truck."

Disgust was evident in Jack's tone. Not that Noel blamed him. Michael had been shocked to discover his Navigator had been stolen, and more stunned still by how it had been used and the damage that had been inflicted upon it.

Noel tore open the flap. "Oh, good. Another poem. 'Starlight, star bright. One's the cause, and one won't fight. If I get my wish tonight, You'll WORK IT OUT and SAY IT RIGHT!'" She gave the note to Jack. "Whatever happened to me being the liaison and you paying the ransom?'"

"We're way past that, Noel." Jack went over the message three times. "I assume he's going to show us something through the window to go with this."

"Inspiring thought, isn't it?" She laid her jacket next to their backpacks on the bed. "What we really need to do, Jack, is gather up the notes, write down everything he's said and done, spread it all out on a table and try to piece together some kind of picture."

"It'll be a skewed one."

"Maybe at first glance, but he's leading us somewhere."

"In circles most of the time."

"He's volatile to start with, but I didn't like what he wrote on Michael's SUV this morning. 'Prisons kill, Jack and Noel.'"

"With the word *Prisons* scratched out. I remember."

"'Kill Jack and Noel'?"

"Kill on one hand," he agreed. "But on the other, 'Love thy neighbor.'"

"Right. Ralph Burnley. A neighbor I knew nothing about until today."

"It's too convenient, Noel. I don't see Ralph as a kidnapper. Just a blowhard with a drinking problem and a failed marriage."

There was piped-in Christmas music, country rock and a sparkly blue garland draped around the door. The room smelled as if it had been vacuumed with an old machine, but it was clean and tidy and there was a Bible on one of the nightstands.

Noel sat on the bed while Jack inspected the bathroom. "Do you really believe Matthew could be behind this, Jack, or do you just want it to be him?"

"I don't know." He came back, sprawled in the room's lone chair. "Probably more want it than believe it. He looks like an ad for the great outdoors. And he wants you back."

"I wish you'd give that up. Until your Christmas party, I hadn't seen him for months."

"When was the last time you saw your other exes?"

"Roberto—no idea. Five years, at least. I saw Damian Lowe last Easter in New York. He's engaged to a dermatologist." She regarded her watch. "It's five to eight."

Jack pushed out of the chair. "Michael got the story on Lowe's Jewelry. We didn't take it over, but we did buy out a rival company and merge it with another we owned. The merger drove prices down and pushed Lowe's out of the malls that had been their mainstay. The Lowe family dissolved the business, then sold their stores and inventory to three other chains."

"Sounds similar to Roberto's story, except the motels and restaurants belonged to his brother."

"Helen called him a rat."

"Noel smiled at the term. "Yeah, maybe that works. I think of rats as slick and dirty, but not really aiming for the big time. Vince was dealing drugs. I have a feeling that was his goal more than making a success of his motel chain."

"Do you know if he's still dealing?"

"If I haven't kept track of Roberto, Jack, you can't expect me to know what his brother's doing." When he hoisted himself onto the window ledge, she accepted the invitation and went to stand between his legs. "I have to say, you have an unnatural obsession with my love life."

"Former love life."

"The only reason I considered marrying Roberto was because one of my sisters and three of my friends were planning weddings at the time. Maybe men don't get swept up in that kind of thing, but women do."

"Except you didn't totally."

"Well, no. For a moment, yes, but overall, I wanted a career."

"You don't think you can have both?"

"I think," she said and pressed a finger to his mouth, "that I'm a good lawyer, and I should be happy with that and not want it all, because I don't know many people who ever get it, but I do know an unfortunate lot who lose one thing in the futile pursuit of the other."

"I imagine there's sense in there somewhere." Jack kissed her hand, then her lips, quick and hard. "Time?"

"Eight o'clock."

He hopped down, and angled himself in front of her. But it was Noel who caught sight of the figure running toward them with something in his hand.

She grabbed Jack's arm and dragged him sideways. Then she waited for the window to explode.

It didn't. Although they waited twenty long seconds, nothing happened. Wind continued to pummel the motel walls. Filaments of red and green light shone through the window from the Christmas tree near the highway. A snowplow ground past.

From his position behind the door, Jack poked his head out.

Noel kept a solid hold on his arm. "Do you see him? Or anything?"

"Not yet."

She envisioned the kidnapper standing outside the window

with his gun barrel pressed to the glass, waiting for them to present him with a target.

But he needed Jack alive if he wanted any money at all. And even if he didn't, he wouldn't want his game to end like that, would he? With something as simple as a bullet to the head?

Jack inched out. Noel went with him. No man stood outside the window, but there was a piece of wet paper taped to it.

Jack squinted. "Can you read that?"

She bent until the printing was at eye level. "It says: 'Take the Bible with you.'"

Chapter Fifteen

Noel's office Christmas party was scheduled for Friday night. Months ago, she'd made arrangements for Helen to close the Winter Valley office at four, and then meet her in Pittsburgh at six. Except now Helen wanted to bring Michael, and he couldn't get away until seven.

Noel didn't mind the delay. Her day wrapped up late in any case. There was always more work to be done. And plenty to think about.

She started with Jack and a fresh cup of coffee brewed by her secretary before she left. "Check your messages," her paralegal added in parting. "There's about ten. But don't be late. You promised Martin Senior a dance and me, three."

The snow had finally stopped falling, the traffic gridlock had been overcome. The city was turning grimy white, but Noel imagined Winter Valley would be beautiful, a Currier and Ives print, especially on her street with its old trees and even older houses.

After leaving the motel, she and Jack had spent most of the rest of the evening holed up in her condo going over the information they had accumulated so far. The notes were like riddles, openly taunting them, but the Bible baffled her. They'd purchased it from the motel clerk before leaving, which baffled him almost as much as their hasty departure. They'd called it a family emergency, tipped him well and spent the next few hours searching for clues among the scriptures.

But not a single phrase or passage had been marked, and there were no messages inside the front or back covers. It was just a standard motel room Bible.

He was getting more and more cryptic, Noel decided. Cranky, cryptic and likely more impatient by the minute. She felt very sorry for Caroline Ransom.

Jack had spent the night with her. Noel hadn't planned it that way, but she'd wanted him to stay—of his own accord and because her place was where he wanted to be. No grand gestures, no big buildup, just the two of them, some Christmas jazz and snow outside the windows, falling in soft flurries.

Inside had been anything but soft. Like before, it was exciting and erotic between them. But there'd been an element of tenderness that had both surprised and unsettled her. It touched an emotional nerve she didn't really want to examine. She'd already tucked away enough emotions concerning Jack.

Ray from Artie's Deli might think *P* words were bad, but for Noel it was the *L* word.

Looking back, she wasn't sure she'd loved any of the men she'd been involved with. Cared about, yes, but not really loved.

The phone rang at her elbow. However, when she picked up, the line was dead. She thought she heard a click but couldn't be sure with The Barenaked Ladies lamenting the plight of unhappy elves on the stereo.

She put her messages on hold for a while longer and took out the kidnapper's poems. Then spent the next hour picking them apart.

When her eyes began to sting, she poured another cup of coffee and drifted over to the corner window.

Even from a fairly lofty height, she could see the street below. There was a man carrying a bag of take-out food walking along the sidewalk. Although he wore a wool cap and a bulky coat, he struck her as familiar. Blond hair stuck out from under the cap. He had a stocky build, and his eyes traveled to her office window several times. It relieved her when he climbed into a car, started the engine and pulled out into the traffic flow.

"Jumping at shadows, Noel," she chided herself. She returned to her desk, regarded her flashing voice messages, then reached for the poems again.

She didn't hear the door open or see the movements of the man who entered. Until he had his fingers curled around her arms and his mouth on hers.

Her response was swift and fiery, more than a match for his sudden assault. When they broke apart, the best she could manage was a shaky, "Hey, Jack. Nice hello."

"I don't want to go to another Christmas party."

Her head was still swimming, her mouth still tasting him. Her lips tingled. "You don't have to go, I told you that last night. This is my deal."

She smiled at Jack's messy hair and the black denim jacket that simply wasn't warm enough for winter. "Didn't anyone ever teach you how to dress for December in the Northeast?"

From inside the jacket in question he produced a single red rose, which he held out to her.

More touched than she was prepared to admit, Noel drank in the scent of the flower. It smelled exquisite. "It's beautiful, Jack. Thank you." She kissed his cheek. "I'll wear it in my hair tonight."

"I can picture that." He looked around at the papers on her desk. "You'll give yourself a headache, you know." He picked up one of the starlight poems, the one she'd written from memory, then hopped onto the desk beside her. "This rhyme seems the most pertinent to me."

Noel agreed. "It's the first one. But the second builds on it. It's also less of a tease, more of an exasperated comment. He's definitely trying to tell us who he is, or at least make sure we figure it out within the confines of his timetable." She indicated the photos they'd taken at the theatre as well as the one the kidnapper had given them. "Why color Tillman's star red?"

"Representative of blood?"

"And that tells us what? That he's going to kill us? He already said it when he wrote 'Prisons kill Jack and Noel' and then scratched out the word *prisons*." Noel ran a speculative fingertip over the velvety rose petals. "I wonder if there are two separate messages here, one a statement, the other a threat."

"You think the word *prisons* is significant?"

"Why not? Why write it in the first place if it wasn't? We should look into that. Who is or was associated with both of us and has also been to prison? And, no, I don't think Matthew's been there."

"But he did shoot a man."

"I'll phone my father this weekend and ask him about that. He and my mother are in Scotland right now, doing a ghost castle tour. It's difficult to catch up with them. My parents aren't great about activating their cell phones on vacations."

"Are they coming home for Christmas?"

"They live in Vermont now, so most likely we'll all go there. Except for my brother. He'll hang out with his buddies in New York."

Jack considered for a moment. "What would you have done, Noel, if our positions were reversed and your brother had been kidnapped?"

She didn't have to think. "No one would kidnap him, so I'd assume he was in on the plot and approach the problem that way."

"Would you have called the FBI?"

"I don't have your emotional block. The answer's yes."

"Do you still think I should?"

What could she say? "I'm not sure what I'd do in your position, Jack. To be frank, I think it's too late to involve them now. We know we're being watched. If this guy even suspected we'd gone to the authorities, he'd probably kill Caroline, then come after us."

"If we knew the guy, we'd be in a better position to guess his reaction." He looked over the papers on her desk. "I have an update on our vindictive accountant, Harry Dexter. He's been skimming for the past six months. He's got a fairly complex system that's been working for him. We'll let him go a bit longer, then catch him in the act."

"After your chat this week, he must suspect you're on to him."

"That's why we'll let him carry on."

"What do you think about him, Jack?"

"Harry's an embezzler, but not a kidnapper."

Noel held up the photo from the kidnapper, together with his second starlight poem. "I wish just one piece of this puzzle would fit into place." She also wished she had more time to devote to it.

She smiled when Jack ran his hand under the hem of her shirt. "So, counselor," he said with a grin. "You going to the party dressed like a sexy lawyer, or do you have a more daring little number stashed under that business suit?"

"It's stashed in my closet, actually." She motioned to a flat wall behind her. "Hidden door. Midnight blue strapless with a wrap." She slid her humorous gaze over his jeans and dove-gray shirt. "You?"

"This is dressed up for me, darling. I don't do suits unless I'm forced to."

He was so completely unpretentious. No wonder he disliked Matthew.

"Okay, tell you what. I have to dress and listen to my messages. Why don't you call Michael and see if he and Helen are en route."

She stepped away before he could disrupt her equilibrium with another kiss.

She had her dress on and halfway zipped when he wandered in. "There's no answer at Michael's office, and his cell's off. I don't have Helen's number."

Turning her back to him, Noel scooped her hair aside and motioned for him to finish zipping. She played her next message. By the time it was done, her dress was open to her waist.

She tipped her head back. "Zip means go up, Jack."

"I like your shoulder blades."

She felt his mouth skimming over them and struggled to steady her breathing. "They're visible even when the dress is done up."

He nipped at her jaw. "Do we have to go right away?"

She let her hair fall and very nearly groaned in pleasure. "I'm a partner, Jack."

"You're so flexible in some ways, Noel, but so rigid in others."

"I'm not rigid." How could she be when everything inside her, including her brain, was melting? She felt her dress slide away to pool on the floor.

"I love stockings." Jack ran a seductive finger around the elasticized lace top. "And high-heeled shoes and sexy bras."

She got the picture and let him draw her back into him. When he nuzzled her neck, she closed her eyes and released a shaky breath. "What the hell," she murmured, and stepping out of her dress, moved into his arms.

It was a good forty minutes later before she managed to get herself reassembled in her lingerie, stockings and evening dress. She fixed the rose in her hair over her left ear, and turned to Jack again, sending him a humorous look of warning.

"This time, zip me up, Ransom, or I'll get the security guard to do it." She hit Resume to play her final messages. She skipped the first when she heard Martin Faber Junior. Then Helen's voice came on the line.

"Noel, I might have something for you. I'm not sure yet, so I won't say, but I'm at the office in Winter Valley and I've just seen someone who shouldn't be in town. I'll talk to you tonight at the party. Don't get excited, because I'm not totally sure who I saw, so it could be a false alarm. Later."

"Someone who shouldn't be in Winter Valley," Jack repeated. "Sounds promising." He circled her waist with his hands. "You sure you want to go out and watch a bunch of legal eagles get gassed and embarrass themselves?"

"You have a grim view of the human race, Jack. It's called unwinding with friends."

"I'd rather unwind with you. Here. Now."

"We're never going to get to that party."

She saw him grin before he whispered in her ear, "Then maybe we should have one of our own." And trapped her mouth before she could protest.

THEY ARRIVED at the hotel reception room very late. Clients had been invited, as well as office staff. Noel sighed when she spied Ralph and Deirdre Burnley.

"This could get ugly," she murmured to Jack.

"Not if Ralph's smart. He kills the deal we've made, and he'll kill himself financially." Jack accepted the champagne he was offered and took a casual look around. "I don't see Railback."

"No comment." She flicked a finger along his black lapel. "I'm too overcome to deny our relationship again."

"Because you discovered I own a tux?"

"No, because you thought to bring it with you and you're wearing it after business hours." And putting himself on display in a way she knew he seldom did. People might not notice the scruffy guy in jeans and work boots, but no one could fail to notice Jack Ransom in black tie.

The crease appeared between his eyes. "I don't see Michael."

"Or Helen." She gave his ear a discreet nip. "Maybe they stopped at his place for a…snack."

"How come when I suggested we draw our snack time out longer, you vetoed the idea?"

"Because I told you, I'm a partner in the firm. And it's Friday night. There's lots of time later for snacks and dessert. Oh, hell."

He glanced over when she sighed. "Ralph Burnley's heading this way."

"So let's head the other. I'm not in the mood for him, Jack, especially with Martin Junior glowering at me over his eggnog."

Turning, she collided head-on with Deirdre Burnley.

"Help me, Noel," Deirdre pleaded. "Ralph thinks I'm having an affair with Matthew."

"I thought you and Ralph were separated." But with a motion to Jack, she let Deirdre propel her toward the powder room.

"We're legally separated, but he's not taking it as well as I expected. Oh, good, Jack stopped him." She relaxed and released Noel's wrist. "I'm sorry. Normally, Ralph doesn't frighten me in the slightest. But lately he's been acting a little odd."

"In what way?"

"He broods a lot, and goes off to his club at all hours."

"Has he been to Winter Valley recently?"

"I couldn't say." Deirdre pressed a hand to her upper chest and gave herself a quick pat. "I'm really quite agitated." Then she curled her fingers. "Winter Valley. That's where you live, isn't it?"

"On weekends, yes."

"North of here?"

"Ninety minutes in good weather."

"So that's the reason." Deirdre's hand dropped as she deflated. "You know, I really have to stop doing this. Matthew wants you, pure and simple."

Noel was getting tired of that observation. "Matthew and I are over, Deirdre. We're history."

"Not in the book he's reading. I wanted to be with him tonight, you know, have a cozy dinner in while Ralph was out. But he said he had to go up north."

Noel's stomach did a quick backflip. "To Winter Valley?"

"He didn't say, and I was too miffed to ask."

Noel turned away, but Jack was still engaged in a heated conversation with Ralph. "Helen wouldn't expect to see Matthew up there. Not when I'm here."

"Tell me honestly," Deirdre said. "Do you want him?"

"No."

"You're sure? I'm not stepping on toes here?"

"No, Deirdre. I want—" Noel stopped herself, but it was close. Jack's name had been on her lips. And she hadn't had to give it so much as a thought. "Damn," she whispered under her breath.

"I can make a play, then, without jeopardizing the offer Jack made to me?"

"You can do anything you want with Matthew, Deirdre." Noel's eyes slitted. "When he gets back from his northern junket."

As the music changed from Christmas waltz to Christmas jive, she caught Jack's eye. He immediately pointed Ralph toward the bar and headed in her direction.

"Of course," Deirdre interjected, "Jack Ransom's not a bad catch, is he? Very easy on the eye. Not that anyone I know would have what it takes to catch him. He's considered rather elusive, relationshipwise."

"Yes, he's very slippery," Noel agreed. "Excuse me, Deirdre."

"What?" Jack wanted to know when he reached her. "Did Ralph hit her?"

"No, she hit me—with a sort of minibombshell." She'd been struck with two, actually, but Noel wasn't prepared to deal with the one she'd set off herself. "Matthew went up north today after lunch. Deirdre thinks he might have gone to Winter Valley."

"HELLO? Is anyone there?"

The kidnapper smiled at the fear in the woman's voice. Her name was Helen Stowe, and she'd looked in his direction at precisely the wrong moment.

She sounded more tremulous when she whispered, "Where am I?"

He opened the door to his dark room, with its cot, paintings and old VCR. "You're here," he said in a cheerful tone. "With me. Oh, and Caroline. Mustn't forget my gold mine. She's downstairs." He closed the door, saw her swallow and squatted so he could look right into her pretty blue eyes.

"Helen Stowe. A plain sort of name, but you're not a plain

sort of woman, are you? Why, I wonder, when you could have been so much more, did you choose to set up your law practice in a backwater town in northern Pennsylvania? It's picturesque, to be sure, but there's so much more money to be had in the city. Especially for sharks like you and Noel."

"Noel's—" She started to say one thing then, quite obviously, switched to another. "Noel will miss me at the party tonight."

"Of course she will." He tickled her chin. "She's a good friend, isn't she? Hmm. Maybe that's part of the reason they're not getting my message fast enough. I mean, let's face it, Caroline's no prize. It's possible Jack doesn't really want her back. Subconsciously, of course. Do you like her, Helen?"

"I've never met her."

"Ah, well, you're lucky, then. But perhaps I made a hasty choice, rushed into the matter willy-nilly. It's difficult, though. Opportunity presents itself, what's a man to do? You plan and you strategize. You think you've got it all worked out, then you realize you've overlooked a rather glaring point. Jack doesn't love Caroline. It's guilt and a sense of familial duty that's driving him. As for Noel, Caroline's a name to her. There's no bond, no affection." His fingers came out to play with Helen's blond hair. He laughed when she shrank from his touch, and removed his hand. "Relax, Helen. I'm not going to harm you. I need you. Yes, I think I really do. Incentive, that's what it's called. I can up the ante now, and the stakes. You're Noel's associate, her very best friend. You went to college together, traveled together, probably got laid together in Martinique."

The flash of anger in her eyes was short-lived, but he liked it. Women like Caroline bored him. Helen might turn out to be much more fun.

Something clanked shut inside him at that thought. Humor whooshed out and loathing in. "I have plans for Jack and Noel," he said, not bothering to disguise the disdainful curl of his lip.

"They'll know who I am very soon. You're part of it now, Helen. You made yourself part of it by being in the wrong place at the wrong time. When it's over and I have what I want, someone's going to be dead. And Jack Ransom'll have to live with that for the rest of his miserable life."

"SHE'S NOT HERE." Michael tugged on his earlobe. "I knew she wouldn't be, but she's not in Winter Valley, and she never showed at my office. She's not answering anywhere. Home, office or cell."

Noel caught his wrist and read his Rolex. "It's almost ten o'clock. Why didn't you call?"

"I thought it might be the roads. They're impassible in some areas."

"The highways are fine. So are most of the routes leading to them." Jack took the cell phone from Michael and gave it to Noel. "Can you think of anyone else to contact?"

Aunt Maddie had been in the city all week, and Noel didn't know the last names of Helen's neighbors. "Mrs. Fisker." She punched the number and ordered herself not to worry. Yet.

"Her car could have broken down," Jack said.

Noel shook her head. "She'd have phoned us."

"Maybe her cell battery died."

"Or maybe," Michael put in, "she's in a ditch somewhere."

Jack glanced at Noel. "Should I tell him?"

When Michael swung his head around to ask, "Tell me what?" Noel nodded. "Go ahead. Mrs. Fisker? Hi, it's Noel."

She had to turn and cover her ear so she could hear. "Sorry, Mrs. Fisker, I'm at an office party. Have you seen Helen today?"

"I saw her around four o'clock, coming out the front door with a man. I thought he was a relative."

Noel inched away from a noisy trio singing about Frosty. "Why a relative?"

"He had his arm around her shoulders."

"Did you see his face?"

"No, he was wearing a hat, a knitted one, and he had the back of his head to me." Mrs. Fisker paused. "He wasn't one of those men who came to see you a few weeks back, was he?"

"It's unlikely. Was he tall?"

"Quite tall, yes. But not heavyset. He was wearing a black overcoat."

"What about his shoes?"

"Oh, I didn't see those."

"Did you notice anything strange about Helen?"

"I thought maybe she'd turned her knee or her ankle. She seemed to stumble a few times, but her friend held on tight."

"And did what with her, Mrs. Fisker? Did they get in a car?"

"Yes. Helen's car. He drove."

Noel's throat burned. "Did you see where they went, which direction, I mean?"

"Toward Maplewood. That's the direction Helen lives, isn't it?"

"Yes, it is." Noel rubbed her temple. "Did you notice anything else about the man? Any features, anything about his clothes or the way he walked?"

"Well, he didn't seem to be having any trouble in the snow. Walked smooth as you please, as if he were gliding through it, and it was no obstacle for him." She halted as if concentrating. "I'm not sure, but I think he had a mustache."

"What's the deal?" With the call ended, Jack steered Noel away from a chain of tipsy dancers.

"We need to go back to Winter Valley."

"Why?"

"Mrs. Fisker saw someone take Helen out of the office. He was tall, walked well in the snow and had a mustache." Her eyes met his. "Just like a certain man I used to date."

Chapter Sixteen

She wouldn't panic because it wasn't in her nature to do so. But Noel was worried. Big-time. She got Jack to convince Michael to go home and wait—to hear from either Helen or them—then returned to her office to change and collect the kidnapper's paraphernalia.

Jack laced up his work boots while she shoved the notes and photos into a brown envelope. She stuck the envelope inside the Bible, tossed the cassette tape to Jack and grabbed her coat.

Jack helped her put it on. "He must have a place in Winter Valley. The trick's going to be finding it."

"Trickier still to find him, if he's in fact Matthew. I'm still not completely convinced, though. Anyone could buy a fake mustache."

"And glide through the snow?"

"Like an outdoorsman, I know, but that's Mrs. Fisker's observation. It might not look like gliding to you and me. Oh, damn, I've got two left hands." She tried to pull on her gloves and realized she was trembling.

Jack caught her by the shoulders, nudged her chin up. "Come on, Noel, she'll be fine. She's tough, right? Like you."

"Tougher than me." Tears threatened to spill, but Noel wouldn't let them. She wasn't going to fall apart. That would be abandoning her best friend. She'd hold together and help her. And

Caroline. She breathed in, then out. "I'm okay, Jack. It was just a moment. Helen's like one of my sisters. We can't let him hurt her."

"We won't." After pressing a kiss to her forehead, he dug the keys from his jeans pocket. "But I'll drive."

She picked up the Bible. "The answer's here. He's given us a puzzle, and that's a thing both of us should be good at solving. We do it every day in one form or another."

Jack's mouth turned down. "I'm okay with puzzles, but this guy's riddles are harder."

"He wants us to solve the ultimate riddle, the riddle of his identity. Maybe we've done that, and maybe we haven't. One thing I've learned as a lawyer is never to draw conclusions until all the facts are in. We don't have enough of those yet. Mrs. Fisker's a sweet old woman who needs cataract surgery in her left eye." She glanced at the window. "At least Ralph Burnley was at the party, so we can cross him off as a suspect."

"Never heard of hired help, huh?" Jack opened the door. "Burnley's in deep financial trouble, Noel. Ten million on top of the sale of his company would get him off more than a few hooks. And get me back for taking over the original tire company."

Noel shoved the Bible in her shoulder bag, then reached for her security card. "You're right," she decided. "You drive. I'm going to review everything this Ghost of Christmas Past has sent to us before he turns Helen and your sister into the very thing he's pretending to be."

Noel kept her head bent over the notes and the Bible throughout the drive. She flipped through all of the pages, then sighed and simply stared at the worn binding. "I haven't got a clue what this is all about. I thought at least he'd put some kind of message on one of the inside covers, but there's nothing except a faded business stamp." She opened it to the first page. "He can't expect—"

Jack glanced over as she paused. "What is it?"

She read the text in the worn blue stamp. "'Property of VSE Motels, Butler County, Pennsylvania.' VSE, Jack. Vince's Sleep Easy. That was Roberto's brother's chain."

He could see her mind racing over the possibilities, starting, no doubt, where he was—with Vince Turano. "Where is Vince?" he asked.

She shook her head. "Roberto's in Europe, but I have no idea where his brother might be."

"Is he tall?"

"Very. The whole family is. We could try New York. He used to talk about wanting to buy a loft in Manhattan. He never did while I knew him."

Jack hunted for his cell, punched up Michael's number on the memory. "What's his full name?"

"Vincent Marcello Turano. He was born six years before Roberto, so that would be 1964."

"The last address you know?"

"In Pittsburgh. I remember the area, Point Breeze, but not the street." She set a hand on his arm. "Get Michael to locate his father. His name's Piero. He lives in Boston, Beacon Hill. He should be listed in the phone directory."

Jack got Michael on the first ring and relayed the information.

"Beacon Hill, right," Michael confirmed. "Piero Turano. Are you ruling out Railback, then?"

Jack slid his eyes to Noel's dark head, still bent over the papers. "Not a chance. But this is the first good lead we've had, so I want to pursue it."

Noel didn't look up as he ended the call, but she said, "They didn't know each other that I'm aware of, Roberto and Matthew or Vince and Matthew."

Jack felt guilty. He wasn't sure why. "Don't you miss anything?"

"Lots. But knowing your feelings toward Matthew, I figure you're not going to let him go as a suspect until the bitter end.

And he did come north this afternoon. But this," she said as she opened the Bible again and ran a finger over the blurred stamp, "has to be relevant. There are no passages marked, and even though it ties in with his Love thy neighbor message, I don't get a sense of connection. It has to be the stamp. Which points to Vince, who might still resent the fact that I wouldn't defend him when he was accused of dealing after he lost his motel and restaurant chains to you."

They were on the exit ramp that would take them into Winter Valley. "Who did defend him?" Jack asked.

"His name's Wilkie. Quite a character. Wears a polka-dot bow tie and green suspenders, in court and out. Imagine a cross between Santa Claus and a leprechaun, and you've got Wilkie."

"Sounds kind of creepy. Was he any good?"

"In his prime, yes. Then he lapsed into senile dementia."

"Where does he live?"

"Pittsburgh. I can find him. Let Michael work on Vince's father. Or I could contact Roberto in Italy."

Jack made no effort to stop the whip of emotion that snaked through his belly. He knew what it was. What he didn't know was what the hell to do about it. "Let Michael try first," he suggested in a bland tone. "He has plenty of quick and reliable connections."

He couldn't read her answering smile and had no chance to ask because they were pulling up in front of her house.

Mrs. Fisker, dressed in baggy pants, matted fur boots and a parka that probably belonged to her husband, waved from the porch, then hastened down the outside stairs.

"I've been watching for you, dear," she puffed to Noel. "Knew you'd come."

She gave Jack a dubious look, which drew another brief smile from Noel together with a quick introduction. "Did you remember something?" she asked the old woman.

"I was getting ready for bed when it occurred to me. It seemed strange when I thought about it. I mean, considering that the sidewalks haven't been plowed yet and all. They drove off in Helen's car." She swept a hand up and down the block. "No other vehicles have come or gone since. And the ones here now belong to people we know. So my question is, how did the man Helen left with today get here in the first place?"

IT WAS A GOOD QUESTION, but answerable. He could have parked in the next block in case someone like Mrs. Fisker happened to notice him. Licensed vehicles were more easily identified than people.

Noel went through Helen's office and her own. Nothing seemed to be out of place, and there were no notes from the kidnapper. She checked her apartment upstairs with Pepper at her side and Jack behind her. Nothing again.

"Figures, he'd leave us in limbo like this when, for once, we actually want a note." She let out a shaky sigh as emotion snuck in again.

"Helen's father was a judge in Pittsburgh," she said. "He had a nervous breakdown when she was ten, and he was never the same again. A lot of the cause was job-related stress, and it affected Helen's entire outlook. That's why she never pursued a career in the city. She started to, then decided smaller was better for her."

"But not for you."

"God, no. I wanted the sun, moon and stars. We lost touch for a while after we passed the bar. She practiced with a firm in Meadville, but she didn't like it much, so she quit and came to Winter Valley. It wasn't her home, but she knew I'd lived here once so it wasn't completely foreign territory. We got back together soon after that, but we didn't become partners until a few years ago when my—" she halted, then shrugged. "Well, let's say when my conscience got the better of me. I decided to try and help some people who really needed help but couldn't afford legal representation."

"So you do pro bono work here?"

She tossed him a smile. "No way. I'm cheap, but I'm not free.

I expect a retainer, however small, and potential clients feel better giving me one. I think they think I'll do a more thorough job if I have some of their money in my pocket. It's kind of like payback for me. Small-scale, but it feels worthwhile. As you know, not every big-time player I defend is squeaky-clean."

His hands moved her hair to the side. "Not every deal I strike shines, either, Noel. Life's not that tidy." His lips grazed her neck. "We'll get them back."

His cell phone rang, and he swore. "Ransom."

There was a long pause while someone, Noel assumed Michael, filled him in.

"Okay," Jack said at length. "If you have time, keep searching. If not, we can contact the brother in Italy."

That didn't sound good. Noel scratched Pepper's muzzle. "Anything startling?" she asked as Jack ended the call.

"Roberto's father's dead."

"What about his mother?"

"She predeceased her husband by six months. Emphysema."

Noel was surprised. "They seemed so healthy and robust. How did his father die?"

"Boating accident on Lake Michigan three years ago."

"I wonder why Roberto never let me know."

"Was your breakup amicable?"

"Well, no. But it wasn't horrible, just stiff and very final. I let him down, and he let me know it."

Before Jack could respond, her cell phone rang.

Noel answered. "This is Noel." She caught Jack's eye. "Yes, I hear you." Her fingers tightened on the casing. "I know you have her. What do you want me to do? Okay, us to do?" Another silence, then, "We're already studying everything. Yes, fine, all right. I'll tell him. Just don't— Damn!"

She hit the End button, then immediately reactivated and punched Star 69. And waited. And sighed.

"He used Helen's phone. He wants us to drive back to Pittsburgh and go over everything he's given us so far. He'll call us at my place in three hours. If we don't answer, either Caroline or Helen will die."

"HE GAVE YOU THREE HOURS to get to Noel's then never called?" Even agitated, Michael managed to prowl Jack's office with grace. "What's his game now?"

"To keep us dangling." Jack felt as if he'd had sand tossed in both his eyes. He hadn't slept since Thursday night, and it was almost 3:00 p.m. on Saturday.

Another weather system was approaching. That was another worry because the side streets were only marginally navigable right now.

"Noel's working the Vince Turano angle through the lawyer who defended him. She knows the guy, so that's our best shot right now." Jack wanted to flop on the sofa and sleep until Noel returned, but for Michael's sake, he remained in his office chair.

"You hungry?" Michael asked with a grin for his friend's drowsy expression. "I could use some fresh air, and maybe we'll get lucky and a certain cross-dressing blonde will show up at the deli—assuming you still want to talk to him."

"It couldn't hurt."

"You sound preoccupied. You're worried about Noel, aren't you?"

"Yeah." But Jack avoided elaboration by searching his jacket pocket for his keys. "I hope this Wilkie guy comes through." He zipped up. "Where's Talberg?"

"You ask me that again, old friend, and I'll think you're falling very hard for this woman."

"Think what you like." Jack opened the office door. "But keep it to yourself."

"She's worth the fall, Jack."

"I know." In the doorway, Jack turned to regard him. "It's not her worth that's the problem."

WILKIE LIVED with his daughter Maureen in a pretty family home on Squirrel Hill. A cockeyed snowman sat in the front yard, welcoming Noel when she arrived at 5:00 p.m.

Maureen led the way up a set of carpeted stairs. "I've heard of you from my father. His mind is dicey these days, but he watches the news morning and evening. When your name comes up, he often points to the screen and says how you sparkled in court."

"I'm glad he remembers me, though I wasn't much of a sparkler when he knew me."

"You said on the phone he took a case you didn't want to handle." They climbed another narrow stairwell. To the attic, Noel assumed and tried not to visualize the famous scene from *Jane Eyre*. "I wouldn't count on him recalling many of the details. He spends most of his day up here working on his miniature Dickens village," Maureen smiled. "He paints a few new buildings every year."

She knocked, stuck her head inside the open door. "You have a visitor, Dad."

It was *A Christmas Carol* in miniature, complete with cotton snow, trees and fairy lights used in two dozen tiny lamps. Foster Wilkie sat amid an array of plaster period buildings, with a strand of silver garland around his neck and his polka-dot tie askew.

He beamed at Noel as she picked her way over to him and shook her hand with vigor. "What a pleasure to see you."

"You know who she is?" Maureen sent Noel a cautioning look.

"Of course I do. Noel Lawson. I believe we're facing off in court on Monday."

Maureen sighed. "Go on in, then, and do your best."

Wilkie drew her forward and pointed to a stool. "So tell me, my dear, what brings you to my humble domain?"

NOEL SPENT TWO HOURS talking to the old man. By the time she emerged from the attic room, her head was spinning and she knew nothing more than before.

After saying goodbye to Maureen, she started for her car. She had her cell phone out and Jack's number punched when she spotted a slight movement in one of the vehicles parked on the far side of the street. It was a Volvo and it sat directly in front of a minivan. When she spied the driver, she aborted the call.

It took her less than thirty seconds to get into her car, swing over to the opposite curb and box him in. She left the engine running, stepped out and walked over to where he sat, trapped.

He opened his window as she approached. "I don't suppose you'd consider not mentioning this to Mr. Ransom?"

"I don't suppose I would. Talberg, isn't it?"

"You have a good memory, Ms. Lawson."

She had a temper, too, which she was fighting quite hard to control. "How long have you been watching me?" she asked and hoped for his sake he didn't play dumb.

"Since near the beginning." He removed his wool cap, exposing very flat blond hair. "I was mostly supposed to keep an eye on you when you were alone."

"So you're not a Peeping Tom."

"I never look in windows." As if inspired, he added, "I have two children, two girls. Because of this extra work, I'll be able to take them to Disney World in the spring."

In court, sentiment didn't stand a chance, but on a snowy street at Christmas time with a headache brewing, her best friend missing, and her emotions in turmoil, the most ferocious thing Noel could do was lean her forearms on the door and ask, "Where's Jack now?"

"I don't know. I'm not supposed to watch him."

A smile flitted across her lips. "Well, I'll tell you, Talberg, he might just come to regret that decision when I catch up with him."

Chapter Seventeen

She had more important things to think about than Jack's be-
hind-the-scenes maneuvering. Noel counted in every language
she knew all the way into the city. On impulse, she drove past
Artie's Deli, spied Jack's SUV and found a parking spot of
her own.

She promised herself she'd be calm about this. Still…

"Hey, Jack."

He smiled when he saw her. "What are you—" Then he swore
when she grabbed him by the hair. "What are you doing?"

"Thinking about killing you."

Michael, who sat opposite him, moved quickly. "I need the
bathroom."

Jack's eyes were steady on hers. "You found something out."

"What I found is a man with blond hair and a Swedish accent. Honest to God, Jack." She released his hair, hesitated, then
gave his mouth a kiss. "You have more nerve than anyone I
know. I told you when we met, I can take care of myself. I don't
need a watchdog."

Jack caught her wrist before she could snatch it out of reach.
"You don't," he said. "But I do."

She regarded him through her lashes for several seconds.
"You needed Talberg to watch me. Why?"

"Because I'm in—" He broke off and made a frustrated motion.

"As the kidnapper got weirder, I worried about you more and more."

"I'm not a feeble woman, Jack."

"You're not Wonder Woman, either. Whether I wanted to admit it or not, I realized we were dealing with a nut. So when I wasn't with you, or when it seemed particularly dangerous, I wanted someone else to be at least close by."

"Did he follow me to the Gemini Theatre?"

"I don't take stupid risks, Noel. He only watched you in your day-to-day life, in case, like Helen, you saw something you shouldn't, or the kidnapper took it into his head to come after you."

She was mollified but still vexed. "I don't like it when people do things behind my back."

He tried not to smile. "Yeah, right, and you've never done that yourself?"

"Certainly not." But she felt a laugh rising. When it bubbled out—probably as a strained form of hysteria—she gave up. "Okay, fine, I've done stuff, too. To Vince Turano, for one." She pushed on his chest with her trapped hand. "I spotted Talberg as I was coming out of Wilkie's place."

Jack sat down and slid his coffee mug toward her. "Any luck?"

"He thought we were going head-to-head in court next week."

"Sounds like a no. Did he remember Turano?"

"Only as a city in Italy. I gave my card to his daughter. She'll try talking to him at one of his more lucid times." She took a sip of coffee.

"There was one thing Wilkie kept saying when I asked him if he knew where Vince was. He said prisons are the only answer for some people's crimes. I thought he was quoting Scrooge, but he said it pretty much every time I mentioned Vince's name."

Jack glanced behind him. Michael reappeared. "Did you get that?"

Michael nodded, took his seat and pulled out his handheld computer. "Prisons. I already checked Pennsylvania and New York. He wasn't sent up anywhere there."

"He wouldn't have been," Noel said. "He was arrested in Michigan. He had several motels there. The warrant for his arrest was issued in Detroit."

"What about this state?" Jack asked.

"Oh, I'm sure he committed plenty of crimes here, but this isn't where he was caught."

"Can you check it out?" Jack asked Michael.

"In time, yes."

Noel regarded Jack. "You know, there is an easier way."

He cast her a sideways look, but said nothing.

"I'm open to easier," Michael put in. "I've got a million other things on the go right now."

Noel held up her cell phone. "I can get Roberto's number from my sister in Philadelphia."

Jack stared at her, then made a disgusted sound. "Yeah, sure, do it."

Her sister picked up on the second ring. "Hi, Ali." Noel kept her eyes on Jack's sulky face. "I need a favor. I have to get in touch with Roberto in Tuscany."

AFTER A PROJECT and development meeting on Sunday, Jack arrived at Noel's condo. New snow was beginning to fall. In a way Jack couldn't recall feeling before, it struck him as oddly festive.

"No answer from Turano?" He wandered around her living space, working the kinks from his neck and shoulders.

"Not yet." Noel rattled cans and bottles in the fridge. "I've left three messages on his voice mail. I have a feeling it was about two or three in the morning when I called the first time."

"Michael's pulling strings with the Justice Department. He might get something on Vince before your ex answers."

Her head popped up over the counter. "You say that like it leaves a bad taste in your mouth. The operative word is *ex,* Jack. Although," she said with a grin, "he was awfully handsome."

"Thanks for that."

"You're welcome. All the notes and photos are on the coffee table if you want to take another stab at solving them."

He really didn't, but he rolled his head one last time and dropped onto the couch.

Noel had written down everything the kidnapper had said to her, so he had that to mull over, as well.

Initially, she'd been told, he'd planned to kill them both. Very nice thought. Then there was Robert Tillman's star, colored red, the Red Touch poem and two cryptic starlights.

"'One's the cause and one won't fight,'" he read. His eyes didn't want to focus, but he forced them. "'If I get my wish tonight, you'll work it out and say it right.'" He looked from one paper to the next. "That line's in both poems."

"Noted and highlighted," Noel said as she strolled toward him with a mug of hot cocoa in each hand and a hopeful black lab at her heels. She even walked sexily in her bare feet, her drawstring pants and her tight white T-shirt. And he didn't miss the glint of her silver ankle bracelet.

He shook his head. "You mesmerize juries in court—that's half your secret, isn't it? Then you hit them with blazing logic and they buy every word you say."

She gave him one of the mugs, then curled up on the sofa next to him. "That takes care of the malleable men, but what about the women?"

"I'm working on a theory."

"Work on the kidnapper's notes instead."

"I have been." He flopped back, poked at the marshmallow with his index finger to melt it. "Unfortunately, my mind doesn't function along irrational lines."

"Makes interpretation more difficult, I agree, but it seems to me he's striving for a simplicity we're not grasping because we're not accustomed to it. What we need is a kid."

He arched a suggestive brow. "You want to have a kid?"

She batted at the hand that trapped her ankle. "You have a one-track mind lately, Jack, and it's on the wrong track right now. We need to think, not make—not have sex."

He caught her slip, as she'd undoubtedly caught his at Artie's last night. It was growing complicated between them. Yet instead of making him want to run the other way, he found himself becoming more and more intrigued by her.

He was in trouble.

He ran a finger inside her ankle chain, but subsided again. "I don't know any kids with a bent for bad riddles."

"I'm guessing you don't know any kids at all, but—" Her cell phone rang, and she picked up. "This is Noel." She listened, then mouthed the name Wilkie. "Yes, I'll come and see your village before Christmas. Vince Turano, Wilkie. Do you know where he is?" She tugged Jack upright and held the phone away from her ear.

"Bad blood," Wilkie was saying. "Got into the white powder. He was very upset."

"Only because he got caught."

"I hate family cases," Wilkie declared. "Always messy. He was mad at me for not winning, madder at you for not helping out. Grabbed me by my lapels and shook me."

"You should have resigned from the case, Wilkie."

"That's what he said. But it was lost from the start. Judge sent Vince to State. Made him furious. Worried me." Wilkie snorted. "I didn't go to the funeral."

Noel glanced at Jack. "Funeral?" she repeated. "Vince's funeral? Are you saying— Wilkie, is Vince is dead?" When he didn't answer, she frowned. "Wilkie?"

His daughter Maureen came on the line. Jack heard her soothing her father.

"Is Vince Turano dead, Maureen?" Noel asked again.

"From what I can gather, he died in prison. I can't give you a year, but as far as I'm aware it was about six months after he went in."

Noel breathed out. "Thanks, Maureen, and thank your father." She ended the call, stared at Jack. "I didn't expect that."

Didn't want it, either, Jack reflected and shoved his hands into his hair to get it off his face. "Okay, Turano's dead. We can verify that. But I was thinking in terms of him being the kidnapper." His brow furrowed. "What are you doing?"

"Calling Italy again." She shuffled papers as she spoke. "Roberto, it's Noel. It's after five here. I really need to talk to you. Please call me as soon as you get your messages." She tossed the phone aside and pulled Jack's hands down. "He's not supposed to be dead. I wanted this to work. Helen's—"

"Fine," Jack cut her off. "Safe."

"You just don't want me to get hysterical."

"I can't imagine you in that state, Noel."

"What about Caroline?"

"She gets hysterical if her bathroom sink's plugged. Helen?"

"She'll be okay."

Her condo phone line rang. She reached over Jack to put the call on speakerphone. "Hello."

"Noel?"

"Roberto." She pressed a finger to Jack's lips. "Did I wake you?"

"I'm not into warm milk and lights out by ten yet, *cara*. I got all your messages. I've been thinking about whether or not to answer them. I don't mean to sound bitter, but you're treading on sensitive ground here."

"I know, and I'm sorry to do it. Is Vince— Roberto, his lawyer told me he died in prison. Is that true?"

"His lawyer isn't supposed to divulge that information. We paid good money to keep the whole ugly affair quiet."

"You paid Wilkie?"

"Of course we did. Him, the prosecution, several of the witnesses, even members of the jury."

"What about the media?"

"The courtroom was closed to them."

"You paid the judge?"

"My father knew another judge, who knew Vince's judge. It didn't lighten his sentence, I can tell you. But it kept the trial out of the papers and off the air. And, to answer your unspoken question, it cost a frigging fortune."

"Did you have a fortune to spare?"

"Actually, no. We had half of one, and nothing by the time Vince was sent up. He contracted hepatitis C. We're not sure if it was before or after his incarceration. He never complained, and no one inside noticed him turning yellow until it was too late." He let some of the venom in his tone bleed away. "I wanted you to do it, Noel. I begged you to take the case."

"It wouldn't have changed anything." Her eyes landed on the coffee table. As she spoke, she uncurled her legs and very slowly leaned forward. "Wilkie was good, better than me in those days."

"No one was ever better than you, Noel."

Jack went forward with her, tried to follow whatever thoughts were zinging through her head.

Something—he couldn't say what—caused his stomach to clench. Icy fingers stroked along his spine. He sensed it in Roberto's voice, a suggestion of fury that bordered on some far more dangerous emotion.

Beside him, Noel pointed to the word *prisons* that had been scrawled then scratched out on the side of Michael's truck. She picked up Robert Tillman's colored star and ran her thumbnail under the initials.

"Damn," Jack whispered before she could set a hand over his mouth.

"What is it, Noel?" Roberto asked calmly.

"Nothing. I'm…sorry about Vince."

"Are you?"

"Of course I am."

"But you're not sorry you didn't take his case."

"It wouldn't have mattered," she repeated. "Whatever I've done since then, I promise you I couldn't have done anything for Vince at that initial—" she emphasized the word just enough for Jack to catch it "—stage of my career."

"You're wrong." The venom in his tone returned. As it did, that icy finger of dread grew spikes and crawled up the back of Jack's neck.

"Roberto…" Noel glanced at Jack, made an uncertain motion.

He mouthed to her to end the conversation.

"I'm sorry, Roberto," she said again. "I really am. About Vince. About everything."

"Oh, you mean everything like my mother's death, because she smoked herself into an early grave? Or my father's, because his motorboat got sliced in half by some rich inebriate's yacht? That kind of sorry?"

Noel drew back from the phone as if it were a snake poised to strike. "I don't want to believe this…" She closed her eyes. "You took her, didn't you, Roberto? You kidnapped Caroline Ransom to get even with Jack, then named me as your liaison so I'd be tied to your plan. Tied to you."

Roberto chuckled, and the sound of it hung like a noxious cloud in the air. With a quick look at Jack, Noel pointed to the Red Touch green poem. The capital *R* and the capital *T. R.T.*

Roberto Turano.

He nodded, and used the side of his hand to make a slash across his throat.

She gnawed on her lower lip. Jack knew she forced herself to lean closer to the phone. "Why are you doing this, Roberto?" she asked softly.

"Oh, because," he whispered. He chuckled again, but the tone was far more malevolent than before. "Because, because." He drew the words out in an eerie chant. Then he barked into the receiver, "Because, Jack and Noel. Because I can!"

Chapter Eighteen

"Don't let him get to you, Noel."

It was the first thing Jack said when she hung up. He didn't understand. It wasn't panic that had her brushing invisible bugs from her T-shirt and pants; it was revulsion.

"God, Jack. I almost married him." She dragged her hair into a ponytail and held it there while she stared at the ceiling. "This can't be right. I'm dreaming. Roberto, a kidnapper? The Ghost of Christmas Past? He was a runway model for big-name designers."

Jack took her by the shoulders and forced her to look him in the eye. "You couldn't have known what he'd become. There's probably a little madness lurking in most of us."

"A little madness?" Her laugh contained no humor. "Get real, Jack. The guy's full-blown insane. And I missed that? How? How could I not have seen it?"

"Because he was probably fine when you knew him. And if not that, then because he didn't let you see it." Jack refused to let her go. "It's possible," he said when she would have protested. "I heard of a guy right here in Pittsburgh who murdered five people over the course of three years and no one—not his wife, or his business associates, or his boss, or any of his friends—had the slightest clue."

She heard him and understood, even agreed to a point. But she was trained to look for the truth behind the lies. That was what she did, tear away the facade and expose what lay behind it.

But she hadn't anticipated a facade with Roberto. She'd been wrapped up in her career, excited at the prospect of joining a prestigious law firm, handpicked by the senior partner, with the knowledge that in a very short time she'd be offered a partnership, as well.

"Oh, hell." She let her hands and her hair fall. "It's all excuses. I should have seen him for what he was, or at least what he had the potential to become, and I didn't. So here we are. He's holding your sister and my best friend hostage. He hates me and, I assume, you. And I can't tell you if he'll trade them for money or not."

Jack steered her back toward the sofa. He sat down beside her, linked the fingers of one hand with hers, and with the other, punched Michael's number on his cell.

"Roberto Turano's the kidnapper," he said, and the flat certainty of it made Noel wince. "He phoned Noel on her house line. Get hold of Gabler and Simms and see what they do with a trace."

Her main line had been tapped early on, Noel recalled, with her full consent.

"He'll have wired the connection through his phone in Italy," she told Jack. "He and Vince were into computers. It would be child's play to him."

"We'll check it anyway," Jack said. Then he turned his attention back to Michael. "See what you can do about tracking his movements for the past five years, but make the last two a priority."

Noel tuned out. She didn't need to hear the technicalities or be reminded about what it was that had driven Roberto over the edge.

Roberto's brother was dead. They'd been close. She'd refused to defend Vince. Wilkie had lost the case. Vince had been remanded to state prison, and Roberto blamed her. He blamed Jack as well, for taking over Vince's motel and restaurant chain, a takeover that had led to an increased dependency on dealing, which in turn had led to his arrest.

The family money was gone, paid out to keep the entire affair quiet. That included, she assumed, any mention of Vince's death.

Because she couldn't bear to be idle, she stood and drifted over to the window. Even the snowflakes dancing outside the glass seemed to taunt her. She should have seen something in him, should have suspected what he could become if pushed. None of this should have happened.

As Jack continued to talk to Michael and the snow fluttered down in large, feathery flakes, she saw it again in her mind. Robert Tillman's star at the Gemini Theatre. Not important for the name, but for the initials.

"Initially." She repeated what Roberto had said to her inside the theatre. Initially, he'd planned to kill them. There'd even been a clue within the threat.

She returned to the coffee table and picked up the photo of Tillman's star. It was glaringly obvious in retrospect. To be fair, however, when approached from the angle of utter confusion, with a hundred or more other suspects upon whom blame could conceivably be fixed, there'd been no reason for her to attach Roberto's name to those initials.

She heard Jack end his call. When he came up behind her, she circled the star with her fingernail. "I should've seen it earlier."

He turned her around, took the photo from her hand and tossed it back on the table. "It's not your fault, Noel. The trial, its outcome and even Vince's death were all hushed up. There was no reason for you, or me for that matter, to suspect the guy."

"Yes, I know." She rested her forehead against his and felt better. "I'm not going to beat myself up for much longer, but I need a few minutes. I almost married a monster. What if I'd said yes, and we'd been engaged when Vince was arrested?"

"Then you'd have defended him, and everything would have been different."

She sighed. "I wouldn't have defended him, Jack. Not for

dealing drugs. For anything else, maybe, but not for that. Anyway, it wouldn't have been in Vince's best interest to have his future sister-in-law acting as his defense counsel, so I suppose the end result would have been the same. Except that Roberto probably would have murdered me in my sleep."

Jack's arms tightened around her. "Does he have a temper?"

"Not a quick one. Roberto tends, or tended, to smolder. When he lost it, he really lost it, but Vince was the true hothead." She brought her own head up. "Helen saw him in Winter Valley, Jack. She recognized him." She frowned. "Why was he there? He must have known I wasn't."

"He might have wanted something from your house."

"Maybe." She cleared the negative thoughts from her brain. "Someone needs to go there, Jack."

"I'll send a couple guys tonight."

"I don't know what he'll do now. He was enjoying himself at our expense before. He didn't sound amused at the end of our conversation today."

"He wanted us to know who he is, and now we do. My guess is he'll carry on as planned."

It made sense. But nerves and fear jittered in Noel's stomach. "Hatred's a powerful thing, Jack. He might want your money, but he might also be willing to sacrifice his own life to ensure we pay for what he views as our crimes." She stopped speaking, lowered her gaze to the coffee table. "The initials are only part of it, two pieces that comprise one element of the puzzle he's given us. There's more here. There has to be." She plopped cross-legged onto the floor. "I feel like my brain's going to explode."

"You need food."

She looked up at him, revived, yet teetering on some kind of precipice she didn't recognize or understand. "That wasn't what I had in mind."

He almost smiled. When he crouched next to her, took her

hand and brought it to his lips, his eyes were on hers and it helped. He helped. He made her feel alive, and he bolstered her flagging defenses. She'd find her strength and her balance again. But she needed to step away from the nightmare. She needed Jack.

"Don't be gentle," she whispered and, wrapping her arms around his neck, pulled him with her onto the floor.

HE'D HAD A TANTRUM, a big one. Roberto looked around the room, at the broken ceramic vases, the smashed Hummel and Doulton, the torn paintings, the shredded upholstery and the black hole that had once been a twenty-seven-inch TV. He didn't remember doing all that, but he must have—unless his ally had gotten here ahead of him, and he hadn't noticed.

They'd figured it out. Finally. They knew who the Ghost of Christmas Past was. They didn't know *where* he was or how involved his plan was, but it was a start.

He'd seen Noel naked. He liked remembering that. She had a tiny mole beside her navel. He'd enjoyed licking it.

Did Jack enjoy doing that, as well?

Spinning, he grabbed a lamp and hurled it against the wall. His chest was heaving. He needed to control that and set his mind back on the plan.

He took the stairs two at a time and kicked the door to his dark room open so hard it bounced off the wall, almost flattening his nose. With a growl, he zeroed in on Helen and glared at her.

Her eyes widened when he reached out to pluck the gag from her mouth. "She knows the truth. He was with her. That means he knows, too." His breath whooshed out. "They're sleeping together, aren't they?" Helen said nothing, so he poked her. "Aren't they?"

"I don't know."

"Of course you do." He gave her a careless shove. "Women tell each other all their sordid little secrets. She's sleeping with him, you're sleeping with his partner and what am I doing?

Waiting for them to realize they're not done yet. They haven't got it all figured out."

Taking her by the shoulders, he hauled her forward until their noses almost touched. "'Starlight, star bright,' Helen. It's so simple a child could figure it out. 'Say it fast, say it right. You'll know to whom you owe your plight.'"

She didn't whimper, but she flinched, just a little. "I don't know what you're talking about, Roberto, and I'm here."

"'Love thy neighbor.'" He enunciated each word. His mustache twitched. "How long do you figure they've been having sex?"

"What makes you so sure they are?"

"Because." He spoke right into her face. "Because she's beautiful and bewitching and she wouldn't give a damn about Ransom's reputation or the fact that he doesn't have a scrap of dress sense. He's only got money." He lifted Helen's chin and squeezed. "Is that the big attraction? Would she have given him a second look if he wasn't stinking rich?"

Helen swallowed. "You threw them together, Roberto."

"Because I wanted revenge. But then, when I saw them at the theatre, I realized I can use this." He broke off, willed his scattered thoughts to settle. "I *can* use it. I'm going to. Yes, of course I am. I want it to be like this. Stupid." Laughing, he released her. "I forgot, in all the excitement." He scratched a finger back and forth under her chin. "Got all tangled up there for a moment, Helen, but I'm straight now." He brought his face back down to hers. "Shh." He tapped his own lips, then hers. "Mustn't say a word to anyone. And mustn't try to escape. I'd have to kill you if you did, and for old times' sake, I want you and Noel to be reunited."

"Are you going to kill her? Us?"

He stood, walked to the door, then turned. "That depends." A slow smile spread across his face. "Someone's going to die, that's for sure. Who it will be is…well, let's call it a spin of the wheel at this point. Unfortunately, Helen, there's only going to be one spin. And the wheel's in Jack Ransom's head."

"LOVE THY NEIGHBOR." Jack couldn't count the number of times he'd repeated the phrase. "Noel believes it's relevant, so it probably is."

"We've established that." Michael sipped his coffee in Artie's Deli while Jack kept an eye out for the blond drag queen.

"It isn't Burnley, unless he's working with Turano, which I doubt."

"There are lots of condos around Noel's, Jack. Conversions and new construction. We could go door-to-door, but it would take days."

"When did Vince Turano die?"

"December twelfth, thirteen days before Christmas."

"And it's what, the ninth now?"

"It's the tenth, Jack." Michael gave his head a baffled shake. "How in God's name do you manage to do everything you do and never know the date or often even the time?"

"Good people around me." Jack glanced up as their sandwiches arrived.

"On the house," Artie said with a grin. "Word around your corporate office is that our lunches are going down well. I'll be taking on extra staff by the end of the week."

"Uh-huh." Jack kept his eyes on the door. "Where does the blonde live?"

"Angie?" Artie asked. "Not sure."

"Do you know his last name?"

"No idea. Do you want me to try and talk to him?"

"No, it's fine." Jack shook him off. "I'm grasping."

"Ah, well, I'll leave you to it and get back to my counter. Your tab's closing in on five hundred, if you're interested."

He wasn't. Not now. Jack held himself still even as he scraped his chair back and stood.

"Do you see something?" Michael twisted around in his seat. "All I see are a bunch of bundled-up office workers."

"And behind them is one cross-dressing blonde named Angie."

"Loving thy neighbor has nothing to do with us identifying Roberto as the kidnapper." Noel was convinced of that. "It has to be pertinent in some other way."

She and Jack were walking in the snow in downtown Pittsburgh. Rush hour was winding down, and a festive feeling had invaded the air. Noel tried to absorb it, but the best she could do was smile at a pair of women laden with boutique bags as they admired each other's new boots.

"I'd love to go shopping right now," she remarked in such a wistful tone that Jack raised a humorous brow.

"You want to try on sexy lingerie for me?"

"That would make me some kind of kinky shopaholic, wouldn't it? Not to mention unfeeling, self-absorbed and the worst possible kind of person. Love thy neighbor," she repeated. "It has to relate to something other than Roberto's name."

"We're going through the condos near yours." Jack squinted at a blond woman across the busy intersection. "I still can't believe that guy got away from me yesterday."

"He's obviously used to running." She saw the sign for Artie's Deli and gave him a nudge with her shoulder. "Wanna try again?"

"Yeah, I'm hungry."

"Big surprise." But so was she, and on top of that, she'd been standing for most of the day. Anything involving a chair would be welcome right now.

"There are the starlight rhymes, too," she reminded him as they pushed through the door and into the crowded delicatessen. "The second one sort of makes sense, especially the part where he says, 'One's the cause and one won't fight,' That's you and me described from Roberto's perspective after Vince's arrest. But the rest is still up for interpretation."

"'If I get my wish tonight, you'll work it out and say it right.'" Jack held a chair for her, then took one of his own. "I'd say it's pretty much been worked out."

"Except for where he's holding them."

"Not at the Gemini. We've had a team scour the theatre twice. The last time was only three days ago."

Noel sat back in frustration. "Well, maybe there isn't anything more. It's just a niggle I can't seem to get out of my head." She looked around. "I don't see your blonde, Jack."

A large man with a pear-shaped body and whiskers like Bluto came to take their orders.

"No Ray?" Noel asked him.

He jerked a thumb toward the back room. "He's working on the inventory with Artie." He lumbered off with their orders.

Noel played with her paper napkin. "Where do you think he's holding them, Jack?"

"The last place we'd expect."

"That would be your place."

He cocked his head. "Here in Pittsburgh, no. But Winter Valley's a possibility." He shoved his chair back, took his cell from his pocket. "I'll call Michael from the men's room." He kissed her and before straightening warned, "Keep an eye out for the drag queen."

Noel found herself smiling despite the circumstances. Did he know he'd kissed her? Did she want to think about the reason or ponder her own reaction to what was becoming an increasingly tangled involvement between them?

"Can't do that and get into Roberto's head at the same time," she decided and fanned his notes and rhymes out in front of her. She uncapped her pen, prepared to circle anything that struck her as incongruous.

The waiter brought the food, grunted when she thanked him and walked off.

She'd never seen him before, didn't really want to again. Ray was better with customers. Although she had yet to meet or see Artie, she assumed he must be people-oriented, as well. You couldn't be much else and own a deli in Jack's working neighborhood.

Propping her chin in her hand, she ran the tip of her pen around the colored photo of Robert Tillman's star. More specifically, she ran it around his initials. RT for Roberto Turano. Well, they'd already established that, hadn't they? Established and set aside. Same thing with the Prisons Kill message.

"Starlight, star bright," she repeated from one of the rhymes. She continued to circle the star that contained Tillman's initials. Initials that stood out because Roberto hadn't colored them red.

"You'll work it out, and say it right…"

Why couldn't she shed the feeling that there was at least one more thing he wanted them to know?

"Say it fast, and say it right. You'll know to whom you owe your plight."

What was there left to know except where he was holding Caroline and Helen?

Robert Tillman's initials appeared to glow within the star. "RT," Noel said softly. Then the haze that had been muddling her brain began to clear. She circled the star more dramatically. "RT." She said it again, and almost jumped because it hit her so hard. "Artie!"

Everything inside her froze. Her pulse roared like thunder in her ears. Her head snapped up and around. "Jack—"

A hand clamped down on her left wrist. "Hey there, Noel."

She swore, breathed in, ordered herself to remain calm. But she didn't look at him when she replied, "Hello, Roberto."

Where was Jack? She searched for him through the crowd.

"There was a line," Roberto informed her. His hand tightened. "Look at me, Noel." Something cold and metallic tapped her leg under the table. "Do it, or you'll be minus one pretty kneecap."

She brought her head around. And for a moment was shocked. Gone was the sleek brown hair and beautifully sculpted features of a runway model. In their place, she saw a riot of tobacco-brown curls and a mustache so shaggy it covered his upper lip.

Small changes, perhaps, but they altered his appearance dramatically.

She held his gaze. "So, what do we do now, Roberto? Or do you prefer Artie?"

He gave her wrist a nasty pinch. "Cool to the last, aren't you, Noel?" He tapped her leg again. "But I've got the gun, your friend and your new lover's sister. We're leaving together, *cara*. No fuss, no struggle. Because I'll blow you away in the middle of this deli, and after I do, I'll turn the gun on myself. Then Helen and Caroline will starve to death, and Jack will have to live the rest of his life with the knowledge that he set the wheels of all your deaths in motion. I don't think even he'd be able to deal with that and continue to function, do you?"

She leaned forward ever so slightly. "Where are they, Roberto?"

He smiled. "You need to love your neighbor a little more, I think."

She might have been able to decipher that remark sooner if she hadn't heard his gun click. "They're in Winter Valley, aren't they?"

"A cigar for the lady lawyer. Up," he ordered in the same breath. "We're going out the front door."

Noel glanced in the direction of the men's room

"God, you're such a book, Noel." Roberto stroked her leg until she stood. He had a smile plastered on his face and his fingers still wrapped around her wrist. "So easy to read right now. Move." He gave her a shove. "Before Jack comes out and sees us." He pressed his mouth to her hair. "If he does, I'll have to make a choice. He dies and you suffer, or you die and he suffers. I think I'd rather kill you, all in all. Feels like it would satisfy me more."

She believed him and didn't fight. But she did watch for Jack and didn't breathe easy until they reached the street. If you could call it breathing with a ball of terror sitting in her throat.

Somewhere in the back of her mind, she thought she'd figured it out. Now all she could do was pray that Jack would do the same thing.

Chapter Nineteen

She was gone when Jack returned to the table. A crease appeared between his eyes as he glanced at the ladies' washroom. Their waiter came over with the coffeepot and poured.

"Where's Noel?" Jack asked him.

The big man shrugged. "I got lots of customers, pal. I don't keep tabs on any one. She want coffee or not?"

"No. Are Ray and Artie still in the back?"

"Far as I know. Man, I got better things to do than watch where people go."

He clomped away, muttering. Jack sat, but he kept his eyes moving. Something wasn't right, he felt it in his gut. She wouldn't have left the food unattended and she certainly wouldn't have left Roberto's notes, poems and photos spread across the table.

The crease deepened as he noticed the black ink that circled Robert Tillman's star. Noel had written something between the man's initials. It looked like a cross, or a plus sign. And below it she'd printed two other letters. *WV*.

His stomach began to churn. He wiped a sweating palm on the leg of his jeans. He was overreacting, had to be. She'd come out of the ladies' room in a minute, and he'd curse himself for freaking out over nothing.

"No pretty lady today?"

Ray's voice startled him, and Jack swung around in his seat. "You didn't see her?"

"Nah. I was working with Artie. Except he's taken a powder and left me on my own. You look kind of pale, Jack. You okay?"

"He's worried about his lady friend, Ray."

Jack turned—and stared straight at the blond drag queen who stood in front of the table with an unlit cigarette between his fingers.

"You've been wanting to talk to me, and I've been doing my best to avoid you. Shall we go outside?"

Jack regarded the restroom again.

The blonde smiled, revealing lipstick-smeared teeth. "She's not there. I saw her leave."

Jack's eyes snapped up. "When?"

"She left with the proprietor while you were gone."

"Artie?" He drew back, took that in and processed it. Then he looked at the photo and the initials Noel had connected with an addition sign.

R plus *T. RT.*

"Damn!" He sprang up so fast he spilled coffee onto the notes. "Artie!"

The blonde watched him through canny eyes. "That's what I said. They left together." He plucked a piece of tobacco from the cigarette. "I recognized Noel the first time you brought her in. How, you ask? Because I know her. Personally. That's all I'm prepared to say on that score. I don't like her, never have. That's a personal matter, as well. But not liking her and wanting to see her dead are two very different things. Artie was walking behind her, Mr. Ransom. Very close behind her. And he had a gun."

THE TRIP NORTH took forever. And there were many better drivers on the road than an exhilarated Roberto Turano.

He kept giggling. Noel wanted to cover her ears, block out the sound, but he'd tied her hands and feet.

He started to sing once they were out of the city. He fishtailed his four-by-four truck wherever possible, but didn't cut anyone off or do anything that might have gotten him pulled over.

"I'll give him some time to figure it out," he chortled. "Do you think he'll manage it, Noel?"

"Yes."

"Me, too, but if he doesn't, I'll give him the answer myself. They traced my phone call the other night, didn't they?"

"To Italy." As she'd suspected, and as Michael had confirmed, shortly after she'd hung up.

"Don't you think that was clever of me?"

"It's what I would have expected from you, Roberto."

"I'll take that as a compliment. My whole plan's been clever, actually. But I won't take full credit for it. I had an ally."

"I wondered about that."

"You wondered, Noel, because that's how your mind works. Jack's moves along different lines. Whose business can I pillage today? Whose life can I rape and or plunder? He destroyed Vince."

"You don't think Vince had a hand in that himself?"

His backhanded slap stung, but she'd anticipated it and didn't flinch. What she did do was twist her wrists together behind her back.

"Just a warning not to push me, *cara*. In your own words, I'm a little insane these days." He winked. "You talked about your Ghost with Jack at the deli. Ray overheard." Roberto faked a gasp. "Oh, my, you missed your dinner, didn't you? And you'll need your strength to get through this, yes you will." Smiling broadly, he reached over her and flipped open the glove box. Drawing his hand out, he snickered and said, "Chocolate?"

"Inside." Roberto shoved her through the door of a small, dark room. "I'll be back."

The door slammed. Noel heard a number of locks click, then spied two separate movements before her eyes adjusted.

"Noel!" Helen maneuvered herself off a lumpy cot and ran to her. "Oh, God, I hate to say I'm glad to see you, but I am."

"Me, too." Noel would have hugged her friend except her hands were still tied.

Helen rested her head on Noel's shoulder. "He had me gagged at first, but then I think he realized that even if I screamed no one would hear me."

"Us," a petulant voice piped up from the corner. "You're Noel, then, huh?"

"Yes. Caroline?"

"Well, duh."

"She's having a wicked stepsister moment," Helen said quietly.

Noel had dealt with witches before. For Jack's sake, and because she was endeavoring to keep her fear under control, she didn't bother with a response and instead studied the woman who was seated like royalty in a shabby slipper chair.

She had a great deal of shiny red hair and even more freckles, a snub nose, a rather attractive mouth—or it would have been without the curled upper lip—and wide set green eyes reminiscent of a hostile cat. The room smelled of expensive perfume, but not a brand Helen would wear. This one had overtones of greenery that were a little too pungent to be pleasant.

When she finished appraising Caroline Ransom, Noel turned back to Helen.

"Love thy neighbor, Helen." She ran her gaze around the small room. "Roberto rented my next-door neighbor's house. That's so incredibly brazen I'm not sure I ever would have thought of it."

"Me, either," Helen agreed. "Especially when there were so many other things to think about." She glanced at Caroline. "He put us together this morning. Until then, I was alone and, I can tell you, terrified. Not that company makes it a whole lot better, but at least it was someone to talk to."

Caroline shifted in her chair. "I was fine with my own company, thanks." She frowned at Noel. "Where's Jack?"

"In Pittsburgh the last time I saw him."

"Is he going to pay your lunatic ex?"

"Do you think he should?"

Caroline worked herself to the edge of the chair and stood. She wasn't as tall as Noel, or as svelte as Helen. And her bone structure wasn't a patch on Jack's.

"Is he going to pay?" she demanded again. "Are we going to get out of here?"

"I don't know."

"You mean—" Caroline gaped. "Are you saying he might not pay the ransom?"

"Oh, he'll pay it. I'm just not sure we're going to get out of here. Not alive, anyway."

"You're a lying whore. He said you were, and he was right."

The antagonism between them was fueling her own fear. If they continued to bait each other, Noel realized, the situation would only deteriorate further.

"Look, Caroline," she tried, "you can call me whatever names you like, but the fact is we're being held hostage by a man who's, at best, mentally unbalanced. You've been with him the longest. Tell us what you've seen, what he's done, how he's reacted to things that have happened and things you've said."

Caroline's mistrust appeared to wane. "I guess that'd be the smart thing to do. He hates you, I can tell you that. He'll give me back when Jack pays, and maybe her." She nodded at Helen. "But I think he has other plans for you."

"You know about Vince, right?" Helen asked.

"I talked to his lawyer," Noel said. "It was Wilkie."

Caroline sniffed. "Some lawyer. First his client gets sent to prison for ten years, then said prisoner catches hepatitis C and dies. Personally, if it were me, I'd blame old Jacob first, then Jack, then you. But since Jacob's dead and Jack's got the money and you're here, you'd be the one I'd vent my anger on. It only makes sense."

Noel's gaze traveled around the room. There was a small dormer window, but Roberto had used steel bolts to secure planks across it, and their hands were still bound. Not that they could have pulled the planks off in any case.

Caroline resumed her seat. "I don't think I have much to worry about, so I'm not going to. He said he'd let me go when Jack paid him."

"He's also insane," Noel reminded her.

"Maybe he just appears that way to you."

"I saw a lot of smashed porcelain and china when he brought me through the living room, Caroline. Broken lamps, a demolished television, shredded upholstery. Believe me, that isn't the norm for this house. He had some kind of fit recently."

"You're just trying to frighten me," Caroline retorted.

"Well, yeah. If frightening you will get you to help us think of a way out."

"I'm too scared to think," Helen said. "Every time I try to come up with something, he bursts in and we have a creepy conversation, then he touches me, and it takes all my willpower not to go crazy myself."

"I know." Revulsion slithered like a snake in Noel's stomach.

"He can't hurt me," Caroline stated. "I'm the money, and he knows it."

Noel wanted to shake her. "You're not listening, Caroline. Roberto's insane. He's playing a crazy game, and the rules keep changing. He gave Jack tainted chocolates, then, the next day brought a homemade remedy to his office. Why? Pure enjoyment, I imagine. And to remind himself that he was in complete control of the game. He said he planned to kill Jack and me at one point, but then he thought of something better. Maybe that was true, maybe it wasn't. The point is, when you're dealing with insanity, you can't put your faith in promises of any kind. I've never been totally convinced it's the money he wants. I think revenge is his primary motivation. He all but admitted it to me on the drive up here. He wants Jack to suffer."

For the first time, a trace of fear invaded Caroline's expression. "He said he'd let me go. All Jack has to do is pay him. He must want the money. Who doesn't want money?"

"A person," Noel said with a shiver, "who, once he has his revenge, might feel he has no further reason to live."

JACK MADE IT to Winter Valley in just over eighty minutes—which was a miracle, considering the blowing snow and icy road conditions. He drove straight to Noel's house and was climbing the porch stairs when his cell phone rang.

"I'm here," he said to Michael on the other end. "Where are you?"

"Halfway between. I contacted her aunt where she works. There's an emergency key inside the gutter at the far end of the porch where the path runs around to the garden. That's Mrs. Fisker's side."

"Her neighbor." Jack turned left, followed the line of the gutter and retrieved the key. Then he paused for a moment, turning it over while he considered an idea.

"Get here as fast as you can," he told Michael and broke the connection.

Inside, he went to Noel's office, but it was tidy and untouched. He crossed the hall to Helen's. There was more of interest in here. Jack ran a hand through his hair as his gaze bounced from her computer to her filing cabinets and over her bookshelves.

Her desk stood next to a large window. On it, he spied a phone, a fax, two paperweights, two open files and a pair of binoculars sitting on top of a bird encyclopedia.

Eyes narrowed, Jack picked them up and then used them to look out the window.

He could see the whole west side of Noel's neighbor's yard.

Not Mrs. Fisker, some other person whose name he couldn't recall. An old man who was engaged to a woman with a walker.

The man was away and his house was being rented, wasn't it? He'd been so caught up in watching Noel cut holly that he'd only heard about half of what she'd told him that day in the yard.

He glanced over his shoulder. He could ask the old lady next door. Or save time and go with his hunch.

He raised the binoculars again. Helen might have been bird watching. Or she might have spotted something far more interesting.

"Love thy neighbor," he murmured, then lowered the glasses when the meaning of it finally fell into place. "Damn!"

Pocketing Noel's key, he ran for the door. Instincts and intellect were a killer combination. Jacob had drilled that into him as a kid. The pair had served him well enough in business; maybe they would do the same now, when it really mattered.

Roberto wanted one of them dead. As he started for the rear gate that led into the yard next door, Jack promised himself it wouldn't be Noel.

"HERE WE ARE." Roberto kicked open a warped alleyway door. "New home."

Old theatre, Noel corrected and would have laughed at the irony of it if she hadn't been working so hard to keep her nerves from fraying.

Jack's men had gone over the Gemini twice. That made this the last place in Winter Valley anyone would think to search for them.

Jack might think of Winter Valley, though. And they'd talked about last places. Assuming he'd gotten the obscure message she scrawled on the star photo at Artie's.

Roberto ordered Noel and Helen to precede him. He wrapped an arm around Caroline's throat and held a gun to her head.

"Not that I don't trust you, ladies," he said with a twinkle. "But

I'm sure you wouldn't want me to blow Ms. Ransom's brains out before the fun even starts."

Caroline choked, then hissed. Roberto shook her. "Shut up and walk." Noel saw his arm tighten around Caroline's windpipe. "Both of you, walk straight ahead." He removed the gun and ran it along Noel's spine. "You're not afraid of ladders, I hope. Only big spiders, right?"

Caroline made a gurgling sound, and the gun returned to her temple. "I said, shut up. We're going down the center aisle, through the little door and into the backstage area where all the ropes and pulleys and cobwebs are. Oops, sorry, Noel. It's only dust. Nothing to worry about. Did you know," he went on in a conversational tone, "that this used to be both a theatre for showing movies and a stage for theatrical productions. Those are plays," he whispered in Caroline's ear. "Thus the pulley system and ladders. Very old, though. Good thing you wore pants tonight instead of a skirt, Noel. Over here, blondie," he said to Helen. "Noel, you tie Caroline's ankles for me while I hold my gun on your friend. How's Railback, by the way?"

"He's fine." Noel debated leaving some slack in the rope but decided against it when she noticed the gleam in Roberto's eyes. Any excuse, she thought and fought back a chill.

"Good girl. Now you wait here." He gave Caroline a rather hard rap on the head and motioned for Helen and Noel to climb. "I'll hang back with my finger on the trigger of the little explosive I've rigged up there. Pull any stunts, and they'll be scraping pieces of your pretty butts off the marquee for a week."

"What are we going to do?" Helen whispered to Noel.

"Wait for an opportunity," Noel returned.

Roberto joined them at the top of the rigging. "Nice sturdy platform," he said and bounced on it. When it creaked and swayed, he laughed. "Well, maybe not."

"Are you going to hang us?" Helen asked.

He jabbed Noel's shoulder. "What kind of gamester would I be if I did that? Stupid question, Helen."

Noel raised her eyes to the rafters. There was a loft area fifteen feet overhead. That was where he was going to take them.

"You're putting Caroline in the cellar, aren't you?" she said.

"Very good." He ran the tip of the gun over her cheek. It was better than his hand. "She's smart, isn't she, Helen? Has it figured out already, and we're not even in place yet. You see, I'm going to give dear Jack a choice. Save you or save his sister. But come to think of it, I'm doing this wrong. Helen should go with Caroline. That'll make Jack's dilemma more difficult. What would you do, Noel? Save a sister you don't really care about and another woman who's little more than a stranger? Or would you say, screw them, and go for the one who's hot in bed? Who knows, maybe he loves you, but I wouldn't count on it. Jack Ransom, like his grandfather before him, loves money above all else. Then again, he is a man, and you are a rather stunning woman. Ah well, we'll find out, won't we? Stop right here." He snaked an arm around Helen's throat now and shoved the gun under her chin. "Tie her feet, Noel, then climb that ladder next to you."

"You wanted to be an actor, didn't you, Roberto?" Noel took the rope and wrapped it around Helen's feet. "You should have pursued your dream."

"Uh-huh. Nice try, *cara*." He was watching her every move with the rope. As much as she wanted to, Noel had no choice but to cinch it tightly around Helen's ankles. He wanted to ensure Helen wouldn't escape while he carried out the rest of his crazed plan.

When she was finished, Roberto forced her up the ladder to the loft. Then he followed her up.

"No closet to lock you in, unfortunately. So I'll just have to attach you to this beam." He kissed her nose. "See any spiders yet?"

She cast a quick look along the beam. "I couldn't have saved Vince, Roberto."

"I don't hear you." He began to sing. "There, done." He gave the rope one last tug, then caught her hair in his free hand, yanked her head back and kissed her.

She couldn't help herself. She bit him. When he jerked back, she saw blood, then felt her cheek explode as he struck her.

"I hope to hell Jack chooses Caroline," he spat.

"And if he doesn't?"

"Roberto shoved his face into hers and leered. "Then I'll have to find another way to kill you."

THE FRONT DOOR of Noel's neighbor's house was unlocked, and there was a note taped to the banister. Jack tore it free and read:

Dear Jack,
Figured it out at last, huh? But of course you're too late to rescue her from here. If you want her, or rather them, come to where the stars hang out on the floor. Come alone. I have a camera rigged. I set it up after your people left last time. Bring anyone with you, and I'll destroy the theatre.

Got that? Good. Now here's where the fun begins. You have a choice to make, Jack Ransom. I'm holding your sister and your new lover in two different places inside. You'll have five minutes from the time you enter the front door to the time I set off my explosives. Five minutes will take you either to the loft above the stage—that's where Noel will be—or to the cellar where your sister will be waiting. Trust me, you can't get them both out in five short minutes. You'll barely have time to free one of them and escape unscathed.

So what do you think? It's after midnight by now, the anniversary of my brother's death. There are thirteen days till Christmas and someone in your life is going to die.

Lover or family member, take your pick, Jack. But remember, COME ALONE. Or we'll all be paying an early visit to the Christmas spirits.

Here's to painful decisions.
The Ghost of Christmas Past

Chapter Twenty

She was going to get out of here. Noel refused to consider any other option. If she did, she might fall apart, and then Roberto would win.

What would Jack do? The question kept creeping into her head. So did the answer. He wasn't responsible for her. She'd gotten herself into this mess with Roberto; she would get herself out.

She'd scanned the long beam when he'd tied her to it. It ran the length of the loft, and while it was rather thick, it was also extremely old.

Old wood was subject to rot, from climate conditions and from insects. Wood bugs, Mrs. Fisker called them. Some of them resembled armadillos, but the most famous were termites.

"Please be infested," she said to the beam.

Roberto had bound her hands above her head, but he hadn't tied the rope tightly enough to prevent her from inching it along the rough timber surface.

How long before Jack showed up? Noel cast a worried look over her shoulder. Ten minutes? Thirty? An hour?

Roberto hadn't been specific in that regard, but she suspected he wouldn't want to wait much longer. If Jack didn't receive his message soon, Roberto would cut the riddle short and simply tell him.

Then he'd wait. And watch. And savor the outcome.

As she inched along the beam, Noel searched for cameras.

She saw none. But she heard something. It started softly and built to a shrill crescendo.

It was Christmas music, she realized, repulsed. A single violin, scratching out a hideous parody of "Jingle Bells." Each note seemed to slice into her brain like the thrust of a stiletto. Roberto wasn't merely insane, he was sadistic as well.

"Should have seen it, Noel," she reproached herself. But she hadn't, and that was that. Her goal now was to find a way out of here, locate and warn Jack and make sure nothing happened to Helen.

Her heart wanted to pound. The longer it took her to reach the end of the beam, the more she felt her control slipping. Terror had been clawing at her since she'd seen Roberto in the deli. His deli, strategically located near Jack's corporate office. Which meant he'd been planning his revenge for a very long time.

What was he doing now, she wondered with a desperate glance into the shadows behind her? Jack's security people had been here and discovered nothing. Assuming they'd been thorough, that meant, at the time, there'd been nothing wired to explode and no cameras installed for viewing.

At some point, Roberto had returned to the city, to continue playing his hand. He'd left for a few hours after shoving her into the upstairs room at Fred Yost's house but not long enough to have done any complicated wiring work.

She'd spotted a boarded-up exit earlier. Possibly, he'd strengthened the supports so the only way into the theatre would be through the front door. He'd have a camera there. That wouldn't have taken long to fix in place. Only one way in meant he'd know if anyone except Jack tried to enter the theater. And if they did…

"Pow," she whispered and gave the beam an urgent yank. "Break."

Nothing happened, frustrating her, but this was the only way. The wood felt jagged. Pieces of it were crumbling off, some damp, some dry, some much larger than she'd anticipated.

The loft floor was sagging, as well, and the sound of it groaning made her heart double-thump more than once. But better the ghastly protest of old wood than the screech of a bad violin. Of course that was why he was playing the music—to terrify her. Revenge was no fun if you couldn't toss a little terror into the mix.

Could he see her now? She had to believe he couldn't, that he hadn't had time to do a complicated wiring job.

She was two feet from the wall, and the floor was making horrible noises. "Please hold," she begged it. "Please break," she said to the beam.

She tested her weight on the overhead wood and heard a crunch. She yanked down hard with her bound wrists. Nothing gave, but there was a lot of snapping, both underfoot and directly in front of her.

She kept dragging on the wood, then tried jabbing upward.

One of the floorboards gave a loud crack, and she stopped dead, half-afraid to breathe. She stared at the wall, found her focus and her emotional balance. She wouldn't panic.

She gave another quick tug, heard a sharp splinter of wood. Something was going to give, but it was a toss-up whether it would be the floor or the beam.

She pictured Jack's face, then Helen's. Roberto would be laughing now. He'd feel certain he'd won. Whatever choice Jack made, someone would die, and he'd have to live with that knowledge for the rest of his life.

Roberto didn't want Jack to die, he never had. He hadn't wanted the money, either, or if he had once, he didn't now. It was all about revenge. Even his own life ran a distant second to the achievement of his goal.

Bracing herself, Noel gave the beam a series of short, jerky tugs. Then, with her wrists, she heaved it upward.

It moved. She was sure she felt it move. Unfortunately, so did the floorboards beneath her.

She shifted her weight. When that board began to crack, too, she hissed in a breath and hauled herself upward until she was hanging from the beam.

The old wood splintered and crunched and finally made a sound like a great, slow groan. She watched it fracture, felt the rope around her wrists begin to skid.

She hit the floor hard. Then watched in shock as the board she'd landed on cracked in two.

ROBERTO HAD TAPED pieces of paper in various places. The first one Jack spotted had an arrow pointing into the theatre. It said Noel. The second, which said Caroline and Helen, indicated an area to the left.

Jack didn't hesitate. He ran into the theatre and followed the arrows to the side of the stage, through a warped door and up a ladder to where the dusty scaffolding was housed.

He swore, caught sight of a movement and ducked. Or started to. Someone collided with him headfirst, nearly knocking him to the ground.

"Jack!"

Noel gasped his name. Before he could gather his wits, she grabbed his hand and began to pull.

"Caroline and Helen are in the cellar. I don't know if Roberto can see us or not. How much time did he give you?"

"Five minutes." Jack had purchased a stopwatch before entering the theatre. "There's three-fifty left."

"It'll be enough."

He didn't argue, just shoved her ahead of him and backtracked through the lobby to the shadowy area where the arrows pointed along a narrow hallway that ended with a door.

"Get out of here, Noel," he said while she yanked on the door.

"Forget it." She started down the stairs. "Helen?"

"Noel?" Helen sounded incredulous.

There were no lights. Jack used his flashlight beam and mentally ticked off the seconds. There were three minutes left, give or take.

He heard a sound behind him and halted on the threshold. "Get Helen and Caroline out," he whispered.

Noel looked past his shoulder, then nodded and continued her descent.

Jack heard the sound again, closer now. It had to be Turano, couldn't be anyone else. He waited until he could feel the man's breath on his neck, then spun and punched.

His fist landed in Roberto's solar plexus. Roberto's elbow whipped up and caught him in the jaw. Through a haze of dizzying pain, Jack saw the other man's hand fumbling to get inside his coat pocket.

Teeth bared, Jack leaped, knocked his hand aside and took him down. Roberto kicked him under the chin, snapping Jack's head back. Somehow Jack wrapped his fingers around Roberto's coat and dragged it off.

Roberto growled and used his foot again. Jack saw a gleam of dark metal, then felt his shoulder explode.

All he could think was that he had Roberto's coat. The detonator for the explosives must be in the pocket. Keep the coat away from Roberto, and everyone should be safe.

Footsteps clattered on the stairs.

Roberto stumbled, swore and dived into the corner. Noel shouted Caroline's name from below. The clattering continued. Caroline arrived at the top, panting and clutching her stomach. She let out a shriek when Roberto grabbed her by the hair and hauled her against his chest.

"No, wait," she gasped. "What are you doing? Jack, where's the money?"

Roberto had both arms wrapped around Caroline's neck. He was sweating and making sharp grunting noises.

Noel stopped on the threshold, out of Turano's line of vision,

Jack hoped. To ensure that, he altered his position. Roberto was forced to turn or lose sight of him.

"Jack!" Caroline cried. "Where's the money?"

"There's no money," Roberto shouted. "What good will stinking money do me? All the people I've ever cared about are dead." He brought his knee up hard under Caroline's backside. "Stop squirming or I'll break your neck."

She froze. Even the fingers that had been scratching at his forearms went still.

"What do you want?" Jack asked him. He tasted blood, but kept his eyes on the man. "Do you want to kill me? Would that make you feel better?"

"No. I want to kill someone you care about." He squeezed Caroline's neck. "I wanted you to choose your sister."

"So you could murder Noel."

Roberto glared at him. "Noel dies, and you suffer. That's how it was supposed to be. Not at first, but later, after I saw you together. I'd kill her, and you'd live with it."

Caroline choked. "You said you wanted Jack's money."

"That's what I said. It was never what I wanted."

Jack noted the subtle movement behind Roberto and raised his hands, palms out. "Let Caroline go, and you can kill me. That has to be worth something."

"Listen to him," Caroline pleaded. "I didn't screw up your family, he did." She glowered at Jack. "Old Jacob screwed me the same way. He was a master screwdriver, and he molded Jack in his likeness. Ahh!" She inhaled sharply when Roberto tightened his hold.

"I want you to shut the hell up," Roberto growled. His expression grew suspicious. "Where's Noel?" Moving swiftly, he whipped his arms from Caroline's throat and whirled. He knocked Noel sideways. He would have knocked her down the stairs if Jack hadn't plowed into him from behind. Caroline screamed and flattened herself against the wall. Noel rolled, caught the rusty spade Helen pitched to her and, scrambling to her feet, swung it like a bat.

The flat end hit Roberto in the face and sent him reeling. He made a single drunken loop, reached for Noel, then lost his footing and tumbled headfirst down the stairs. There was a cry, a crunch of bones and, finally, a moan that ended with a raspy breath.

Caroline covered her mouth and slid down the wall. Jack attempted to hold himself upright, but pain burned a path from his jaw through his shoulder and straight to his knees. If Noel hadn't run to catch him, he'd have joined his sister on the floor.

"Good one, Ransom," she whispered. She searched for and located his cell phone. "He had the detonation devices in his coat pocket."

"Yeah, I guessed that." His vision blurred. "Why do I feel so fuzzy?"

"He shot you, Jack."

"What? When?"

"I don't know, but he got you in the shoulder." She rested her forehead against his hair. "The gun's in the corner. Roberto must have lost his grip on it, or you kicked it away."

"Missed that," Jack murmured. "Stupid."

Caroline's hysterical screams faded out. He felt Noel pressing something to the spot that burned even more than his jaw. "Tell Michael," he said when he realized she had his phone. "No cops."

Then he dropped his head onto her shoulder, and the whole grisly Christmas nightmare turned black.

Epilogue

"How is that handsome man of yours, dear?" Mrs. Fisker rushed down the stairs of her front porch, carrying a covered basket and a dented thermos. "I made you some food for tonight. I'm so glad you're not hurt. A nice man with a ponytail told me that all of this is going to be taken care of quietly, seeing as it involves two high-profile members of the community." She popped the thermos inside the basket and pushed the basket into Noel's arms. "Imagine, Jack Ransom coming and going from your place all this time and no one knew a thing about it. He'll recover, I'm sure. You and Helen, too. And that other woman."

"We'll all be fine," Noel assured her. She debated, then asked, "Tell me something, Mrs. Fisker. When we talked several days ago, you said you hadn't met the people who rented Mr. Yost's house. Not him or her."

"That's right, dear." She raised her hands to her lips as if praying. "I'm glad now that I didn't. Imagine old Fred not bothering to ask for references. I talked to him this morning. He's flabbergasted by the whole affair."

"He's not alone." Noel gave the woman a hug. "Thanks for the food."

"You tell Mr. Ransom that no one will hear a word about this from me."

Noel waited until she was out of earshot before smiling slightly. "Wanna bet?"

But it didn't really matter because, one way or another, some portion of the story was bound to leak out. Toss in equal measures of speculation and gossip and it would make for a fascinating tale to be told around numerous Christmas tables in Winter Valley. Maybe in Pittsburgh, as well, although in the grand scheme of life there, this was only one of many unpleasant headlines.

She heard Helen and Michael talking in Helen's office when she went inside. She left them alone and climbed the stairs to her apartment.

When she spied Jack on the sofa, she sighed. "I thought you were in bed."

"I'm bored," he said and, with his head resting on the back cushions, sent her a steady look. "That better not be chicken soup."

"If it is, it's well-intentioned." She plunked the thermos on his lap. "Is Caroline still here?"

"For the moment. Her ride's en route."

Noel chose her words with care. "Do you still plan to keep the details of the kidnapping quiet?"

"Yeah, like that's gonna happen."

"Okay, then, as quiet as possible—and I said the details, not the whole gory incident. I don't think," she added, perching on the arm of the sofa, "the police have a problem with Roberto's death. Fred Yost's house and Roberto's apartment near the deli were loaded with evidence. He gave old Fred the name Jacob—I knew I'd heard that name more than the usual number of times lately—and set up his Winter Valley headquarters upstairs. He desperately wanted revenge. If he got caught after the fact, it didn't matter."

"Only the game was important."

"Winning the game was important. To that end, he plotted his strategy step by deliberate step."

Jack regarded her through his lashes. "What aren't you saying, Noel?"

She drew a bolstering breath. "He had an ally, Jack. He admitted it to me on the drive to Winter Valley."

He regarded her for several long seconds, then his eyes moved to Noel's guest bedroom where Caroline was waiting for her ride to Pittsburgh. "Right from the start, do you figure?"

"I'd say so. Do you want me to talk to her?"

"No." He roused himself from the cushions, careful not to jar his injured shoulder. "This one's all mine."

"WHAT'LL HE DO to her?"

Helen poured Noel a cup of tea in her office. Michael had gone to the Winter Valley police station to see how matters were proceeding, and Jack was still in with his sister.

Noel added milk and sugar and leaned a hip on the windowsill. "Probably not a whole lot." She sent her friend a small smile. "Guilt's a powerful weapon, and Caroline wields it well."

"She's a witch in the wickedest sense." Helen dunked one of Mrs. Fisker's shortbread cookies. "I'd be sorely tempted to press charges if I were Jack."

"Yes, but you're not, and neither am I. She was out of money and extremely resentful of her older half brother. On the other side, Roberto had a workable agenda already under way. He was going to make Jack and me pay for what we'd done to his family. Enter Caroline, an integral part of the plan he'd been formulating. He talks to her and, surprise, surprise, realizes she hates her brother. It's a stroke of luck. Even unbalanced, Roberto knows how to charm a woman. He feeds her lies—or maybe it was the truth at first—until it occurs to her that they can help each other. She wants money, and she believes he does, too. He tells her he does."

"Except he doesn't," Helen said. "He's lying and she's buying. Then, when she discovers the truth, she panics."

"She didn't figure it out until right near the end." Noel was certain of that.

Helen tipped her head to one side. "How did you know?"

"Mrs. Fisker," Noel told her. "And you."

"You'll have to elaborate just a little, hon."

"Mrs. Fisker told me a while ago that she hadn't met the people who rented Fred Yost's house. Not him and not her. She'd seen them three or four times, but hadn't spoken to them. How many kidnappers do you know who walk around with their hostages in tow?"

"It could have been some other woman, a girlfriend or a friend friend."

"I agree, but then I saw you and Caroline together inside. Your makeup was smudged, your hair wasn't brushed, your clothes were wrinkled."

"Don't remind me."

"He didn't put you together until the last day. When I saw Caroline, she was clean, polished and wrinkle-free."

"Ergo, she'd been grooming herself." Helen smiled. "I'm so glad you were on my side."

Noel glanced upward. "It was still only a strong hunch at that point, but it made sense. I don't think she'll bother to lie about it."

"Why bother when you've got a fat wad of guilt in hand?"

"Wayward siblings store that kind of thing up."

"As your own brother has proved to you and your sisters many times over." Helen kissed her cheek. "Whatever Jack does with Caroline, I hope it involves a different continent and a one-way ticket."

Noel looked out at the picture-perfect snow on the street outside and didn't know what to hope for.

SHE WAITED DOWNSTAIRS until Caroline's friend arrived from Pittsburgh to take her home. He resembled a young Elvis, and he was driving Caroline's blue Mercedes.

Jack was standing at the window when she returned to the apartment. The lights on the Christmas tree sparkled and winked, and only the smell of Caroline's perfume overspray marred the scene.

"What did she say?" Noel asked from across the room.

"What you'd expect. She denied it—for about five seconds. Then she started to cry." Jack looked back at her. "Jacob never did cut her much of a deal."

"It sounds as if he didn't cut her any deal at all." Noel strolled up behind him to play with the ends of his hair. "I can't say I like her, but I think I understand why she turned out the way she did. People need to know that other people have faith in them. It's no wonder the businesses she attempted to manage failed."

Jack stared out the window. "I'll give her money. She wants to go to Paris. She has a friend there who works for a fashion magazine. Maybe she'll get involved in that."

"Roberto used her, Jack. The resentment that had built up inside her over the years would have been a veritable gold mine to him. All he had to do was string her along with the promise of a big payoff."

"Yeah, well, that's Caroline's deal." He turned his back on the Christmas scene and draped his good arm over her shoulder. "What about yours? Are you all right?"

"I'm fine. It'll take a while to sort out the whole Roberto-was-my-lover thing, but I'll get there." She felt as if she was halfway there already, just having the nightmarish aspects finished. "At least he won't have to suffer. I don't know if you've talked to the coroner yet, but Roberto broke his neck when he fell down the stairs. It was a quick death."

"I guess that's merciful."

"It's poetic justice." She outlined his lips with her finger. "What about the deli?"

"Roberto bought the place just under two years ago. He's been running it as a profit-making business since he took it over. Whatever else he was, he knew the food industry."

"That would be Vince's influence. I never saw Artie, Jack. I should have realized that and wondered why. He was one of the people who catered your Christmas party, you know. Michael arranged it, knowing your penchant for a certain kind of sandwich. I didn't see Roberto there, but obviously he slipped in and out."

"With your scarf." Jack kissed her nose. "Tell me, did you ever see the blonde up close?"

"The cross-dresser? No. Why?"

For the first time since Roberto's death, Jack smiled. "Think office nemesis, Noel."

She did, then stopped and raised surprised brows. "Martin Faber Junior?"

"One and the same. That's why he ran when I approached him at the deli. He thought you'd seen through his female guise and sicced me on him."

"I never got close enough to really look at him." She tried to imagine him in makeup. "Faber Junior, huh? So it was business suits at the office, and women's clothes on his own time."

"Some people like to live out their fantasies, Noel."

"At least his didn't hurt anyone. And he did it in your neighborhood rather than his own. He must have been shocked the first time I showed up at Artie's." She smiled. "A secret life. That's so cool. I didn't think he had it in him."

"I promised to keep his secret. Junior helped me find you, Noel. I'll always be grateful for that."

"So will I, Jack. Don't worry. His secret's perfectly safe. Who knows, maybe it'll become the basis of a friendship between us." She grinned. "Or not."

"You have a mean streak, lady."

"Only a little one." She pressed her lips to the crease between his eyes. "What happens to the deli now that Artie's gone?"

He stroked the hair from her cheek. "I think Ray can run it, don't you?"

"From my point of view, he pretty much already did. You going to buy it?"

"It could be arranged."

"And the theatre?"

"Already in the works. It's worth restoring—although the rotted wood did us a favor in the end… Why are you looking at me like that?"

"I'm thinking that you and Roberto have something in common—and, no, I don't mean me."

"What, then?"

"Games. His were totally unstable, but you enjoy playing your corporate games as much as he loved playing his. You say your grandfather coerced you into becoming what you are, but I think you'd have done it anyway, eventually. What you didn't like was that he forced your hand."

He stared at her. "Am I supposed to agree with any of that?"

"Food for thought." She tickled the nape of his neck. "Okay, so we've got you and Caroline, Ray and Junior settled. Now it's my turn." She drew back just far enough to look him in the eye. "Have you got any plans for Christmas, Ransom?"

His lashes dropped a little. "You know I'm not—"

"Big on Christmas. Yes, I do know that." She sent him a sly look. "But don't you think that maybe it's time for a change?"

His eyes narrowed further. "Are you propositioning me, Ms. Lawson?"

"Well, yeah."

He regarded her for a long moment, then grazed her cheek where Roberto had struck her. "I think I love you, Noel."

Angling her head, she moved her mouth close to his and whispered, "I think I love you, too, Jack." Amusement entered her tone as she brushed her lips against his. "Strange feeling, isn't it, for a couple of relationship-challenged people like us."

"Any idea what we should do next?"

"How does Christmas in Vermont sound?"

"With your family?"

"You don't need to look so panic-stricken. They're nice, normal people. My sister just had a baby girl, so you can ooh and aah over her with the rest of us. There'll be turkey and stuffing and probably half a dozen snowball fights. My sisters are all bringing their husbands or partners so there'll be lots of guy time as well. You might get hit up for work—I think Ali's husband is between jobs right now—but you can handle that. There are sleigh rides on Christmas Eve, skiing any time you want, and five cozy fireplaces at my parents' lodge. And if you're good," she added, giving his stomach a poke, "I might be coaxed into putting a candle in the plum pudding for your birthday."

The humor that flitted through his expression took root in his eyes. "Only a fool would say no to all that." He touched his brow to hers. "The Ghost of Christmas Past might be dead, but Christmas Present's not looking bad from where I stand."

"As for the future, we'll leave that one alone for now." Wrapping her arms around his neck, Noel let the feeling of the season wash over her. "Merry Christmas, Jack."

"This time," he said, "I think it just might be."

As he covered her mouth with his, Noel thought she glimpsed three hazy shapes outside the window. Then they were gone, and there was only her and Jack and the hopeful promise of their Christmas Present.

Holiday to-do list:

- wrap gifts
- catch a thief
- solve a murder
- deal with Mom

Well-respected Florida detective Maggie Skerritt
is finally getting her life on track when a
suspicious crime shakes up her holiday plans.

Holidays Are Murder
Charlotte Douglas

HARLEQUIN
Next

HN21

Available December 2005
TheNextNovel.com

HOMICIDE DETECTIVE
MERRI WALTERS IS BACK IN

Silent Reckoning
by Debra Webb

December 2005

A serial killer was on the loose,
hunting the city's country singers.
Could deaf detective Merri Walters turn
her hearing loss to advantage and crack
the case before the music died?

Available at your favorite retail outlet.

www.SilhouetteBombshell.com   SBSR

If you enjoyed what you just read,
then we've got an offer you can't resist!

Take 2 bestselling
love stories FREE!

Plus get a FREE surprise gift!

Clip this page and mail it to Harlequin Reader Service®

IN U.S.A.	IN CANADA
3010 Walden Ave.	P.O. Box 609
P.O. Box 1867	Fort Erie, Ontario
Buffalo, N.Y. 14240-1867	L2A 5X3

YES! Please send me 2 free Harlequin Intrigue® novels and my free surprise gift. After receiving them, if I don't wish to receive anymore, I can return the shipping statement marked cancel. If I don't cancel, I will receive 4 brand-new novels each month, before they're available in stores! In the U.S.A., bill me at the bargain price of $4.24 plus 25¢ shipping and handling per book and applicable sales tax, if any*. In Canada, bill me at the bargain price of $4.99 plus 25¢ shipping and handling per book and applicable taxes**. That's the complete price and a savings of at least 10% off the cover prices—what a great deal! I understand that accepting the 2 free books and gift places me under no obligation ever to buy any books. I can always return a shipment and cancel at any time. Even if I never buy another book from Harlequin, the 2 free books and gift are mine to keep forever.

181 HDN DZ7N
381 HDN DZ7P

Name _____ (PLEASE PRINT)

Address _____ Apt.#

City _____ State/Prov. _____ Zip/Postal Code

Not valid to current Harlequin Intrigue® subscribers.

Want to try two free books from another series?
Call 1-800-873-8635 or visit www.morefreebooks.com.

* Terms and prices subject to change without notice. Sales tax applicable in N.Y.
** Canadian residents will be charged applicable provincial taxes and GST.
   All orders subject to approval. Offer limited to one per household.
® are registered trademarks owned and used by the trademark owner and or its licensee.

INT04R   ©2004 Harlequin Enterprises Limited

eHARLEQUIN.com

The Ultimate Destination for Women's Fiction

For **FREE online reading**, visit www.eHarlequin.com now and enjoy:

Online Reads
Read **Daily** and **Weekly** chapters from our Internet-exclusive stories by your favorite authors.

Interactive Novels
Cast your vote to help decide how these stories unfold...then stay tuned!

Quick Reads
For shorter romantic reads, try our collection of Poems, Toasts, & More!

Online Read Library
Miss one of our online reads?
Come here to catch up!

Reading Groups
Discuss, share and rave with other community members!

For great reading online, visit www.eHarlequin.com today!

INTONL04R

HARLEQUIN®

INTRIGUE®

KELSEY ROBERTS
CHARMED AND DANGEROUS

When FBI agent J. J. Barnes is assigned to a high
profile investigation, the last person she wants
to be paired with is the arrogant Cody Landry.
But after succumbing to their heated passion
J. J. must make a choice…back out now or
risk her heart with a possible suspect.

Also watch for

THE LAST LANDRY, March 2006

Available wherever Harlequin Books are sold.

www.eHarlequin.com   HICAD